T0153178

Acclaim for Felice Picano

"Felice Picano is a premier voice in gay letters."—Malcolm Boyd, *Contemporary Authors*

Felice Picano is "…a leading light in the gay literary world… his glints of flashing wit and subtle hints of dark decadence transcend clichés."—Richard Violette, *Library Journal*

"Felice Picano is one hell of a writer!"—Stephen King

"Picano's destiny has been to lead the way for a generation of gay writers."—Robert L. Pela, *The Advocate*

"These stories [*The New York Years: Stories by Felice Picano*] are as well written and immediate as any contemporary gay fiction."—Regina Marler

"With *True Stories*, Felice Picano enhances his status as one of the great literary figures in recent gay history and does so with wit, verve and as much panache as we've come to expect."—Jerry Wheeler, *Out in Print*

Also available from Bold Strokes

The Lure

Late in the Season

Looking Glass Lives

Contemporary Gay Romances:
Tragic, Mystic, Comic & Horrific

Visit us at www.boldstrokesbooks.com

TWELVE O'CLOCK TALES

by

Felice Picano

A Division of Bold Strokes Books

2012

TWELVE O'CLOCK TALES
© 2012 By Felice Picano. All Rights Reserved.

ISBN 13: 978-1-60282-659-5

This Trade Paperback Original Is Published By
Bold Strokes Books, Inc.
P.O. Box 249
Valley Falls, NY 12185

First Edition: April 2012

THIS IS A WORK OF FICTION. NAMES, CHARACTERS, PLACES, AND
INCIDENTS ARE THE PRODUCT OF THE AUTHOR'S IMAGINATION OR
ARE USED FICTITIOUSLY. ANY RESEMBLANCE TO ACTUAL PERSONS,
LIVING OR DEAD, BUSINESS ESTABLISHMENTS, EVENTS, OR LOCALES
IS ENTIRELY COINCIDENTAL.

THIS BOOK, OR PARTS THEREOF, MAY NOT BE REPRODUCED IN ANY
FORM WITHOUT PERMISSION.

Credits
Editor: Stacia Seaman
Production Design: Stacia Seaman
Cover Design by Sheri (graphicartist2020@hotmail.com)

for Ross Crowe
with thanks to Harlan Ellison—who doesn't want any
and in memory of Arthur C. Clarke

CONTENTS

Preface   1

Synapse   5

Duel on Interstate Five   13

Spices of the World   19

Eye   31

Food for Thought   57

Love and the She-Lion   75

A Guest in the Heavens   89

Swear Not by the Moon...   111

The Gospel According to Miriam, Daughter of Jebu
and Anna, Wife to Johosephat, Mother of Joshua   125

Absolute Ebony   131

Room Nine   155

One Way Out   177

The Perfect Setting   203

PREFACE

In a way, this book is one that I've been writing for many years. My family is from Rhode Island, and the city of Providence is surprisingly rich for being the residence of masters of supernatural fiction—among them Edgar Allen Poe and H.P. Lovecraft. My much older Aunt Lillian and Uncle Bert lived midway between the residences of both men, and they knew the latter author briefly in his last years. Whenever I stayed with them during childhood summers in the early 1950s I would read volumes of both authors' works, both at their home and at the local library on College Hill.

Poe of course is a classic, although in truth he is rather spottily known. Some of his best work is not the half dozen poems and tales he's known by, but instead longer works like "The Gold-Bug," "The Unparalleled Adventures of One Hans Pfaal," and the utterly mad *The Narrative of Arthur Gordon Pym of Nantucket*. Those were the tales that stuck with me, and rereading them recently proved them to be wonderfully subversive and gaga.

Unlike today, at that time, Lovecraft had virtually no reputation as a writer outside of faithful readers of *Weird Tales* magazine in the 1920s and 1930s. That he does today is partly thanks to the staunch and persistent efforts of Arkham House in Sauk City, Michigan, which reprinted everything, even the poetry, in editions usually limited to a few thousand copies. But also thanks to the San Francisco Hippie Rock group H.P. Lovecraft and their eerie hit song "The White Ship."

Today his books are fittingly part of the huge Library of America series. Rereading them, I'm always surprised how fittingly he uses the odd geography of Rhode Island—half-water, half-land; and of the latter, half-city and half-rural—in his stories and novels. At that time, however, most of Lovecraft's titles were out of print and unobtainable. By the way, a handful of movies were made out of Lovecraft's works in the 1970s based on his books, too. Most are odd and bad, but some are very surprisingly true to the source and even watchable.

Later in life, once I was writing fiction myself, I was fortunate enough to come into contact with two master authors of Science Fiction, Arthur C. Clarke and Harlan Ellison. Individually, and entirely unprompted, they reviewed my books, praised them, and encouraged me—and so unwittingly they set me on the path that would end up at this volume, and with my sci-fi trilogy *City on a Star* still being written.

In a way *Twelve O'Clock Tales* is an homage to those unique and astonishing talents: Poe, Lovecraft, Clarke, and Ellison. As well as to M.R. James, Walter de La Mare, Ambrose Bierce, Nathaniel Hawthorne, Edith Wharton, Henry James, Saki, Algernon Blackwood, etc., all of whom I've read and still read today.

For people who keep track of things, *Twelve O'Clock Tales* is my fourth collection of short stories, following *Slashed To Ribbons in Defense of Love* in 1983 (reprinted as *The New York Years* in 2003), *Tales From a Distant Planet* in 2005, and *Contemporary Gay Romances* in 2011 (also Bold Strokes Books). The 2005 title was published by French Connection Press in Paris, France, and had a very limited distribution, although the book is still available for sale in the U.S., and I'm including two of its most praised stories here.

Although I am primarily known as a novelist (and lately also as a memoirist), stories are my favorite way of writing fiction, whether it is a 1,750 word "amusement in prose" (the second story here), a 35,000 word novella, or anything in between.

When I can know, sense, or even merely get a hint about an ending while I'm writing, I think I'm simply a better writer, certainly a tighter one. Doing that with a novel usually means a five- to ten-year period of gestation before I even begin, and equal years of commitment on the other end. With stories I can start and end in a few sessions, or in the case of longer works, do so within a month. Any more time than that and it becomes something else.

My first story was written when I was twelve, and my first published story (collected in *Slashed to Ribbons*) was written as far back as 1972. I've now written almost fifty shorter stories, of which (with this volume) now forty-seven have been published in one form, format, place or another, from magazines and newspapers to anthologies to online magazines. Very early on I wrote "strange" stories: My second "finished, adult" story, in fact, could have easily fit into this collection.

Among the stories here, a few included here were popular: "Absolute Ebony" has been published several times in mainstream magazines and other people's collections, ditto with "Spices of the World" and "One Way Out," and it's amazing that readers find them fresh and relevant. Another tale, "Love and the She-Lion," was second runner-up as "story of the year" for the late, lamented *Story* magazine.

The other tales are recently written, from 1995 to 2011, and brand new. Most of the stories here are strange, a few comical, and others rather sinister. They came from different places and times—a Hebrew backwater in B.C.E. Israel; a California highway some fifteen years from now; an unnamed New England rural area, time unknown; East London around 1950; New York City, etc., in as far as I can determine the 1970s. Other places are difficult to determine: the Midwest for two of them; for one, the British Midlands. One takes place in Venezuela, a country I've never visited, was never in any way interested in, and maybe thought of a total of three times in my life.

Reviewing my recent nonfiction collection, *True Stories: Portraits from My Past*, Thom Nickels pointed out that among those relationships were several which dealt with experiences that cannot be explained, and that I dealt with them as objectively and honestly as I could. He was surprised, saying it's seldom done and mostly frowned upon in "literature."

Since I—and people around me—have actually had such unexplainable experiences, I believe they are valid loci and foci for writing as well as discussion. Anyone who denies to my face that the "unseen world is all around us" is usually met with a laugh—if not a giggle—I know better. And the more it is written of and discussed, the less it will be demonized; the more it might be understood.

Unfazed, my intrepid publisher, Bold Strokes Press, has issued *Twelve O'Clock Tales*, so named because around midnight is when I sat down to write most of the tales, and it's a good time for you to read them too…Boo!

Felice Picano

SYNAPSE

So, Annette…Do you mind if I call you Annette? I mean we can't keep up this dopey fiction of 'Mom' and 'Son' anymore, can we?"

She stared at me across the table, so I went on.

"You keep asking the questions. So now I'll tell you."

There was a new look, of panic, on her face. But I went on anyway.

"You see, unlike your husband Mike or your son Lyons, you *do* keep asking the questions. And they're the right questions, Annette. They really are. For example, who is this kid sitting at your kitchen table? You *know* I'm not your son, Scotty Alcock, aged fourteen. You've known that for a while now, haven't you? Even though that's exactly who I look like and sound like."

A sob escaped her, and she quickly closed it back with a hand. Her eyes were an odd mixture of fear and desire. Desire to know—and now!

"Not when I first showed up in the hospital, maybe. And maybe not even when I first came home. But soon after. Right?"

She shook her head, and I knew she meant yes, even if it looked like no.

"Then the books. The computers. The kids coming by from school. None of Scotty's old friends. None of those losers! Not the ones who left him to die, alone, hanging out of that car that they crashed and left him to die in."

Another sob that she caught just in time.

"No, instead, the new school friends. The smart ones. The good-looking ones. The ones going somewhere in life. And then the school itself. Those amazing report cards. Those stunning grades on those papers. Those teacher-parent meetings. Mike was sure it was a miraculous change. But you knew Scotty better than Mike, didn't you, Annette? You knew he'd never be that bright, didn't you? Never be that capable of change, would he, miracle or not?"

Sob number three, caught like numbers one and two.

"So who am I?..."

"Who are you?" she asked. I could barely hear.

"I'm the guy driving the other car. *I'm the one who died!*"

She removed her hand long enough to ask, "How?"

"I'm not entirely sure how. Wish I *was* sure, because then we could all make a pile of money on this, you know, transferring minds from one body to another. But I don't really know, Annette. I've got some theories. They involve the series of treatments I'd been taking. Purely experimental. Part of my partner's and my so-called business at the Geldhover Laboratories a couple of states away. I'm sure you read in the papers or heard on TV after the car accident that I was a quote distinguished scientist, unquote. Well, I was. And technically it's beyond you, but maybe not. You're not stupid. They were combinations of electrolyte solutions that I'd been injecting for about two months. In themselves nothing too unusual.

"But at the particular time of our accident those solutions were holding in stasis a variety of unstable molecules that my partner and I had constructed, little atomic-sized 'computers,' for want of a better word, that under certain chemical stimuli would act in certain primitive yet useful ways. Line up in certain rows, say. Or stand up and wave. Or produce a simple electric charge. Or even an atomic charge. Nano-techs, we called them. You could probably think and figure out how they could be useful in, say, NASA programs and suchlike."

"What were they doing *inside* you?"

"Well, Annette, the truth is I was stealing them. My partner had gone behind my back and sold our little inventions to a secret arm of the United States Air Force, and when I discovered this fact, completely by accident, by the way, I felt completely betrayed, not by the sale, but by who was getting them. I would have liked Lenovo to get them, or Microsoft. Before he could deliver them, I injected whatever I could find, which was all of about two sets on hand. Then I cashed out my bank accounts and took off. I'd been on the road for about twenty-six hours when the collision occurred.

"Oddly enough, those Nano-techs inside me not only kept me wide awake and driving all that time, but they aided my vision, and they enhanced my memory, and they also sharpened various visual and judgmental abilities. For example, I saw the car with Scotty and the other two boys coming from far, far away, and saw that there was a chance it would arrive at the highway approximately when I did.

"Naturally I continually altered my speed to ensure that would *not* occur. But I didn't count on the fact that the boys were drunk—sorry to have to tell you—really drunk, and out of control, and that the driver, that boy Alton, he kept drunkenly changing the speed of the car. So that didn't work out as I planned.

"As for the exact mechanism of it all, well, I think *you'll* have to take some reponsibility for that, Annette. What I mean is the cell phone you insisted Scotty keep nearby all the time he was away from home.

"When I came to after the crash, I was still in my old man's body—I like to think of it now as my Mad Scientist's body—a foot or so through the windshield of my car. But your son was *all the way through his*, meaning he had not been wearing a seat belt, and I could see that he'd shot right over the air bag, which had opened in time to catch only his feet. The two cars had hit almost head-on: my driver side to his passenger side. Clever Alton was able to swerve the main damage away from himself at the last minute and thus toward your Scotty. The little bastard.

"The two cars kind of crunched together, and folded, up into the air. Your son's face was about four inches away from my face, Annette, so I can report that he was still pretty much unconscious, but that his pinned and lifted right hand was tight up against his right ear, and he had that cell phone there and it was turned on: matte green lights on that LG-3 screen. I heard more than saw the other boys hightail it away from the car. One of them—Zach, I think—asked, 'What about Scotty?' And Alton replied, 'He's dog food.' Then they fled on foot.

"And we hung there, folded up maybe eight, nine feet in the air, while the two cars smoked and things started dropping out of them slowly down to the macadam below. I don't know what: pistons, cogs, brake rotors. Whatever.

"Then Scotty opened his eyes, conscious for a second. And we just looked at each other. Two poor bastards!

"That's when the thunder and lightning began. Of course, in that big, wide-open-plains space, our heaps of metal were the only lightning target for miles and miles around, and Scotty's phone was the especial target. The first bolt struck the back of my car and it jolted my section down maybe two inches, until my nose was just brushing the bottom of that phone. The second lightning strike, well, all I saw of that was stars, green, red, blue, and yellow, just like in the comics. I'm guessing that strike hit me and the phone and Scotty, and those twelve little molecular computer-thingies inside me. It went kinda 'twang' like a giant guitar string. You know, the bottom string? *Terwwwaaangggg!*

"When I came to, I was in the intensive care unit in the hospital, and the rest is history…I'm very sorry for your loss, Annette."

She started crying then, and I comforted her as best as I could. When she was done, she got up and used some paper napkins to wipe her face. She leaned against the brushed metal of the big new Norwegian dishwasher and she asked in a tiny voice: "Now what?"

And like the gentleman that I am, I said, "That's entirely up to you, Annette."

"What's that mean?"

"Well, it means I can just leave."

"You can't just leave!" she said. "You're a fourteen-year-old boy! Remember?"

"I'll 'run away.' Fourteen-year-old boys do that all the time."

"Your father will kill me if he finds out I just let you go…I mean Mike will," she corrected. "As it is, well, he suspects…all isn't completely right between you and me."

"He'll get over it after a while, Annette. Kids vanish all the time. Why not get pregnant again. That'll distract him."

"Is that what you want? To just disappear? What do I call you? I can't call you Scotty! Especially now."

"I know. Annette, to be honest, I don't know what to do. Not yet. It's taken me this many months to adjust to everything that's happened. Don't think it was easy, any of it…"

"You mean deceiving us?"

"If I'd told the truth right off, where do you think I would be?"

"Locked up!"

"At the least…Everyone has a right to survive."

"No, you're right about that," she admitted. "It was survival. But what about the past?…Are you married? Did you have children? Grandchildren? Should someone know…?"

"No. No. And no, *no one can ever know!*"

She sighed. "Then you probably ought to just stay here. Grow up. Go to college. Mike's already putting money away for you to go to college. He never put away a cent for Scotty."

"I'll pay you back. I'll make sure I pay my way around here!"

"How? You keep forgetting! *You're fourteen years old!*"

"Even fourteen-year-olds make money nowadays! Via computers. The Internet. Think about it, Annette. I don't know how, but I'll pay my way…I'll sell a patent."

"You mean, I'll have a brilliant son?"

"Another brilliant son. Lyons is smart."

"In business."

"Then he'll help me…Where did you come up with that name for him, anyway?"

"A tea bag. In the hospital. I had tea after he was born."

"Look, we don't have to decide right away," I said. "But if you want me to go, I'll understand. Really, I will, Annette! The truth is I don't want to be where I'm not…you know—wanted."

She sighed and turned and began pouring coffee for herself.

"It's not like I intended this to happen," I defended myself.

She looked up at me, holding a mug up.

"I would *love* some. Black. Two sugar."

When she sat at the table again, she said, "So…what was the letter about you brought home from school? Even if you aren't…*him*, I suppose I still ought to see it."

I brought it out from my little netbook case. She looked at it, not comprehending. "It's from the track team?"

"You see, Annette, this is a good body I've found myself in," I said. "I know Scotty didn't go in for sports or anything, but he could have easily. And as this body heals, we've all become aware of its potentials."

"We being…?"

"The therapists. The doctors. The coaches at school. Me, especially. We all think it could be a *great* body."

"A great body?"

"I have several reasons to believe that those Nano-techs came with me into Scotty. In my crazier thoughts, I think the only reason I'm here at all is that the Nano-techs saw a way of surviving and doing a lot better than in my original body. When that lightning struck and a channel opened up via the cell phone…they took the channel, and took *me* along for the ride."

"Trading up?" She seemed only half-skeptical.

"Or selection of the fittest…"

"And they took your brain because…? I see—it was the fittest brain."

"Of the two of us, yeah. A better chance at survival."

We sipped our coffee.

"You don't have a cookie or two?" I asked.

She dragged over the Oreos and we munched, unhappily, sometimes side-glancing at each other.

"Now, don't take this the wrong way, Annette, but I also think the Nano-techs have somehow enhanced themselves beyond what me and my asshole partner—pardon my French—did."

"What do you mean?"

"Well, in the ICU when I was hooked up to computer monitors for three, four days? I swear I think the Nano-techs migrated back and forth through the tubing into the machinery, getting stronger, perhaps even learning stuff."

"Oh brother!…Okay, I'll bite. How does this translate into track?"

"This afternoon I clocked off the charts for my age group. Off the clocks for high school, period."

"Showing off?"

"That's just it, Annette. I wasn't showing off. I wasn't even trying. I was just running like my physical therapist asked me to do and I was thinking about other stuff. And then I noticed them all gathering and excited, so I fell back a lot and pretended I had no idea what was happening."

"So you're what? What's it called—bionic too?"

"I'm thinking maybe the Nano-techs operate a lot better in a growing, healthy young body like this one than they did in a decaying seventy-seven-year-old body like I used to have."

"Why track?"

"Well, track to begin with. The coordination is pretty simple compared to other sports. When I get stronger, of course, I thought I'd switch to throwing, tackling, jumping. Maybe even football!"

"Brilliant *and* with a team letter! Mike will kiss your feet," she said. "He'll become your agent, your manager. Hell! He'll divorce me and spend all his time with you."

"You're overreacting, Annette."

"Am I? Well, I can tell you something I would have never told Scotty. Mike's pretty much past heterosexuality, except maybe socially and because we're married. He's back to when we were eleven years old. He lives, breathes, works with, plays with, and hangs around with men and only men. When his mom calls once a year, and this is a woman who blushes at the word 'prostitute,' he refers to her as 'Guy.' New woman in his office came complaining to me at the annual office picnic that she couldn't seduce Mike. I wanted to say, 'Get in line.'"

"Come on."

"Mike discussed his colonoscopy with Lyons three months before, during, and after the test. Lyons is seventeen! When did I find out? When the doctor's bill arrived. I almost didn't open it. Mike said he didn't want to bother me with it. Since when? He used to bother me about a hangnail!"

She sulked, adding, "I mentioned this to a coupla other gals. They said I should be happy. 'Me too. *Fine*-al-*ly*,' one sang."

"So maybe me doing all this sports stuff might be a help with keeping Mike around and all?"

"Well, it'll keep Mike focused more on the family. Since your... since Scotty's accident, he's been here three times as much as in the past five years."

"So it could be a *good* thing?"

"I don't know. I. Don't. Know. But I do like looking at you," she admitted. "Idiot that I am. Seeing you heal and get better looking. You *are* better looking, you know. It's not just Scotty."

"Yes. I decided to fool around a little with that last facial surgery Scotty needed, the big one? *I* kind of subtly redirected the doctors, giving them photos of Mike when he was younger. It was partly to help you...you know, separate from your son. And partly to establish myself as different from your son in school," I added, lamely.

"A younger Mike...Well, I do like it. Even though I know you're not my son inside there. But...I still need something to call you. A nickname or...what was your name? Professor Paul something or other?"

"Paul Allen Duclose. French in origin."

"Duclose. I'll call you Duke," she said, trying it out.

"People will think I'm a dog."

"No. They'll think we have a special bond. And we do, don't we?"

"Unless you tell them the truth."

"*Who'd* believe me?" she asked. "*I* don't believe *me!*"

She handed me a another few cookies and slowly pulled one apart. As I watched her lick the cream off one side, she stopped and mumbled, "Synapse."

"You mean the area between two nerve cells in the brain?"

"Yeah. I remember that word from high school biology, because it was my only wrong answer on my final exam. Kept me from getting a perfect score, that word," Annette said. "That's probably where those Nano-techs got into Scotty? Through the synapses."

"It's as good a theory as any," I admitted, promising myself to check it out much more thoroughly. Like I said, Annette wasn't a stupid lady.

"@$%#&# synapse!" she concluded.

So Annette and I became friends, never close, always a little wary, but friends. Allies at times. Never enemies.

With Lyons it would be different. And with Mike! But that's another whole chapter. Right before the one where I became a great football star, a scientific genius, a Wall Street Mogul, and *then* took over the world as Benevolent Dictator for Life.

DUEL ON INTERSTATE FIVE

A t 5:17 a.m. my Solara Convertible woke me up.

"What's going on?" I asked, groggy as hell. I'd kicked down an Ambien-Dopo 75 at 1:00 a.m., intending to sleep through until Downtown Sunnyvale, with an injected Caf-kick-up for a 9:00 a.m. meeting at Paleo-Genetech's Main Office.

"Emergency," Sol reported. "Stranded individual."

"Here?"

"A few klicks up the road."

"Unsmear the windows," I ordered and they became transparent again. Very few overhead floaters. The in-road tracking beams were standard for Ay-Eye Transport. I couldn't make out much outside, not even an incipient dawn.

"Sol, where the hell are we?" I had to ask.

"Interstate Five. Thirteen miles off the Hanford Exchange Route 198."

"In other words, nowhere."

"Nowhere!" she confirmed.

"So how the hell could there be...?" And I thought about it: stranded.

"One individual. Female. Young," Sol reported, then, "According to the California Motorist By-Law Amendments of February, Twenty Twenty-four, any stranded motorist must be..."

"...picked up by the next available vehicle," I continued. I'd actually read the goddamn amendments and passed the stringent, recently regiven motorist's exam, being one out every ten drivers who took it and passed and could thus be privately driven.

"She's been there eighteen minutes," Sol reported.

Meaning we were the first vehicle in that time on this interstate. Even given that it was 5:00 a.m.…it seemed that even fewer people were driving than a few months ago. That had been the state Senate's intent, after all, in passing the law.

"So stop for her," I ordered.

I sat up, the front seat folded up to normal for me, and I heard and smelled Sol vacuum and perfume the backseat area, getting it ready for company.

"Aren't you glad I restocked the bar and fridge in Van Nuys?" Sol asked.

Nine minutes later Sol slowed, and there at the side of the road, sitting on two large silver robo-bags, was the stranded young woman.

I let Sol announce what was going on and got an irritated "Yeah, yeah" from her as she ordered Sol to open the trunk. The bags rolled themselves over and flipped themselves into the gaping trunk (servo engines at each wheel leaves a trunk the size of a sixties Eldorado's). The strandee got into the backseat. She was young, pretty, and pissed off, wearing a half-chain, half-silk facial veil and what passes among the North Hollywood Junior Set as trendy clothing.

"Your host," Sol announced, "is Mizz…"

Both Sol and I expected at least a thank you.

What we got was "Well, just as long as you stay up there and keep your hands to yourself."

To which I turned and very personably said, "I don't do women. So you're safe, girlie!"

That earned me a surprised glare. Then she settled in.

"This is nice. What is it? A Twenty-four?" she asked.

"Latest model. Twenty Twenty-six," Sol announced while I looked the strandee over. She was very pouty. Boob job. Medium-priced Valley face job. Who knew what other work?

"We're headed to Silicon Valley by way of the 152. We can leave you off anywhere between here and there and/or put you onto public transportation."

"I'm going to Emeryville," she said in annoyance.

I figured she was headed up to shop at the six-hundred-store mall there. Either that or get work there.

"We'll put you on a Coastal Cal Rail at Sunnyvale," I said. The sooner the better, I thought.

"What happened to your vehicle, miss?" Sol politely asked. There was no such thing in sight.

"Jacked!" she said.

"We'll call the local authorities," Sol said.

"Don't bother, it was legal. Sort of. I lost it a duel."

"You lost your vehicle in a road duel?" Sol asked. I kept staring. She didn't look to be on any of the newer meth derivs. What the hell would make a young woman road duel in this Obama-forsaken county? I couldn't help myself from asking:

"You lost in a road duel with a local shit-kicker? What were you driving? An Escalade?"

"No, it was a post-production high-revving Prius. A Twenty Twenty-two. The dueler was good. Actually *they* were good. It was a double-duel."

Then she looked right into Sol's visual unit and said, "You could take them both easy with this boat."

"Road dueling is against statutes eighty-six ay and bee, as well as being totally contraindicated in amendments thirty-six and forty-four," Sol said.

"Bite my labia!" was the strandee's response.

"Let's go, Sol," I said, chuckling.

Sol wasn't giving up yet on conversation. "What do you think, miss? Will Chelsea Clinton take the presidency?"

"What?"

"Or will it be Governor Lohan?"

"I hate that old bitch!" was her response. "Both of those old bitches!"

I resisted the impulse to say that she might someday be an equally "old" bitch.

"What kinds of high do you have in here?" she asked.

"Three percent alcohol."

"I'll need a gallon for a buzz! Okay, give me some."

At 5:45 a.m. Sol announced, "Two vehicles on an intersect course from the right on a two-lane unmarked road."

The dueling duo, looking for a little more action.

"We'll just miss them. Or...? We could make contact in seven minutes and thirteen seconds," Sol reported.

"Slow down to meet them," I said.

"That's the guys I dueled," the strandee said from the backseat.

One of them was driving a souped-up-looking Civic Hyper-Fuse, painted glittery bronze; the other was in a cut-down Sonata with nothing stock about it: matte gray-green, like one of those institutional trash cans you see outside a hospital.

"We're being hailed," Sol reported.

"Put them on split screen," I said, and looked into the monitor.

From behind me, I heard the strandee say in an insinuating voice, "You can take them! They're nothing but bullshit!"

Two young men I guessed to be maybe eighteen with big hair and the current "frozen" hairdos and nothing in the way of upper-body clothing to hide their hard flat pecs and abs appeared on Vid, smiling and joking.

"Hey! SoCal Vehicle and Citizen! Care to race?" the blonder of the two said.

When I half turned I could see our passenger had moved herself out of view. Hmmm. Ashamed? Or something else? Did they have a not-so-nice history?

Sol took over and gave them all the legal manual stuff against dueling.

"Yeah, we know all that," Blondie replied. "But we've never raced such a superhotredmojo Solara Semi-Pro like yourdownself, babe!"

"I'll take this, Sol."

Into the Vid I said, "Hello, boyz. Are you sure you're old enough to drive? You even have licenses?"

That riled the dark-haired one. He had the more kissable mouth. But I liked the blond's armpits.

He smiled and said, "We're totally legit! Ask your Sol."

"Well, Boss, they've slaved some pseudos that are fully legit," Sol announced, to neither of our surprise.

"What's the prize when I win, boyz?"

"You get one of our superslickcinnabon cars, is your prize, in the unlikely event."

"No thanks, what else you got?" And before they could act surprised, "How about your cherry, yo Blond One? Or has that already been picked by your Horny Hick-Daddy already?"

Astonishment, extreme anger, then a bit of guile crossed both faces.

Blondie recovered first. "Can I see what my future lover lady looks like?" he had the extreme gumption to reply.

Sol sent my standard film-clip résumé with voice-over: quality all the way.

"Oh, so I'm gonna be ravished by some totally together Hollyweird Babe Mogul!" was Blondie's response. "Well, if I gotta go…"

Using "ravished" was a nice touch, I thought.

"I swear I'll be gentle. At first."

"Then let's have our cars draw up a dueling contract!"

"Sol, do it."

From the backseat suddenly I heard, "Don't. These guys fight dirty. They've got throw hooks and jet-nets and even have those extendable wheel cutters. They trashed my car and almost killed me. Don't do it!"

"Did you hear that, Sol?"

"They seem reprehensible, at best," was Sol's comment.

"At best. Amend the contract."

"They don't want your car," she continued from the backseat. "They've got some hack shop and—"

"Sol," I interrupted, "is that contract ready?"

"Drawn up and witnessed. Now I need your handprint. There we go, ma'am."

"Really, guys! This is a nice car. Don't do it," she insisted.

"What'll happen to you, if we lose? Raped again?"

"Just let me out somewhere," was her answer.

"Right here. Before the race," I agreed. She'd gone from all she-devil to all-snivel awfully fast.

"It's your funeral!" she said as her bags tumbled themselves out and hobbled away. I waved at her. Sol sped up to meet the two cars.

The two boyz were revving and I slid up between them. They smiled and gave fingers up. They even let Sol announce the take-off.

We all took off, and then Sol slowed down and they sped up and laughed and howled and we could hear them over the Vid screaming and laughing.

That was when Sol lifted off the ground, put on her thrusters, and boom, before you knew it, we were at the finish line.

In fact, I was standing outside Sol, waiting for them at the finish line when they skidded to get off the road and onto the soft shoulders of the northbound eight-laner.

Alas for them, Sol had already seeded the road between us with little tire-damaging units so we heard their cars go plop, plop, plop, plop. The vehicles skidded into very bad spun-out stops.

The two guys exited fast and began to make a run for it, in opposite directions. That's when their car nets shot out and grabbed them both, one by the belt, the other by the foot. That had been written into the race contract too, although I guess they didn't read Sol's fine print. They were thrown to the ground.

The two were all netted around and kind of stunned when I reached them.

"Sorry, boyz. But you lost!"

"You cheated," the dark-haired one said first. I pulled his net over to the open trunk where Sol hoisted him in, asking if he was comfortable as she injected him with a non-lethal narco. He would be held in reserve for later on.

Blondie was sputtering and spitting when I reached him. It took a bit more to get him into the recently vacated backseat, but then Sol *is* a convertible.

He was injected, and Sol took off, with me back there too.

"You young guys really have to get off your Vids and *read* more! Especially read more carefully your car news," I lectured mildly. "The Twenty Twenty-six Solara is all new! With loads of extras!"

"You're not really going to do what you said, right?" Blondie asked, his voice beginning to slur with the injection.

"A contract's a contract!" I said and began to remove not the netting, but much of his already road-torn denim.

Three hours later, when we dropped the two of them off at the Sunnyvale Coastal Cal rail station with paid tickets back home, they were almost fully awake again.

And an hour later, it was as good a business meeting in Sunnyvale as I'd hoped it would be.

As we were stepping out of the building the CFO said, "I can drop you off at the airport."

"I drove," I said and pointed to Solara.

"Isn't driving kind of old-fashioned?" he asked.

"It is," I admitted. "But sometimes I'm an old-fashioned kind of gal. And then, how else can you interact so closely with the local wildlife?"

SPICES OF THE WORLD

The little square he had been directed to lay unfashionably northeast of St. Paul's Cathedral and Ludgate Hill, a forlorn small plaza with an unclipped, irregular common and a few dilapidated wrought-iron benches deeply set in weeds. Row houses glowered on each side, four landings tall and built in the era of the Reform Act, displaying—at least in their exterior detail—that the area had once been populous, and more than likely genteel. Generous oyster shells of water troughs for awaiting carriage horses, arabesques of concrete balustrades cracked here and there and so poorly mended their iron framework showed through, other details of external trim—pilasters and false Doricisms—in pretentious abundance. All had fallen into an inexorable slow disrepair. Only one of the surrounding rows looked recently painted, and that a bilious brown. The other three slabs of buildings peeled coats of *fin de siècle* canary to reveal previous coats of Prussian blue, questionable lavender, even the original dusky brickwork.

The minute they arrived at the address David had given, the cab driver called out that he would wait. Doubtless, he sensed as strongly as David that this was hardly the type of neighborhood a well-dressed passenger would wish to remain stranded in. As soon as David stepped out of the Austin Princess and looked about, he couldn't be certain whether or not he'd imagined quickly hidden stares from behind grimy windows through curtains unironed for a decade. When he turned to the driver for confirmation of what he thought he'd seen, he was met by the indifferent headlines of a lurid daily scandal sheet.

V.R. Bardash, Spices of the World, was only one of several shops dug into below-street-level openings on the southern—and gloomiest— row of the square, and the only one still open for business. Signs in English, Arabic, and what he took to be Urdu and Pali script declared the place and its wares: "Peppers, Salts, Cumins, Corianders, Gingers, Turmerics, Nutmegs, Cloves, Chilis of All Varieties, Sizes, and Powers" read its enigmatic advertisement, causing David to wonder exactly how many different sorts of ginger and clove actually existed.

He pushed open one of the filthy, narrow, mullioned doors into a tiny, narrow shop. The single room seemed lighted by two high windows that opened to God only knew where—certainly not onto the streetside, which had been without any apparent venting. In the strong, sharply defined late-afternoon sunlight, the air seemed so filled with particles of dust he immediately began to cough before realizing it wasn't dust but instead the powdery emanations of hundred of spices that he was breathing: a cacophony of odors so overwhelming as to stop him briefly, his hands still on the door handle, exhaling forcefully to retain a clear head.

Tall, mostly bare, sagging wooden shelves on either wall dominated the shop. About halfway down their great height and centrally placed as though to spotlight them, three or four small, cellophane-wrapped packages huddled together, their garishly printed boxfronts and indecipherable writing declaring them unquestionably of Eastern provenance, if in no way explicating their contents. Two long, sagging deal counters fronted the shelves, extending virtually from front to back of the shop. These were less sparsely laden, with small sacks, their hempen edges rolled back to reveal brown lengths of vanilla beans, knobs of mahogany-colored cloves, baby cannonballs of nutmeg and allspice, twisted tiny tan mannequins of ginger root, and long yellow strips of dried papaya and other fruit, unrecognizable to David in this form. The extremely limited floor space was reduced to a single, nearly impassable aisle leading to a discolored paisley curtain, which no doubt opened upon an office or living quarters. Knee-high rucksacks of other spices—among them giant balls of green peppers, but most of them unknown to David and more than a little otherworldly in shape and hue—crowded about his legs, more or less tripping him into immobility by threatening to spill over with each step he took attempting to brush past.

In the fortnight since the letter from Lahore arrived with its urgent request from the Mazudrah family, David had been all over London and several of its more squalid suburbs attempting to locate his old friend—and failing most emphatically. Something indefinable besides the actual contents of the fractured English of the communication had suggested that Rajinder was in serious trouble, political trouble perhaps, something to do with Sikhs and sects and bombs and assassinations half a world away. How this could be, David wasn't certain. Although he hadn't seen Raji in almost four years, surely the clever, overintelligent philosopher who could minutely dissect Kant and Wittgenstein, who derided nationalism as "the folly of the senses in our century," couldn't have changed so utterly? Could he?

So far, David's quest had not answered that question satisfactorily. On the debit side, there had been that slender, red-nosed, whining barrister, Monica something-or-other, who gushed close to an hour about Raji's work with the Ealing factory workers, only to admit she hadn't seen or heard from him in months. Not to mention that arthritically deformed, garrulous railway man in East Grinstead with whom Raji had boarded as recently as six months ago, and who'd insisted to David that there was "no wog born good as the lad," despite his intimations that Raji's bedsitter had also been a meeting place once a week of several unsavory types. "They told me they were studying the niceties of the Mahabharata, whatever that is," the old railway pensioner had said. "But some of them toffs didn't look like they read more than the pony listings, if you get my drift."

On the plus side, David would have to place Mrs. Arrowhead, an aging, pincushion-shaped secretary of the United Baptist Mission to the heathen, where Raji had worked almost two years. She'd been unstinting in her praise of young Mazudrah—"Such a good example to the neighboring West Indians he was. Liked his tea strong, always a sign of a God-fearing man. After he came to us, we had no more break-ins or vandalisms." Mrs. Arrowhead said she'd been delighted when Raji took the post in the bursar's office at Brighton College, even though it meant the mission losing him. Ian McQuith, head bursar at the seaside institution, had nothing but praise for the young man, insisting that without Raji's help they would never have reorganized their past decade of files. Yet even McQuith had wondered aloud over some of the more "sinister types—actors and suchlike" at the college in whose company Raji was often to be found. And Mrs. Arrowhead had insinuated that she hadn't ever discovered the methods whereby Mazudrah had intimidated the local toughs from harassing the Mission.

A checkered recent past, David had to admit, quite different than what he'd expected of his brilliant pal. And now, all leads to Rajinder's whereabouts seemed to have ended as though he'd evaporated into the sky, as the prophet Elijah was said to have done, taken up in a chariot of fire. David had thought to hire a private investigator. But if for some reason—good or otherwise—Raji was in hiding, a stranger's inquiries would send him even deeper into hiding. Whereas word of David looking for him ought to be far less threatening. Even so, the search had been long enough and sufficiently fruitless that he'd fallen back to this address, the first one Raji had ever had in England. Should this fail, David would have to concede defeat and write back to Lahore with the bad news.

Although he'd jangled the shop bell as he'd entered, no one had responded. David cautiously stepped back and once more roughly rang the bell, peering into the dusty corners to see if any object reacted.

He'd just decided the shop was abandoned when the paisley curtain was furled back an inch from one lower edge and a large pair of frightened dark eyes looked out at him so briefly that he'd scarcely gotten over his surprise when the face was gone again.

"Hello? Anyone here?" he called out. "Mr. Bardash?"

The curtains ballooned out a bit before a small stout figure stepped out and made a sketch of a salaam: the owner of the dark eyes—or rather of a remarkable pair of pistachio-colored eyes, large eyes, childlike eyes.

"Good afternoon, Sahib!" the man's voice fluted in a ridiculously high register for an adult. "Can I be of assistance to you in your purchase of many spices?"

"I was looking for Mr. Bardash, Mr. V.R. Bardash," David said, watching the turbanned, rotund little man pick his way toward him easily enough through what had recently seemed impossible-to-get-around paths of overflowing sacks.

"Deceased!" the man chirped, joyful as a robin at daybreak.

Before David could react, the man moved deftly behind a nearby counter and smilingly sung out, "I am Mr. V.R. Bardash's nephew, R.J. Bardash. Perhaps you will not be too unforgiving if I offer to assist you in your selection of spice purchases, taking the place of my distinguished uncle. I cannot pretend to his vast knowledge of each and every variety, alas," he twittered merrily, "for I have not personally journeyed to all of the many spice islands in the several hemispheres whence they derive." He all but sparkled as he added, "Yet I will attempt my greatest endeavors."

"Actually, I'm not looking for any spices."

"Not looking for any spices." Bardash giggled, as though David were clearly making a joke.

"Fascinating as they seem to be," David conceded. "I'm actually looking for a person."

"Fascinating indeed are spices." Bardash twinkled. "This, for example. I wonder, can you tell me what it is?" He held a longish well-dried-out gourd, slightly bent in the middle and speckled brown against a more general ecru color.

"Why no, I'm afraid not."

"Neither can I." He sniggered. "It has been in this shop for years. Since I was a boy. Mr. V.R. Bardash knew what it was. But he would not tell. Even as he lay breathing his last, I pleaded, 'Uncle, esteemed uncle, I beg you, tell me what the object is, in what it consists, what it contains.' He would not tell. I thought perhaps *inside*." Bardash shook the gourd and something did seem to rattle within. "Ought I chop it open, do you recommend?" he sang out in countertenor, making a machete-like motion with his tiny fist. "Or is it better to leave it as it arrived, unchopped?"

He seemed to hesitate, as though David could answer him. In fact, David was about to say yes, by all means, chop it open to see what's within, when the shop owner interrupted.

"Yet…if I chop it open, I may not be able to sell it. And who knows if what is within will then go quickly to rot. But perhaps one day some distinguished person like yourself will step into this ship, see the object, and cry out, 'Aha! There! That'—whatever its name will prove to be—'that is *exactly* what I've been searching for!'" Bardash's eyes glittered in merriment and potential profit. "And then I will know what it is, and I will still be able to sell it. Don't you think?"

Unable to follow the little man well enough to know what to think, never mind how to answer, David merely said, "Perhaps you have a point there. I was asking about Mr. Mazudrah. An old friend of mine. I believe he used to lodge with your uncle. At least this was the name and address he gave. Mr. Rajinder Mazudrah?"

"Then again," Bardash giggled, "what if no one does eventually come into the shop to identify the object. What then? Eh? It is possible, you will admit. Even likely, given the fact that as yet no one *has* come in to identify its properties or better still, to purchase it."

David was beginning to feel as though some test were being proposed to him, a code whose secret he did not know. Once more he was about to say yes, that by all means Bardash ought to chop open the blasted thing, when the diminutive, round spice merchant wagged a doubly beringed index finger at him.

"What then? I'll tell you! Then I will still have the ambiguous pleasure of possessing a mystery. There is much pleasure in possessing a mystery, don't you think?"

"Yes, of course there is," David assented, relieved he'd not fallen into the trap. "Very wise of you indeed. Now, about Mr. Mazudrah? You know him?"

"The name is not entirely unfamiliar."

"Rajinder Mazudrah is his full name. Or at least, all of his names he provided us with." David felt suddenly on uncertain ground. Had Raji another name? A middle name? Or more than one? Had it been a kindness, a courtesy on his part, to merely give out the usual Occidental two names, instead of a string of them as he might have in his country? And what if there were some honorary title he'd also possessed, all unknown to David, who, having failed to provide it to this man now, was in fact insulting Raji or offending both countrymen?

Only slightly daunted by these new questions, David decided to go on. "Mr. Mazudrah used to work as a tailor for my father before he went to university in Manchester. Mr. Wechsler. Of Wechsler's Fine Haberdashery on Regent Street? Say four years ago?"

"An estimable business, haberdashery," was Bardash's cryptic response.

"We were friends, Raji and I," David tried. It was possible this fellow thought David was a constable or government copper in plain clothes, and that Raji was in some sort of official trouble. "He used to board with your uncle, he told us. Or at least at this address. He gave my father this address."

"Alas!" He seemed genuinely affected. "I myself did not reside here with Mr. V.R. Bardash four years ago. But upon a neighboring square. With my cousin, Mr. L.S. Bardash."

"I see. I must find Mr. Mazudrah. It's a matter of some importance."

"I think not," Bardash chirruped happily.

"You think not what? That he's here?"

"Oh, you are an *amusing* gentleman. Who could be here but myself?"

"Naturally, I didn't mean to imply that you were hiding him."

"*Most* amusing gentleman." Bardash tittered into his tiny, fat fist.

"You do know of whom I'm speaking?" David felt he had to ask.

"Yes, surely, I do. Mr. Rajinder Mazudrah, who used to live with my uncle some four years ago or so, or nearby, who used to work for your father, Mr. Wechsler, of Wechsler's Fine Haberdashery upon Regent Street."

"Good," David concluded, somewhat relieved, until he realized that the spice vendor hadn't told him anything about Mazudrah that he, David, hadn't already a minute past just told Bardash. "Perhaps, perhaps I ought describe him?"

The large pistachio-hued eyes twinkled in merry agreement.

"Well, first of all," David began, "Raji was, well, somewhere between yourself and myself."

"That cannot be," Bardash sputtered, "for then we would see him!"

"I meant, of course, in height!" David clarified. Was it language or intelligence that was at issue between them? "In height," he repeated, "he was neither short, like yourself, nor tall, like myself." Equally inane: Such a description might signify any of a million men in London. "Lightly complected, he was," David went on, a bit more unsteadily, "like yourself. Or rather, not so olive-complected as yourself. Yet not so ruddily complected as myself."

"Yes? Yes?" Bardash urged, all ears.

"Well, I don't know what else." What else indeed. That in age, Mazudrah was somewhere between the two of them, as he appeared to be in ethnicity, and… "You are certain you know the man of whom I speak?" he again asked.

"With such a description, how could I not?"

"Then, perhaps, you could tell me where Mr. Mazudrah might be. It's rather urgent that I see him."

"I think not," the little man sang out.

"You think not because you don't know? Is that what you're saying?"

"I wonder," Bardash held up a small brown knob of a thing, "if you can perhaps tell me what this object is?"

"You're saying you don't know where he is? Or that you do know and you won't tell me?"

"Neither, Sahib." He seemed offended now. "I clearly said neither of the two."

"But you clearly said, 'I think not.'"

"Indeed, Sahib. And did you take that to mean that I know of Mazudrah's whereabouts and yet will not tell you?"

As David no longer knew what he'd meant, he merely gaped at the Asian, who once more picked up the small brown object.

"It is perhaps somewhat like this object," Bardash mused, his voice restored to its more usual chirruping manner. "I beg you, hazard a guess what it might be?"

Indifferently, David said, "I haven't a clue."

"A Jerusalem ar-ti-choke!" He tittered. "So many things we may not know because they have in some manner changed. And how should you know a dried ar-ti-choke when you come upon one? No, believe me, Sahib, it is far better to possess a mystery. Even an ambiguous mystery. Far more valuable," he trilled.

"Is there *anyone* who might be able to tell me where Mr. Mazudrah may be now?" David tried and as the little man merely smiled and rolled the obscene, dried artichoke from one hand to another he added, "Are you trying to say to me that Raji is transformed in some dramatic and unrecognizable manner?"

"You are *truly* an amusing gentleman. I was simply speaking of ar-ti-chokes. I wonder, can you tell me what this other object may be?"

"You needn't be afraid for his sake, you know. We were great friends," he added.

"Were you indeed, Sahib?"

"I mean to say, we were great friends at one time."

"Four years ago, you said, Sahib?"

"Yes. But we never had a falling-out or anything of that sort, you understand. He merely up and left."

"Up and left, Sahib?"

"Just up and left. Although I assure you we were *great* friends."

"So I understand."

"One remains friendly after four years, you know. Even after one has just up and left, you see. It does happen. He wouldn't be purposely hiding from me, therefore. There's no earthly reason for him to do so. He hasn't an idea I'm even here looking for him, you must grasp. There would be nothing in the world to even suggest that after four years, upon some whim or other, I'd suddenly come looking for him, would there now? Would there? *Would there*, I ask you?"

David's head throbbed with possibilities he'd never before entertained, thoughts which had come spewing into his mind simultaneous with his absurd bout of self-defense. What if Raji was actively hiding from him? What if he didn't wish to be found? By anyone? What if all this was some sort of blind? A smokescreen? And he, David, a complete ass to have come here, to have tracked him this far, to this ridiculous shop with this inane spice seller?

"Of course not, Sahib. Not if you say not," Bardash sweetly enough answered. In his hand he now held a small repellent greenish object, sort of a cross between a dried-out lizard and a hairy plant. "I wonder, Sahib, if you can tell me what this object is?"

David could only stare. Three objects. Three tests. As in some mad Oriental tale. David had already soundly failed the first two. Gaping at the object before him, he knew that once again he wouldn't be able to even hint at what it was—some rare medicinal root? Some large, specially preserved caterpillar?—and failing to answer that question too, he would be ridiculed, humiliated, and who only knew, perhaps asked to identify another and another more outlandish even than these. Before he could reach across the counter and throttle the little beggar, he spun around and was outside the doors, leaping up the steps, and into the square.

Inexplicably—how long had he been in the shop?—the cab was gone. The square abandoned.

He could have sworn the driver had said he would wait for him, had put up a newspaper and begun reading the telly listings. And now he was gone! David was certain he saw a sari behind one of the curtained windows flash orangebright into and out of view on the floor directly above V.R. Bardash, Spices of the World.

An appalling thought crossed his mind. That last object…was it… could it possibly be…a scalp? A human scalp? Raji's scalp?

He turned to face the shop doors' grime-stained windows. They didn't seem in any way different; yet, as a result of his going in through them and meeting Bardash and asking questions and being asked questions and…they were now quite ghastly different. As though some dark deed carefully withheld until these past few minutes and his arrival here could no longer wait but must be accomplished with all haste, and with utter ruthlessness.

He rushed down the steps to the shop door and shook the handle. It was locked, damn it. And though he rang the bell and rattled the door and could hear the shop bell echo shrilly within, no one answered.

When he finally, defeated, ascended back to the street, many curtained windows in the row above the shop were filled with veiled faces openly—mockingly, he was sure of it—staring down at him.

Suddenly, and with an unshakable certainty, David knew he would never see his friend again. He thought he should shout something at them all, that he was going to find a bobby, a dozen bobbies and half of Scotland Yard, and come back until he found Raji. But as he watched, all the curtains fell closed, shades dropped. Filled with horror and despair, he turned and began to walk away, feeling the curtains once move a half inch open behind him, the shades lift a bit, the eyes once again observe, watching, laughing.

Hastening now, and damning his legs for moving so slowly, barely able to restrain himself from breaking into a full run, certain that if he dared turn and look back, there would be footsteps behind him, men in poorly wrapped turbans and filthy *dhotis*. His breath came on tighter, a stitch had begun to rip into his side. And now he did begin to run, to run until he was approaching the end of the infernal row, and around an accursed building, out of the hellish square.

He dashed across a narrow lane and dared himself to stop, to stop, and look back. Damn it! He wouldn't be made a fool of by some despicable Pakis.

He steeled himself, stopped, and turned, panting like a cur. A dark figure he'd not noticed collided with him.

"So sorry!" David uttered, courtesy rising mechanically to the occasion.

The man who pulled away was short and turbanned, with a flowing bright *dhoti*.

"I wonder," the voice said in a remarkable basso voice. "Could you tell me...?"

David didn't remain for the rest of the question, didn't even look at the questioner. He was running, running, running now for sanity, for his very life, down the narrow lane and into the next street, running directly into the blaring horn and brightly red bonnet of an oncoming omnibus.

EYE

This morning's edition of *El Nacional de Caracas* noted the death of astrophysicist Jose-Martí de Rigoberto y Alain with a long tribute to his many accomplishments that the earlier Internet obituary glossed over in its effort to be timely.

With Professor Rigoberto's death, my twelve-year-old promise to him and to the others in the Puruana Laboratory has come to an end.

Professor Umberto Ventano died four years ago in a rented single-engine Cessna, somewhere around the Iguaçu Falls in a still not adequately explained flight and fatal accident. Dr. Santiago del Cuerco went missing from his home in Maracaibo a year after, leaving a garbled note that suggested that his sanity had fled some time before he physically decamped. He's since been declared legally dead.

We had all promised never to reveal what happened in that laboratory we all shared overlooking the pellucid lapis waters of the *golfo* during the first few days of July 2001. More precisely, our promise concerned the small, prismatic torus of unknown material and origin that we discovered in connection with the El Tigre Meteorite—so named because it was first spotted in its descent over that jungle area.

The meteorite was seen shooting across the sky and then falling spectacularly—witnessed by many thousands in the cities of Caracas and Maracay, the towns of Valencia, Carora, and Calimas. It was recovered by the Venezuelan Coast Guard on the shore of the Golfo de Venezuela and sent to our laboratory in Puento Fijo for analysis.

I wrote "our" laboratory, although it was Professor Rigoberto y Alain's lab. The other two men had already worked with him: del Cuerco at NASA in Houston a decade before, Ventano for ten months at the Pasadena Jet Propulsion Lab even earlier. So I was the newcomer, just graduated with a master's degree from the University of Venezuela's College of Applied Physical Sciences and still far from completing my Ph.D.

When the meteorite arrived at the lab, del Cuerco joked, "Here it is, Georgie-Boy"—my given name is Jorge—"your Ph.D. thesis itself, in person, all wrapped up with ribbons and bigger than life."

One reason for the sensation caused by the meteorite was its size. Most meteorites that reach Earth in one or more pieces are small. Showing video clips of it falling not an hour after the event on national television, the nightly weatherman had described it as "a green-gold flaming moon!" So it seemed, photographed by many as it fell at around ten p.m. on a beautiful balmy night on May First, one of our bigger holidays. So many people had been out in the streets that it was widely witnessed.

When recovered, the object measured some four and a half by six meters, and weighed close to three tons. It was of a dark brown and charcoal gray color, with a few small streaks of what appeared to be ferrous red.

El Tigre had spent most of the two months before its arrival in a completely sterile lockdown in some undisclosed location, thanks to the vigilance—del Cuerco said due to the paranoia—of the Venezuelan Armed Forces and the Academy of Science. We were assured that it had been already subjected to a wide range of preliminary chemical, physical, and biological tests. All of which proved it to be totally inert and safe to be handled "without extraordinary measures required."

Our job was to distinguish El Tigre's exact composition and any special properties it might contain. It was a fortuitous task for us because of the fame of the meteorite. But not a terribly difficult task, since recovered meteorites tend to be pretty similar. Their makeup falls within a small number of acceptable parameters familiar to any high school student with Internet access. Even so, when it arrived, every magnet in the lab immediately went screwy and all of them were removed.

All this to explain Professor Rigoberto y Alain's decision to allow me, the youngest and least experienced of the four, to work with El Tigre. He and the others were already involved with other projects they deemed more interesting. So I received what they thought of as the rather humdrum object.

It remains unclear to this day why after this two-month period of time El Tigre reacted as it did, although I've developed a few tenuous theories. Over the decade and more since, on the rare occasions that two or more of us happened to be in a room together—at some party or conference, say—we would invariably speculate upon this question, among so many other ones; del Cuerco most often, and at times with the most bizarre notions that he would present with a great cackling laugh. But after all he was the most affected by its arrival.

Lest this preamble seem to be mere procrastination, I'll announce what is to follow: the taped journals I myself as a new lab assistant faithfully kept, day by day, at the end, and sometimes in the middle of, each workday. With them any other writing from the others in the Puruana Lab that I later learned of or had access to—e-mails, etc.—for the six-day period involved.

I wish to reiterate that the meteorite did *not* provide my thesis subject. And also wish to state again that I never spoke about El Tigre or what had happened to us to anyone outside of the Puruana Lab nor even *inside* the lab after that first week had passed—unless, that is, one of the others first brought up the subject.

❖

July 2nd, 2___

"El Tigre" arrived yesterday and was set up in the larger of the two rooms that represent the outer chambers of the laboratory here. Because of its name, I expected the meteorite to look somewhat extraordinary—perhaps even tiger-striped. It does not. It looks like any other meteorite that I have seen in a museum: dark, inert, un-intriguing.

All of us except Prof Rig were out when it arrived last night, delivered by some cohort of the Armed Forces which had held it, and so I was the second of us four to see it in person, right after I arrived in the morning. I peered in at it through the separating triple-paned glass.

When I had gotten over my initial disappointment for its extreme ordinariness, I met with the others in the little breakfast room. Over packaged desserts and the strong Dominican coffee that Prof Rig prefers, I received my instructions.

"As you know, Jorge," the prof began, "the Americans found what they claim to be fossilized proto-annelids and/or pre-bacterial life from Mars on that meteorite that dropped onto Antarctica a few years back. It's still in doubt what they actually found. An ice sheet that extensive is supposed to be a natural sterilizing room…But who is certain! Your job will be to photograph El Tigre entirely, using ordinary and first-level micron cameras, and also to dust it, and remove anything that appears to be extrinsic. After we have completely mapped it, square inch by square inch, we will decide where and using which methods we can take extremely thin slices of it to look at more closely under second-level, or even the electron microscope."

"It looks damaged," I remarked. "There appears to be a very thin centrally running fissure equally from each vertical side on what is now the top, and all down the left side right to the plinth it rests upon, and possibly even beneath."

"Really?" Prof Rig asked. "I didn't notice that last night. But it was so late and they made such a fuss that I never got that close to it."

"It landed where, exactly?" Ventano asked. "On a sandy beach, I heard."

"A beach almost directly across the gulf from the lab here. Saltwater sand can be a fairly sterile medium," Prof Rig said. "Of course, not as perfectly so as antipodean glacial ice. The Armed Forces tells us that El Tigre was physically contained and removed from its landing site within twenty minutes of its touch-down. They were afraid of UFO nuts and looters. They also secured and tarp-covered the arrival spot."

"Georgie-boy is going to be hunting for pre-Cambrian life!" del Cuerco said, and corrected himself, "Pre-Solar life!" before stuffing himself with his third McDonald's apple fritter.

I joined the laughter of the others at this quip.

However, soon after I followed orders and self-sterilized completely. I then put on what passes for Haz-Mat gear in the lab before I actually stepped into the room holding El Tigre, my awkward tent-like outfit dangling with various sterilized cameras and measuring tools. I must have looked a sight!

From ten fifteen a.m. to two p.m. and again after lunch and siesta, from four p.m. to seven, I photographed El Tigre and dusted it. It was a boring job, worse than routine. Except that when I was done for the evening, the hairline crack I'd noticed looked somehow wider. I decided to measure that crack in four places, all of which I then tagged, and I noted these measurements down for Prof Rig to check over.

I looked at it under the micron electroscope and it looked geologically apt: nothing special at all.

July 3rd, 2___

The media greeted us as we arrived this morning, Prof Rig first in his big Chevrolet sport utility, shortly after del Cuerco zoomed up in his silver Mercedes coupe and Ventano noisily arrived on his futuristic-looking motorcycle. I was ignored arriving in my little old sedan.

Besides reporters and photographers from Telvisora Nacional, Televisia and Radio Caracas Television, there was a news team truck from our local television station as well as from Television de Zulia.

For two hours they had us posing, having us re-arrive at the lab in our vehicles, sitting at our little communal breakfast, inside various offices, at blackboards showing the trajectory of El Tigre along with allegedly relevant formulas and information ("for the Science Nerds," a pleasant enough dyed blond female TV reporter explained), and finally, and most crucially, posing next to El Tigre itself.

The Puruana Lab has two Haz-Mat suits, and I and Prof Rig began suiting up and we were photographed alongside El Tigre—from the outside corridor looking in. But even this wasn't enough for the media, and no sooner had we left and unsuited than we returned to find them busily videotaping and photographing Ventano and del Cuerco inside and along with El Tigre and without the Haz-Mat suits. The two of them were joking around, leaning all over it, del Cuerco licking the surface and giving a thumbs up for one photographer, and engaged in other nonsense.

I could see Prof Rig's little pointed beard trembling with anger at this foolery and he managed to get the media away from the meteorite fairly rapidly, and our colleagues soon left off their antics and went back to their offices.

Editor's note: Late at night, when my children are long abed and my wife too is sleeping, I remain awake sometimes an hour or so remembering it all. And every time, my memory comes back to this moment, this unexpected and conscious disregard of the Lab's sterilization procedures, this direct contact of human flesh with El Tigre. I cannot say it is responsible for what occurred. That would imply an intelligence or activity in something that seemed merely material. Even so. It may in some way explain, if not what happened to us, then at least what happened to Ventano and del Cuerco in years after, and why two formerly completely staid and reputable scientists became so extreme in their behavior as to end up as they did: one dead in a plane accident, the other vanished.

After the media had left, the others went to work and Prof Rig and I spent about an hour and half going over the forty-five photos I had taken of the meteorite, which I meanwhile had scanned and downloaded to the Mac.

We settled on two areas that looked to be "flaking," either as a result of the trauma of El Tigre's atmospheric descent or as a by-product of some other unknown event(s) while in transit. One of these was completely surface in location. But the second one he decided upon was within what seemed to be a natural indentation at the top, and in fact near where I had first noticed the running crack yesterday. Prof Rig was especially anxious that I obtain that slice of material.

I once again suited up and went into the room containing El Tigre.

The first thing I noticed was that the fissure I had noticed the day it arrived had unquestionably opened further. All four points I had tagged it were now twice as wide. I thought this notable and planned to tell Prof Rig at the first opportunity.

I had brought with me tools for the removal of the "flakes" of material we had decided upon. The first one was removed easily and in fact seemed to be just that, some previous ferric "rusting" that had flaked sometime earlier or in its last aerial transit.

Prof Rig and I looked at the material together, once I was back out, using the micron electroscope. It appears geologically appropriate, not special at all.

I mentioned the widening of the fissure and he looked at me and said, "They probably leaned on it too hard in their lust to be on television." I didn't know how to take that quite unusual criticism, and so I did not respond.

He was meeting someone for lunch, and the others had already gone out for theirs, so I remained in the lab, lunching on a sandwich and fruit I'd brought. I napped for twenty-seven minutes in the breakfast room.

They were all back and in their offices when I woke up. I had coffee, suited up, and went back in to room with El Tigre to remove the second piece of material.

In those two hours, the fissure had widened yet again, its rate of widening seemingly increasing. But of course this could only aid me in locating a more interior area to remove a slice of El Tigre for our electroscopes, just as the professor wished.

After I had done so, getting a slice of rock from inside the newly opened fissure itself, I looked at the slice under the simple magnification we had in that room. When I glanced back at El Tigre, I could have sworn that I noticed a glimmer of color coming from within that fissure, i.e., from inside the meteorite.

I changed my position for another look and the color was gone. I tried to locate my original position but could not seem to recover that gleam or glimmer—both words being too strong to describe the very dim, somewhat ultraviolet-like hue that I thought I had seen. I concluded that the effect must be a trick of the glass in the helmet of the Haz-Mat suit I was wearing, along with the fluorescent lightbulbs high up in the room, which I had noticed at odd times flickered. I said nothing of it to Prof Rig when I brought in the second slice, but I did mention the increased widening of the fissure.

He was pleased by both slices and said he would look them over carefully. He sent me to my office to fill out my daily report. He remains now with the slices under the electron scanning microscope. I guess he's searching for bacteria fossils.

Fine with me. I'm about to leave. I've got a date in town with a young woman I've been interested in since I first saw her.

July 4th, 2___
10:45 a.m.
Surprisingly, I was the only one here in the lab all this morning. Prof Rigoberto sent me an e-mail that I only read once I arrived here today

in my old Datsun, reminding me that he would not be in the lab before noon, as he had a doctor's exam in town. I have no idea where del Cuerco or Ventano are.

The professor said he had found some "anomalies referring to color and possibly also to composition" in the second slice of El Tigre that I'd taken yesterday and he wanted me to look it over. And, if the fissure had widened, to go back and take another slice of material as deeply located as possible.

I went into his office and looked at the two slices. As he mentioned, the second one indeed seemed to have a slight tinge of that same ultraviolet glow I thought I had seen inside yesterday. So perhaps it wasn't a trick of the light as I'd first thought. No hint of any fossilized proto-life, however, in either slice.

Ten minutes ago, I suited up and went into the room with El Tigre. The fissure had widened to eleven centimeters, i.e., three times what it was on yesterday evening. I could place my entire gloved hand into the fissure from the top surface. The glow I'd seen before was now present, as before, if of even deeper origin and somehow suffusing more what I could see of the interior. Are those even the right words to describe it?

I did as Prof Rig had requested and carefully made a very deep inroad into El Tigre twenty centimeters in, and using the utmost care, I removed the material in a thin slice. When I held it up in its tiny forceps, it had that same odd glow. I looked at it in various kinds of artificial light and it still had the glow, although it was now not ultraviolet, but also had hues of violet, green, and indigo.

I brought it into Prof Rig's office and placed it in a sealed plate. Then I unsuited and returned. Del Cuerco had come into work and asked me what I was doing. I told him, and together we looked at the slice of material under triple magnification. He muttered something unintelligible and would not repeat it when I asked him to. I received a strong impression that he was hungover from a night of drinking; it wouldn't be the first time.

Prof Rig has just phoned to say he won't be in at all today. He reacted badly to an injection of B-12 and something else his doctor gave him—is he one of those Doctor Feelgoods? They do abound in Caracas.

I told him about the fissure and the multicolored glow. He requested that I look back at El Tigre at 3 p.m. and if the fissure has widened further that I take a another interior slice, going as deeply in as I can.

I'm not sure why I'm making this entry, probably because I'm nervous. Prof Rig is not here. Del Cuerco is, but he's hungover, and Ventano called to say he'd be in later.

10:22 p.m. Yes, p.m.

Prof Ventano is sitting here with me in his office as I am still somewhat shaken by the events of this afternoon. I've had a half glass of brandy and am calmer. Possibly the most astounding aspect of it all is that it is 10.22 p.m., since what happened seemed to me to take place over perhaps ten minutes, at most.

Whereas, according to Prof Ventano and Dr. del Cuerco, I was gone over seven hours!

Ventano had just arrived at the lab. I met him in the corridor all suited up at 3:05 p.m. and I went back into the room with El Tigre. He was standing in the corridor looking in at me when he got a call from his mistress, which he admits absorbed most of his attention as they were arguing over some private events of the most recent weekend. Yet he said he was also, if not with his fullest attention, watching me.

I will first relate what happened in the room. Then Prof Ventano will add what he witnessed.

I entered with my usual tools for taking interior slices and I was extremely startled to see the prismatic glow I'd noticed before was suffusing the entire top surface of El Tigre. As I neared it, I immediately noticed that the fissure had considerably widened.

When I looked into the interior I immediately saw that the light and colors were coming from an object embedded in the interior, some fifteen centimeters from the top.

If I was astonished then, you may imagine my further astonishment as the object began slowly rising, with no apparent noise or strain. As it did, I could make out its shape, a torus or solid ring, its color, prismatic as I said, albeit at first in the green-blue-violet range, and its size was no bigger than my gloved hand. I couldn't even speculate on its composition.

It rose so slowly yet so continuously that I turned to the glass separating me from Ventano and gestured to him. He was arguing and looking away, so I tapped on the glass.

When he looked at me, I gestured at El Tigre and shouted and then mouthed the words, "There's something inside. It's coming up." I gestured to indicate something rising slowly. Ventano did not understand and so I located a piece of paper and wrote down what I meant and held it up to the glass.

He read it and glanced at the meteorite and yelled, "I'll suit up and come in."

He hung up the phone and ran to the storeroom.

I turned back to El Tigre. I could now see the object's top edge over the top of the meteorite. It was continuing to rise. I turned to see where Ventano was, then back to El Tigre. He wasn't coming. Had he taken another phone call?

I could not stop looking at the meteorite. The object now had risen halfway up.

I rapped on the glass, hoping to urge him to hurry up. No luck.

I looked back at the thing, and now the object was up almost its entire length.

I went closer, and sure enough, although I couldn't say why or how, it was still moving. It had managed to rise so that all but a very tiny portion of it was still touching the interior.

I turned back to the glass and corridor and pounded on the glass. Where was Ventano?

I looked back and the object looked as though it was clearing the surface. I swore I could see its bottom edge clear the rock interior.

Thinking it was clearly a manufactured and not a natural object, given its perfection of shape and its utter amazement of color, my fear was that if it fell onto the floor, it would crash and break into a million pieces. It did look that fragile. And I would be responsible for destroying something of unknowable significance. That must not happen!

I looked back once more for Ventano. But he was not coming. Then I turned and grabbed at the torus to keep it from falling.

Professor Ventano's statement was found in an e-mail he sent to Professor Rigoberto y Alain on July 4th at 3:45 p.m.

Something has happened to Jorge! He was inside with El Tigre, working, when a sudden glow illuminated the interior of the thing. He got my attention and I went to suit up. When

I returned, I saw him reaching for some non-natural object at the very top surface. As he did, an enormous silent explosion of light and color occurred, stunning me and blinding me for at least three minutes with its strength and luminosity.

When I was able to see again, El Tigre was there, but not Jorge. I was suited up and I went into the room carefully, and there was a large fissure opening up inside El Tigre to maybe an arm's length in depth. But Jorge and whatever he had been reaching for were gone.

I searched the room, then left and unsuited and searched the lab's rooms and offices and closets and the lab's exterior too. No Jorge. Del Cuerco had been sleeping, but with my shouting he came running in. He joined me in the search. Please phone and/or advise!

I turned and grabbed at the torus to keep it from falling and I managed to get my gloved hand around it to hold it still. Just then there was a sudden burst of light so great I was forced to shut my eyes despite the Haz-Mat suit's colored and tempered helmet glass, and to keep them closed at least thirty seconds.

When I opened my eyes the torus was still in my hand. But—and here I can do nothing but write the truth—but I was no longer inside the Puruana Laboratory. Instead I was on what seemed to be a small, concrete or rocklike ledge, about a meter and a half from a vast wall of the same material.

I looked forward to the wall. I looked up and the wall extended almost as high as I could see. I turned slowly to the right and the wall extended almost to the end of my vision; I turned left and the wall extended very far, maybe a half a kilometer, and then met another similar wall at more or less a right angle. I looked down and the wall extended as far down as I dared lean over to see.

The term "fly on the wall" suddenly had meaning to me. Except that the wall was not exactly vertical but the top of it leaned over a few degrees, and of course, as I looked down, it sloped inward from my perch. Also, I slowly made out other little balconies like the one I stood on, extending maybe two meters wide and another two deep. Perches, rather, as they had no railing or support at the open end.

I was, of course, astonished. But also I suspected it might be merely a hallucination caused by touching the torus. So I moved forward and touched the wall with my other gloved hand. It was roughly surfaced and clearly not natural but instead constructed. As I came near I could see extremely straight, albeit oddly angled, shallow fissures and concluded that the wall was indeed constructed, not natural, and it was composed of irregularly triangular bricks.

I tried turning my back to the wall and managed to get a shoulder of the Haz-Mat suit against it. It was definitely hard—real. From here I could make out a large open space of a distance difficult to ascertain but perhaps a kilometer exactly opposite this wall and perch, where there was another, similar, wall with perches, equally high, wide, and angled in from the top. So if it was a hallucination, it was an extremely detailed and consistent one. Also, there was sky and atmosphere, but it was oddly colored; pale chartreuse is the closest I can come to its color.

When I turned again, to look in the other direction, the still iridescent torus I held flat out brushed the wall. As it did so, a large space opened up in the wall, not at all jagged and so, I assumed, purposefully made. I supposed this to be an entry or ingress.

I peered into what seemed to be a chamber, long and narrow and high. The coloring within was an even denser and perhaps even smoky or misty version of the outside air.

I am not particularly afraid of heights, but this was such an odd place to be, a tiny fly on a Herculean wall, that I admit I was uneasy. I stepped cautiously into the chamber, still holding the torus in front of me.

Immediately apparent was that the walls also were constructed and, how do I say it, somehow textured in many layers, one over the other, what artists call pentimento, I believe. The interior wall and ceiling coloring was all shades of tan and brown, and the ceiling appeared rounded where the vertical met the horizontal. Like the outer wall, these were at slightly askew, not at right angles to the floor nor to each other, and the chamber was a bit like funhouse walls at a carnival. Also textured out of the sides of some of the walls were seats or ledges or benches, at irregular heights, but all of them large enough to hold a man sitting or perched.

Smaller and more roundly textured protrusions seemed placed

upon the chamber walls, some with odd sticks or other rope like excrescences.

When I got too close while trying to inspect one of them just above my head, the torus I was holding brushed the wall and it opened up again as the chamber had from the outside, this time into a window to another space.

I was not prepared for the enormous size of this new space, an interior courtyard of the same oddly angled walls but now in some sort of ziggurat fashion with ramps going up and down. Nor was I ready for the sudden noise, nor the unceasing motion of what seemed to be dozens of dark, unclearly seen, shapes, all clearly animated, and all shrieking or screeching.

There is no other way for me to explain this.

I withdrew just as one or two of the figures suddenly noticed me through the opening and rapidly approached in what might have been a curious or a threatening manner. I didn't stick around to see which it was.

I quickly strode to the other opening of the chamber leading to the outside perch, and as I rushed toward it I somehow struck the torus against a side of the opening, and again a great light swamped me and I fell to my knees.

When I opened my eyes I was back in the laboratory and the torus was at the top surface of El Tigre where I first had grasped it. I was maybe a meter away from the meteorite, on my hands and knees, upon the room's tiled floor.

I heard loud knocking against the glass, and when I opened my eyes and looked, I saw Ventano out there in Haz-Mat gear but without the helmet, his hands thrown up, and he was screaming something.

Just then del Cuerco came running into the corridor. Ventano pulled on the helmet and rushed into the lab room. He came over to where I was trying to stand up, and grabbed me by both arms, shouting, "Are you okay? Are you okay?" and after I'd nodded and yelled back that I was okay, he pulled me out of the room.

Del Cuerco had his office set up so that no sooner was I unsuited than he led me in, sat me down on his sofa, and began giving me a physical exam: eyes, ears, nose, throat, lungs, heart. Everything but a electrocardiogram, and he would have done that if he had the nodes and machinery there. The upshot, clear from his relieved reactions, was that I was fine.

Ventano was there too, and they both pulled up chairs and peered at me closely.

"Where were you?" Ventano asked.

"The strangest place imaginable," I told them. That's what the tape recorder they had turned on confirms that I said.

"Where?" del Cuerco asked.

"I have no idea."

"Can you describe it?"

I described what I have just spoken into this tape recorder. After I was done, I drank some bottled water, and Ventano said, "That only sounds like the activity of a few minutes. What about the rest of the time you were gone?"

When I looked puzzled he showed me their watches and then opened the curtains. It was a clear starry night outside. That's when he told me how long I was gone—and most crucially that I had been gone.

"The torus," I said. "It began when I took hold of it to keep it from falling."

"It didn't fall. It's just sitting there," del Cuerco said. "Come see."

We went into the corridor leading to the windows leading to the room I'd been in with El Tigre, and there the torus sat or hovered not quite atop El Tigre's surface.

Professor Rigoberto arrived just then and I repeated it all for him.

By then it was midnight and Prof Rig said he was feeling better after napping most of the day and so he would stay up and keep watch over El Tigre. We should all go home.

July 5th, 2___
11:15 a.m.

The only indication I had that the others at the laboratory were concerned or at all unsure of me last night was that del Cuerco followed me in his Mercedes coupe all the way home, and waited while I parked and went into my apartment building. Only then did I hear him roar off into the night.

I was exhausted but starved and made toast and covered it with peanut butter and marmalade, eating maybe five sandwiches of that and drinking almost a liter of milk. I slept dreamlessly.

When I arrived at the lab this morning, Professor Rigoberto y Alain was on the phone, and he remained on the phone much of the morning. He called me in and had me read over a transcription someone had done from the tape of what I told Ventano and del Cuerco late last night. He'd made red pencil question marks that he wanted me to confirm. I did so.

After he hung up the phone he asked me to once again describe the "animated shapes" that I'd seen in the interior of the structure. Were they man-sized? More or less. Could I describe them better? Did they have arms, legs, a distinct head, a neck? I thought so, but told him my vision had been very fuzzy because of the dense atmosphere and the interference of the Haz-Mat helmet glass.

He then asked why I'd withdrawn. How threatened did I truly feel? I had to admit not that much. The animated shapes might have just been curious.

He led me to the corridor outside the chamber holding El Tigre. Ventano and del Cuerco were inside suited up. They were filming, taking various measurements, I don't know what else.

"I sent your report by fax to the Academy of Science at Caracas. Dr. Nuccio responded by saying that you were hallucinating. When I mentioned that you were physically missing for over seven hours, he changed his approach. He wants me to go in and grasp the torus, just as you did."

"Someone has to repeat the experiment," I agreed. "Or else it's bad science."

"They wanted each of us to try it!"

"I agree," I told him.

"Except that Ventano pointed out that you may have already inadvertently formed some kind of chemical or physiological bond with the torus that provoked it to become operational. It may not work again with another of us. So we decided that I will suit up go into the room and grasp it. And you will be suited up waiting nearby. If nothing happens, you will come in and grasp it along with me."

"Fine."

"I told Dr. Nuccio you would agree. We're going to do it at the same time as you did yesterday. Just in case that is a factor. Agreed?"

I agreed. He looked at me and half smiled. "What an adventure, eh, young man? And on your first job."

"What an adventure," I repeated.

Ventano and del Cuerco exited finally and unsuited. We all met in Prof Rig's office and they related their findings: the torus and El Tigre were unchanged since last night. They began unloading their measurements into the Mac, and when they were done, del Cuerco began cackling.

"Well, as we all suspected," he said. "The light spectrum being emitted by the torus falls into a fairly unique range. We'll send out the formula to various labs and observatories and see what they can come up with. You said that the air was pale chartreuse?" he asked me. "But it had no distinctive odor?"

"I couldn't smell it. Not through the Haz-Mat helmet, no."

"We've dusted your entire suit, but it seems you were there for too short a period of time for it to have left any traces."

"What are you expecting to come up with?" I asked.

"Well, we know the torus is not from here." Prof Rig laughed. "And given the colors you mentioned, the meteorite does not derive from Mars, which has a distinctive pink to red atmosphere that every lander has photographed and relayed back. So it must be from elsewhere."

"Methane is yellow," I said. "So are some sulfur mixtures and metal sulfates. And also I recall some ammonium carbides and perhaps aluminum sulfides?"

Del Cuerco smiled. "Where in the solar system is it yellow? A moon of Saturn? Titan?"

"Enough speculation! Back to work," Prof Rig declared and we all went back to our desks.

I'm waiting to go back to El Tigre. I'm not sure how I feel about it.

11:49 p.m.

At three o'clock this afternoon, both Prof Rigoberto and I were suited up in our Haz-Mat gear and entered the room containing El Tigre meteorite.

I remained at the back wall; Prof Ventano and Dr. del Cuerco remained on the other side of the triple-paned glass out in the corridor. I was filming from a small digital camera inserted into the helmet of my

Haz-Mat suit and so was Ventano from a larger camera. He was hoping to catch the actual vanishing moment and point, if the professor does vanish as I supposedly did yesterday. We've also fitted both cameras with a flash filter, which should instantly go into effect if there is a bright flash as happened twice yesterday.

At 3:03 p.m. Prof Rig went up to El Tigre. At 3:05, he grasped the torus. Nothing happened. He continued holding it, released it, then grasped it again. Still nothing happened. He then gestured to me and I placed the third camera, a video, onto a stand he had earlier set up inside the room but opposite where he and del Cuerco would view us. This would provide a triple perspective.

At 3:07 I went over to El Tigre where Prof Rig was holding on to the torus with his right hand. I moved to his left and grasped it too.

Once again there was an explosion of light and color, for which both of us were prepared this time.

Only a few seconds passed before I opened my eyes. Same yellow-green atmosphere, and we were standing side by side on a rocklike perch once more. This time, however, I felt that we were in a different spot than before, higher up on the outside wall outside of the huge edifice. I could easily make out the top of the wall above, but not at all below.

Ventano had cleared the internal mics between the two Haz-Mat suits and we had tested them in the office.

"This is the place," I now said to Prof Rig. "But we're higher up and I think further away from that corner." I pointed to where the two vast walls met.

"Amazing!" he said, and I realized from his awed tone of voice that none of them had believed me before, at least not completely.

It was awkward, both of us holding the torus, but we managed to turn about fully on the perch and Prof Rig said, "Look!" pointing with his free hand across from us where, as before, there was an identical wall and perches.

We could make out the roof line there and depressed in a bit what looked like a natural overhanging lip that extended as far as the eye could see.

"It's a natural canyon, I believe," Prof Rig said. "And these two long edifices were built in underneath the cliff edge. Astonishing!"

I stand maybe three inches taller than the professor, and I could see something above the natural lip opposite very far along its length of wall. It seemed to be a mountain peak. I mentioned it to him.

We turned carefully around again and he said, "Now we go in."

We put the torus against the wall and it opened an entry for us as it had before for me.

This chamber seemed to lead to another but was essentially the same as the one yesterday. As we stepped in, we felt a sudden and enormous tremor and both of us put up our free hands to hold on to the wall. Two sudden very large jolts occurred, following by a rolling motion.

"Earthquake!" Prof Rig said. I'd never experienced one before. "That's new," I replied.

Our opening was still intact and we peered outside. The edifice wall opposite us on the other side of the canyon appeared to be have been riven through. Huge fissures appeared running crazily in all directions. We could make out two little perches angled over steeply.

Another tremor occurred, this one sharp and loud. Those angled perches fell and more crazy rifts occurred in the opposite wall.

"We must see if this one is also compromised," he said calmly, and so I stepped out again onto the perch and looked around. But no, I couldn't see anything like cracks on this wall. Were we too far away? Was it only affecting that cliff wall on that side of the canyon?

We went back into the chamber. "Is this how it looked before?" Prof Rig asked, and I looked about and concluded yes, and we took photos of it all, going close-up on the strange protuberances I'd seen at eye level, and the stick-like objects and the rope-like objects too.

All this took five minutes by my watch. Because I'd been so taken by the time discrepancies we'd all noted before, I wanted to be precise about everything this time.

He then asked me if I was "ready," and I said yes, and we placed the torus against the inner chamber wall and quickly stepped back from the window that soundlessly opened in the wall.

Here the internal ziggurat shape and ramps going up and down were very apparent; we could actually see where they ended in a roof area not high above us. As with across the canyon, there was a space of maybe ten meters between the roof and the overhanging rock cliff edge.

More crucial was the almost chaotic movement of those dark, animated shapes I'd seen before. To begin with there were scores of them this time. Then too, many were rushing about in what seemed to be a true panic, carrying objects, running into each other, grabbing each other. As before I couldn't make them out any clearly, but this time I did see that many of them held out a torus similar to the one Prof Rig and I held.

He tried stepping out onto the open way that seemed to lead to the ramps, and he fell back as another two or three rushed past him, racing up the ramp. From this close up and because there were so many of them, it became clear that they had three upper limbs growing out of or attached to a clavicle, shoulder area. Also that they had a single thick middle lower limb beneath a cone-shaped torso or trunk that was propelled along as though by some built-in mechanical motion from below; whether it was manufactured or not, I couldn't tell, because they were moving so quickly and also because there were much thinner, more flexible bottom limbs that wrapped around, supported, and aided the forward motion of this single limb and that also—if any of them would stand still long enough—might also be a prop or support. As they shot by us we could see they had heads of a sort, but nothing like a neck, and I couldn't make out hands at all, just moving, grasping fingers, or perhaps they were even tentacles.

"Look how they're using the torus," the professor said and pointed. I could see those who reached the roof locate a spot they searched for carefully, then become statue still for a second, as though settling in, then raise up the torus with that upper limb not busily holding objects—treasures? heirlooms? The torus opened a window in the rock ledge above them. Then they were somehow projected there, and we saw them through that hole on the surface of the cliff before they rushed off.

The noise they made, as it had been before, was high-pitched, horrifying, and tumultuous, so that we had to shut off the speakers inside our helmets.

But the cause of their panic was clear enough as the floor beneath us was jolted strongly three times in a row, with a sickening rolling motion in between. Peering into the chamber, it was clear the outer walls here too were now badly cracking and might be about to fall.

Once we felt a slackening in the number of the many shapes going past us, Prof Rig motioned me to go out and up a ramp with him. We began ascending the ramp way up the interior ziggurat.

The higher we went, the more evident it became that the huge edifice below us was already damaged beyond repair. Once we got onto the roof, distant sections of it began to collapse and fall. Clearly we had to do something fast.

We tried looking down to find those spots on the roof the shapes had located, but it was nothing but a swirl of textured layers with no rhyme or reason.

Now we were beginning to panic as the section we'd just been in, where in fact we had entered, fell with a crash, leaving an enormous gaping hole in front of the ziggurat ramp, which now we saw exposed some hundreds, perhaps thousands of meters down.

We'd barely understood this when two of the dark animated figures shoved up past us and pushed us off the spot where we were standing. We barely kept our balance. One came so close that I could for the first time actually make out a face. I was horrified by its strangeness, as it must have been horrified by mine. But the two of them stood together, holding one torus almost above them, and went still, as the others had, before a hole was somehow pierced in the rock ceiling above and in a second they were gone.

Prof Rig had not looked them in the face as I had. Concerned to see what they had chosen, he'd looked down at the roof and then up at the ceiling.

"I've got it. I understand," he shouted. He pulled me alongside him almost two meters. He located a certain swirl of texturing on a roof below our feet, a roof that was starting to collapse in vast chunks all around us, and he pointed up, where he shouted there was an identical texture.

"I hope you're right," I said, and we stood still and held the torus up to the under-ceiling swirl, and suddenly we felt as though encased in some transparent tube.

"Look!" he shouted and I did, and that ceiling swirl was now open to the sick yellow sky above. Before I could reply we were up there, beyond the roof, and I could see the ground beneath us was now the cliff. As I'd guessed, it ran alongside a canyon that was maybe twenty kilometers long. Across from us, the mountain peak I'd seen a hint of before was huge, and worse, it was shuddering, before one entire side of it collapsed.

Beyond us, the animated shapes were rushing to flee along the cliff to some interior area. The ground beneath us began to rise and fall so suddenly that we could barely keep our balance.

"We've got to get out of here!" Prof Rig shouted. "How did you do it before?"

In the midst of a cataclysmic collapsing landscape, all I could recall was that I had struck the torus on its thinnest side, which I'm guessing had negated something. I told him so, and we went over to a jut of rock barely holding together and struck the torus.

Nothing. A second cyclopean tremor shook us, surely destroying the ground under our very feet. Then the light came and blinded us.

Relieved, we came to together, still holding each other. It was deep night and I recognized the Southern Cross constellation at the horizon. I never before so loved seeing a clear, starry, Venezuelan night.

It took us a few minutes to locate the Puruana Laboratory some four hundred meters below the rocky outcrop where we had somehow alit.

I checked my watch and it read 3:28 p.m. We'd been gone only twenty-one minutes.

In the lab, Ventano and del Cuerco told us it had been over eight hours.

The torus was where we had grasped it earlier, slightly hovering over El Tigre meteorite.

This time there were two of us to relate the experience, as well as my camera, to show what we had seen and witnessed.

I found myself once more ravenous and ate all of what del Cuerco had been saving up in the way of packaged cookies and little cakes in our breakfast area.

I'm so exhausted I simply have to get some sleep now.

July 6th, 2___
Ten minutes after noon.

I just woke up and went out of the breakfast room. The others were confabbing in the office. Prof Rig looked tired but also very excited. I could see images playing on the Mac evidently downloaded from the camera in my Haz-Mat helmet, and Ventano and Prof Rig and del Cuerco were commenting excitedly about each one as the professor explained what they were looking at.

I made some fresh coffee, ate what looked like freshly delivered pastries, and returned to the office and also looked on and listened.

When there was a break in their talk I said, "It's an eye! The torus. It's a kind of activating eye that can open…I don't know how… windows and doors in solid material. I believe that during the disaster we witnessed our torus somehow became embedded into a chunk of that ceiling ledge, and when the ledge collapsed or was shaken apart, it was somehow or other thrust into space. The colors of El Tigre, once you scrape off the burn-surface, should be identical to that rock ceiling, to that that cliff edge that we stood on."

I'm not sure how I knew that, but I did, and I persuaded them. Soon Ventano was suiting up and going out to the chamber where the torus still hovered, and he did a careful surface abrasion of El Tigre. What he came back with did in fact look similar to the cliff we'd stood on.

The second thing I said that startled them was, "I saw one. Close up. This close. Face-to-face."

Slowly but surely, the next day, with the assistance of an illustrator, I was able to show them what it looked like: del Cuerco said it resembled a much larger white-faced vampire bat, without fangs.

"Go over your report," Prof Rig said, "and I will go over mine. Dr. Nuccio will be arriving in an hour or so to hear us out."

Dr. Nuccio is the head of the National Academy of Science and I can hear the noise of the rotors of his helicopter landing. He is coming into the lab now with three other men.

July 7th, 2____
3 p.m.

There has been a terrible incident in the lab. I was out with Dr. Nuccio and his assistant, and Professor Rigoberto and two other people from the academy, having lunch in what passes for a town here in Punto Fijo.

Prof Rig's cell phone rang, then Nuccio's. They heard the story simultaneously and jumped up. I managed to filch whatever pasteles had just been dropped on the table for desert (why am I so hungry?), and we all took off back to the lab in two cars.

The video camera we'd set up yesterday afternoon in the lab now goes on when ever anyone enters the lab, and it caught everything, including sound.

The latter mostly consisted of del Cuerco shouting, "No! No! It musn't! It cannot! Not yet!"

We see what he is shouting about: the torus slowly descending until it is no longer in sight, evidently headed into the core of the interior, once again.

Del Cuerco said that he was passing by the triple-paned windows when he noticed it. He said that it was happening so quickly that he didn't think he'd have time to change into the Haz-Mat suit. So instead he rushed into the room and tried to grab the torus.

Del Cuerco didn't ever tell us what had motivated him to do it. We'd already told him that we now believed that the source of the torus no longer existed, and that we believed we couldn't ever return. Prof Rig had even speculated that we'd not actually been there but instead within some kind of representation of the event, some four-dimensional video tape loop the torus has somehow reconstructed for us, since where it had taken place had collapsed, had been utterly destroyed by that huge earthquake or enormous volcano burst or whatever it was that we'd seen and experienced.

Even so, del Cuerco had rushed over to El Tigre, shoved a footstool against it, bent over, reached down into the suffused ultraviolet interior, and grabbed onto the torus.

It had not risen, as he'd hoped. It had continued to descend, and then it stopped. As he tugged and grabbed at it (luckily with only one hand) and shouted in dismay, the interior rock had begun to close around the torus. Before he could withdraw his hand it had closed solidly upon it, almost, he said, as though it had flowed molten for a moment, while he'd watched it happen in some sort of stupefied wonder.

He'd been too stunned to even feel pain. He claimed he hadn't. But suddenly he couldn't feel anything at all at the end of his upper wrist. The rock interior had fully closed, the fissure and any trace of it were no longer there. The meteorite looked as it had before, when it had first arrived.

When the shocked del Cuerco had lifted his wrist away, it came away without the left hand. It was an absolutely clean cut, raw, red, a patchwork of blood vessels, nerve endings, severed muscles, and as-though-lasered-through bones. As he looked on, it seemed to instantly cauterize itself, with a sort of film that slowly opaqued as he watched.

It's only then that the video camera shows him falling off the stool backward onto the floor.

That noise was what Ventano heard.

He is seen rushing in, looking at El Tigre, looking at del Cuerco, who is on his back on the floor and holds up his handless wrist in astonishment.

July 8th, 2___
10 a.m.

Fifteen minutes ago, Prof Rigoberto y Alain asked us into his office where Dr. Nuccio had set up a teleconference call from Caracas on the monitor of the Mac.

He began by telling us that El Tigre would be removed from our lab within the hour by the army, which was already on its way. The meteorite would be taken away to an undisclosed location.

He requested us to give up all notes, tapes, CD-ROMs, videos, photos, handwritten and computer keyed-in data and information on El Tigre and on the entire past six days.

Hearing that, del Cuerco sobbed loud enough for Dr. Nuccio to pick it up on his end.

"I'm terribly sorry for all of you. Especially for you, Santiago, my old friend," Nuccio said.

"But…But…something did happen here!" del Cuerco said. "It did! You can't deny it."

"Santiago, please! I know you're upset. And you are right to be. But listen to reason. If any thing at all is revealed about El Tigre, it must all be revealed. The object is dangerous. Surely you must see that as well as anyone. It cannot be allowed to become a public spectacle. Who knows what else might happen?"

Del Cuerco grabbed me with his good hand. "You, Georgie-boy! Tell him. You were on some other planet. You saw one of them. Face-to-face."

"I'm sorry, gentlemen," Dr. Nuccio said. Then, "In compensation, you will all be rewarded, in various appropriate manners, but believe me, you will be richly rewarded by the National Academy. It will be done as discreetly as possible, so no one suspects anything. And I must ask you to not ever speak of this again. I must have you promise not to ever speak to an outsider about it."

After the visual link had closed down, we heard him speaking a bit, and then the audio too was shut off.

So it is all over. As though it never happened. As though El Tigre never arrived here.

This concludes the journal of Jorge Rivas Y Clark.

That's the last entry in my audio-taped journal.

It was the day after that that Prof Rigoberto requested that we promise to never speak about El Tigre to anyone outside of the lab. Del Cuerco handed in his resignation later on that day, muttering, and he left exactly after the required thirty days. Ventano found something else to interest him and he too left, a month later. I took over their projects at the lab.

Two months later, Dr. Nuccio called me to his office in Caracas and offered me two excellent fellowships, each of them leading to a Ph.D. and to a tenured university position. I took one of them, and I married that young woman I'd been dating, and we moved to Caracas, our large, wealthy and vibrant capital. I never looked back.

I heard that Prof Rigoberto received a cushy position in the Houston Lab, office of the extraplanetary group that NASA and JPL set up in tandem. He remained in the U.S. until his recent death at the age of seventy-nine. Nuccio died before that.

I'm not sure if I would have ever written about all this if not for a very minor incident that happened a few weeks ago. It occurred during one of my long vacations—one of the perks that come with my new job. My family and I were in Maracaibo, and somehow or other, Diego, my youngest, had gotten hold of a catalogue at our hotel for the local natural history museum and begged me to take him and his sister.

I looked at the catalogue, and among its various attractions, it claimed to be exhibiting the El Tigre meteorite.

Curiosity got the best of me, and so I took the children, while their mother went shopping.

They were very excited to see the huge meteorite that had fallen in their country before they were even born. I don't know what their mother had told them, but they vaguely knew that it was connected to their parents first meeting and getting married.

Diego especially loved the meteorite on display, and he took many photos of it with his new camera. He loved most the so-called tiger-striping across its side and the various theories given for why the meteorite possessed them. As for El Tigre's origin, the flyers we picked up supplied a wide range of not terribly off-the-right-track possibilities presented. Evidently the information about the color of the atmosphere that I'd first noted had already gone out to dozens of scientists before the total information shutdown occurred. Iapetus, a small moon circling the planet Saturn, has become the most popular choice of where El Tigre came from. Based on various criteria that seemed to be not entirely arbitrary, the time of El Tigre's origin was given as between seventy-five and a hundred thousand years ago, when that little moon apparently underwent its last volcanic-tectonic activity.

I, of course, understood. It was another meteorite, one less publicly known, from some other place, some other country, perhaps from another continent.

What was the difference to the public? No one had seen the real El Tigre after it had landed, except a few army personnel—and us.

That night I was awakened from a dream in which everything was crumbling around me with the greatest noise and shaking I'd ever experienced, and in the midst of this cataclysm, an absolutely fear-stricken face like no face I'd ever seen before suddenly arrived a few centimeters away and shoved me off its preordained spot. It and its companion then pointed a small iridescent torus upward and vanished through the hole it made in the ceiling above.

FOOD FOR THOUGHT

B ecause he was a telepath and a little sensitive following their most recent landing, Andy was awakened last.

In fact, it was hotly discussed whether he ought to be awakened at all.

Bim thought not. She'd still not gotten over the hysterical panic-state Andy had been in when he'd returned to the *Dallas* after that Deneb 3 affair. She'd had to shoot him up with every conceivable fungal-soma-to derivative in the dispensary. And when those hadn't done much, she'd fallen back to more primitive phenobarbs before Andy had finally calmed down.

Roy thought Andy *should* be awakened. He pointed out that Deneb 3 was unique: Its nonsense-thinking and speaking inhabitants probably would have made Lewis Carroll pop a gasket. He reminded the others that before the *Dallas* had arrived, all relations since the disastrous first landing on the planet had been negotiated through mobile computers who couldn't understand the difference between simple non-rationals like a human crew and real wackos like those on Deneb 3. Andy was the first human, Roy pointed out, certainly the first T-p, to visit the Denebians. And he'd eventually come down from that experience, hadn't he?

Patsu also voted no. She was second officer and an improbability addict, which had carried weight before in their group decisions. This time, however, it had become common knowledge among the crew that Patsu was operating with less than her usual objectivity. Andy—admittedly the best-looking genital male on the Dallas—had only made it in Playby with Patsu one time, claiming that she gave off heavy hostile-death thoughts during the sex act. Since everyone else on board had Andy in Playby at least a dozen times, they were convinced that anything Patsu might have to say would be colored by this apparent rejection, and who knew, possibly jealousy.

Hill, the oldest-seeming of the crew (with all the time/space screw-ups, who could tell real age anymore—after a few years "out" the crew looked younger than their great-great grand nephews and nieces) and by his seniority as much as by default more or less the captain of the *Dallas*, reminded them that Andy had, after all, saved them and the ship, and probably the Company's entire operation in sector 657 of NGC-345 when he'd telepathically defused and then resolved the !Koh-Mantra Crisis, two trips back.

Willow, Andy's friend and most constant Playby mate, also voted yes. So did Ho Wang and Native—whose name was just one part of his claim to be distantly descended from some Old Earth aboriginal group. Native explained his vote: "We've already sent ten fly-overs across this new planet's surface, and they don't show a single living creature down there. Andy will be as calm as a disconnected 'droid."

"What about the Swamp Moths on Epsilon Vega?" Patsu asked. "They were conscious and communicative and never showed up on our fly-over reports."

"But they were a *positive* experience for Andy," Hill argued. "Remember how he taught them how to play infrared chess? All we can see downstairs is plants. Flowers, vegetables, trees, grass, and more of the same."

"Sounds great," Ho Wang said, "after some of the hellholes we've been to lately."

"Temperate climate," Willow chimed in. "Breathable atmosphere. Water. The works. We could picnic for a month."

Hill agreed. It was the first stop so far on the trip that looked even vaguely habitable. "The Company will like it."

It was a little planet, only size 4 in the Company's catalogue, the eighth world out from a double star system of a medium-sized redSun and small white-blueSun. It had a solid, metallic core, extremely slow-shifting continents, was composed of 81 percent land, the rest non-saline water; but with a mantle of real rock and real dirt. The fly-overs had already shown the crew wonderful vistas below, and—as Native said—they had found no animal life on land or water large enough to be detected. But to be classified for colonization and/or exploitation, the planet needed to be landed on, actually tried out by humans. And for an official landing with a designation-status imposed, the human crew had to include one T-p. Company rules. Tried and true after centuries. No ifs, ands, or buts.

"It's your funeral," Patsu warned and voted no.

She and Bim were outvoted by the six others. Andy was awakened.

He surprised Patsu by asking if she'd Playby with him and Willow after chow-down. She'd been enjoying Ho and Willow for the last few days with Andy asleep and had pretty much decided she'd have to give up being in a trio.

"We'll be in Playlounge five," Andy said, smiling. "Bring a few Super-Qs, will you?" Patsu always kept a large supply of the recreational hypno-stimulators on hand as all the crew liked them in Playby.

"And, Patsu," Andy added, "don't feel guilty about voting to not awaken me. It's too typical as behavior to be out of character."

❖

"Well, Andy," Willow asked when they first stepped out of their lander and onto what seemed to be a ten-kilometer ellipse of short-leaved, perfectly manicured green lawn, "do you T-p anything?"

Andy didn't. Not a thing. Of course, he heard the various thoughts of the eight others, all thinking furiously, as they always did upon first planet-fall. Howard wondering if he'd forgotten a needed instrument gauge, Hill still thinking furiously about his recent Playby with Roy, Native nurturing fantasies that he'd soon leave this spot and encounter landscapes similar to that of Wyoming, wherever that might be—some area from his tribal collective history, Andy supposed. By now, Andy was able to channel the entire crew's fairly predictable thoughts into a single murmuring noise—something like radio static. He'd been a T-p long enough to be able to deal with the Big Brown Buzz, which was how all T-ps among themselves and at their silent, active, infrequent, bi-decade conventions referred to the general, barely acceptable background tele-noise of their surroundings.

"You are scanning, aren't you?" Willow asked.

"Of course I'm scanning. My range is only about a hundred

kilometers in surface atmosphere at this density and composition. I still don't T-p a thing."

Which was odd, Andy thought. Almost unprecedented, in his experience. There was generally some kind of T-p noise, at one frequency or another, comprehensible or not.

"Well," Hill said, frowning a bit, "you might T-p better once we're out of your way. Let me know." He knew the Company would like a perfectly empty world for once. No pay-offs, no negotiations with greedy inhabitants. "The rest of us are going to explore," Hill added.

Exploration was pretty much what the crew did all the rest of that day. It was fairly primitive exploring compared to what the *Dallas*'s computer/sensor backups had already achieved though scores of particularized fly-overs previously sent out. But in a way more essential. The planet might look like a paradise, but if the Company was going to stake a claim here, it had to be proven to be completely inhabitable by normal humans. No more expensive surprises like on Tau Ceti 12, which the *Valparaiso* crew had found a while back, now famous, or rather infamous, in Company annals.

There too, the planet had been beautifully, utterly comfortable for humans—an Eden. A month of landing and visits with the charming, hospitable Cetian humanoids had been an experience to be savored by the crew for years after—it was so rare. All the more of a shock when one crew member, stuck on board the observing ship with punishment-duty for the entire planet-fall duration, had decided to play back some of the luckier crew members' wandering infra-sound and ultraviolet video recordings. The planet proved to be not what it seemed; instead it was nothing more than a thick sheet of some kind of plankton floating upon an unstable lava ocean. And the Cetianids were neither graceful, beautiful, nor humanoid, but instead a sort of omniphagic bacteria with extraordinary control over their appetite and extraordinary telepathic ability, powerful enough to confuse humans and sensors, and with the ability to create perfect tri-dimensional illusions. Their evident aim in so wonderfully greeting the *Valparaiso* had been to encourage a large colony and thus assure themselves of a good-sized human population they might then feed upon at their leisure. A plan thwarted by one disgruntled crewman with time on his hands who'd saved not only the crew, but possibly thousands to come. The story had been told across the galaxies, and even Patsu referred to "the *Valparaiso* factor" whenever she wanted to explain exactly how improbable improbability could be whenever living beings were involved.

The *Dallas*'s planet-fall crew broke up into groups of two, except for Andy, naturally, whose efficiency demanded he be alone. Each of the others was to cover a sector previously mapped out by fly-overs. During the previous charting session aboard the ship, they'd already designated areas with fanciful names: the apparently sparkling (bi-carbonated) fresh water area was referred to as Lake Champagne; the extensive north-south chain of deciduous forest was titled the Peppermint Wood; the enormous, apparently self-cultivating oval and elliptical fields of what appeared to be wheat and rice, they called the Pita Basket and the Rice Bowl. The crew members snapped into their little planet skimmers as though they were on holiday.

All but Andy. His skimmer also glided over enormous pastures, across giant plains filled with huge and healthy specimens of what looked like natural wheat, corn, carrots, string beans, all sorts of fruit orchards, none of it terribly different than the Old Earth varieties grown on the *Dallas*'s own conservatory—the basic food staples of all Company colonists, no matter where they ended up settling. Few of these human origin foods had ever been found indigenous to any New Home planets, although most of them had been seeded and eventually found to adapt well to new environments without too startling genetic differences. Like Proxima Centauri 16's bright azure wheat fields and baked breads that all the tinting and bleaching in the universe couldn't keep from retaining a bluish cast. Or the melon-sized raspberries and blackberries of Spica's single planet, or the tiny, naturally pickled, pineapples grown on the sulfur fields of Io.

Here, everything looked right. The coloration more or less correct, the size about right, the various species laid out similarly to the way Native did it on board the *Dallas*. No obvious anomalies like mangoes growing next to potatoes. Still, something about all this plant life bothered Andy. What was worse, he couldn't exactly pin down what it was.

Perhaps it was merely that he hadn't picked up a single thought. With the other crew members off on their own skimming missions and way beyond his T-p range, it was the first real tele-silence Andy had enjoyed in months, in fact, since his affair on Company Depot Lounge #2 with another T-p who'd also learned how to turn off transmission.

In a sense, this was even quieter. With Branca, Andy was never certain whether or when she'd suddenly turn on or not. And when he and Branca argued, it had quickly descended into an all-out T-p mental war, devastating to both of them for days after. Here, there wasn't a hint of a thought.

Having nothing to do but listen, Andy managed to skim his section in a few hours, then decided to set down for a snooze in the warm sunlight. It might be hours more before Willow and the others returned to the planet-fall base. They'd relay any anomalies at that time, and naturally Andy would check them out.

He selected a grassy knoll beside a glassy-looking rivulet. In the distance he could make out thousands of untouched acres of bright green mature corn stalks. It was so warm here, so quiet, he napped outside the skimmer on an inflatable. For the first time in what seemed to be years, Andy fell asleep instantly without having to slowly tune out the Big Brown Buzz.

He awakened as the smaller, white-blueSun was setting. According to previous calculations, the redSun would remain above the horizon another twenty minutes or so to color the landscape with warmth. He remembered Ho saying that tomorrow the two suns would exchange positions, and the redSun set first.

He'd overslept. Everyone but Bim and Howard was at the lander by the time he skimmed the dozen kilometers back to their planet-fall spot. Andy's own lateness went unremarked, either verbally or T-pically. While waiting for the last two-person skimmer to arrive, the others were busily enthusing over the planet, vying with each other for delighted descriptions of the day's explorations. They all agreed that the planet was the company find of the decade. Definitely temperate weather: not a hint of polar weather; no sign of seasonal changes either. It appeared rich in geological diversity: Their instruments had confirmed the fly-over's ores, minerals, and metals galore. It was also filled with naturally growing foodstuff no matter where you turned— from artichokes to kiwi fruit, rhubarb to honeydew—and in the right proportional quantities for human consumption. The forested areas, the lakeshores, the grass meadows, the low-humped hilly ranges that separated the good producing areas, were spacious enough and more than pleasant enough to provide built-up areas for millions of potential colonists without a bit of crowding. The planet was rich, beautiful, accommodating: undoubtedly that rarest of Company catalogue designations—Class A. Even the normally restrained Willow thought so. The *Dallas* crew was certain to receive the Company's highest bonuses for finding it.

"Where *are* Bim and Howard?" Patsu asked in exasperation what all the others were thinking. The redSun was setting now. The grassy plain before them turned scarlet, then purple under its atmospherically intensified glare.

—Are not—popped into Andy's mind.

"Who thought that?" Andy asked aloud.

"Thought what?" Hill asked.

Andy wasn't foolish enough to say the words. So he ignored Hill, waited until the others were busy, then went behind the lander's antenna dish. The system's amplified blind side would block out most of their thoughts. Not knowing whom he was addressing, or who had previously addressed him, Andy T-p'ed an emission that asked, "Where are Bim and Howard?"

To his surprise, an answer came back:—Are not—

Only this time the T-p wasn't obscured by the Big Brown Buzz. Andy heard it clearly, and it definitely didn't fit the frequency pattern of thoughts of anyone on the *Dallas* crew.

—How do you know?—Andy T-ped.

—Know—came back on a higher band than Andy had ever received on, and—paradoxically—on a lower band too than any he'd received on.

—Where are Bim and Howard?—Andy T-ped.

—Orange Wood—

—Who are you?—Andy asked.

Silence. Then a high-pitched giggle.—No distinction!—

—What?—Andy T-ped frantically.—Who?—

—No distinction—came back, just as he'd heard the first time, followed by a another fit of giggling.

—Where are you?—Andy tried, and slowly spun about in place to see in what direction the giggling came from. It seemed equally forceful from every sector of a 360-degree revolution. Must be some sort of a tele-sonic distortion.

—Where are you?—Andy tried again.

But he couldn't raise the T-p signal again. He pondered a

few seconds, then found Willow and Hill and told them what had happened.

"Bim and Howard were in the J-L sector," Willow said, "It's daylight there for another hour or so."

"Let's send the others back to the *Dallas*" was Hill's decision. "We three will go in skimmers to take a look."

"Knowing Bim," Willow commented, "she's probably so busy eating forbidden fruit, she's forgotten the time."

They located the so-called Orange Wood easily enough once they'd arrived in the middle of K sector: it was an enormous citrus orchard—millions upon millions of trees in full fruit. And, after a short while, they spotted the abandoned skimmer. It had landed, which was against company rules. But then all of the *Dallas* crew had already admitted to having broken that rule: This planet was just too damn inviting not to take a closer look.

As they circled in skimmers, Andy opened his T-perception to its widest reception range, trying for any hint of Bim or Howard's thought frequencies. Nothing came back. They'd have to land and search on foot.

Hill located Bim first. She was about fifteen feet off the ground, her long hair entangled in surprisingly rugged orange tree branches. It was evident that she'd decided to climb the tree—why, none of the three could say, as the fruit looked as full and rich in the lower branches as in the higher ones—and a branch supporting her feet had given way. In her drop, several lianas had twisted around her neck, strangling her. Below Bim's dangling body, a pyramid of oranges half as tall as a person had been shaken to the ground.

While cutting her down, they had a difficult time trying not to step on or slip on the fallen fruit. Hill took a spill. And in so doing, he revealed Howard, beneath the pyramid of maybe a thousand fallen oranges. His hands were frozen in front of his face in a vain, final effort to keep them off him. His mouth was stuffed with a large, juicy-looking Valencia. He must have been caught in the same bizarre accident as Bim. Perhaps he'd gone to save her and slipped and fallen, and then been suffocated? Although they remained looking around for another twenty minutes after recovering the bodies, neither Hill nor Willow could find any trace that the two deaths had not been a complete—if admittedly odd—accident.

"T-p anything?" Hill asked Andy.

"Besides you guys? No. Not a thing!"

❖

The following sidereal day, they again landed on the planet and broke up into couples for skimmer exploration. Again, Andy was alone.

The deaths of Bim and Howard had depressed everyone on the *Dallas* sufficiently for Hill to declare an unprecedented eight-hour Playby with double doses of Super-Qs for distraction. Even with the drugs, Andy had caught down-mood peripheral flashes from several crew members. The Company had psycho-selected the crew for low grief levels and synergistically mixed them for the lowest possible loss quotient. Even so, they'd been together a while, and every one of them had one reaction or another to the sudden change.

For Andy, as significant as the deaths was the giggling T-p voice that had refused to identify itself. Now, as he sped in his skimmer over his assigned sector for the day, he openly emitted, trying to locate the T-p voice again. No luck.

As had happened the previous day, Andy finished his work rapidly and set down the skimmer, opened an inflatable, and rested in the bright, warm, afternoon sun from the binary suns—far from any trees. A gentle breeze played over his body, wafting the scent of ripening peaches from an orchard that stretched before him. Clover and an odor like sweet marjoram added their light perfumes from the meadow into which he'd skimmed. Once again, Andy relaxed deeply in the complete T-p silence. But he didn't make the mistake of falling asleep again.

Good thing too. Otherwise he might have been awakened with a jolt. As it was, he sat bolt upright when he heard Roy's and Patsu's thoughts.

—Hey—Andy T-p'ed back.—Get out of my sector! You're in T-p range!—

No response followed, so he called the lander itself for a radio relay to their skimmer. Willow had remained there at planet-fall. She told Andy he was wrong. Roy and Patsu were way over in sector X-Z, eleven hundred kilometers away.

But Andy had *heard* them T-p. He now wondered why.

—You still there?—he T-p'ed them.

Giggles. The same ones as yesterday.

—Where are they?—he T-p'ed the question.

—In flower—

Despite the surrounding giggles, the tone was less than amused.

—Are they…*not are*?—he T-p'ed, remembering the construction put on yesterday's tragedy.

—Not yet!—followed by a cascade of giggling.

Andy didn't like the sound of that at all. He jumped into the skimmer and set it for their sector, calling Willow from the air, telling her he was going after the two. She said not to. Hill and Native were in Sector T, much closer. They'd go look.

Andy arrived back at the lander just as Hill reported in. He and Native had found Roy and Patsu unconscious, but still alive—and completely stoned out among a sea of poppies. The pale purple and white blooms they'd been walking through were able to explode their morphinid alkalis into the surrounding air. Roy and Patsu had been felled in minutes. Native had gotten punchy on the stuff the second he stepped out of the skimmer. Hill put on a protective mask, but he was a bit dizzy too. At least they were all safe now.

❖

"That's it," Hill declared, once the crew had all arrived back at the lander. "This planet is off-limits."

Patsu and Native argued that even Old Earth possessed its natural dangers—poisonous plants, feral animals, earthquakes, landslides, floods, tidal waves. They simply have to recognize what exactly constituted a hazard here. More exploration was required to do so.

"It's not as though we're being consciously attacked or anything!" Roy agreed. "It's partly stupid mistakes leading to equally stupid accidents."

"What if it's a pattern of them?" Hill asked. "Patsu, give me the improbability statistics on nine people in two days. Two killed and two nearly killed."

Patsu did a quick calculation and came up with a high figure. Too high for mere chaotic improbability. Too high for Hill's liking.

"Let's face it, crew," he said. "Despite Andy's extremely limited

T-p contact with someone or something or other, the planet itself seems quite barren of intelligent life. On the other hand, it does seem to be equipped with what can only be called a rather subtle, but effective, self-defense system. For all we know, it already belongs to someone. It's their farm world, perhaps, or their garden world. And we're the intruders. I say we leave."

"I'm not sure how limited the T-p contact was," Andy argued. "It had to be awfully strong to interconnect me to Patsu and Roy from so far away."

"How intelligent would you rate the voice that T-p'ed you?" Native asked.

Andy couldn't say: too little conversation.

"What exactly did the T-p say?" Willow wanted to know.

Andy repeated both "conversations," which even he had to admit were both of very short duration and most primitive. And the giggles. In terms of time spent during the entire T-p'ing, Ho Wang calculated the giggling occupied about three-quarters of the messages Andy received. Ho speculated that it was some sort of semi-consciousness. Perhaps even a 'droidlike alarm system.

Which was possible, Andy had to admit. But why then did he still intuit a larger intelligence? Because he did. He couldn't explain why.

The others listened to his arguments, and as he spoke, Andy T-p'ed them, carefully sorting each one's reality from wish fulfillment. They were coming down against the planet, against him.

Hill didn't need to T-p the crew to recognize that despite their high hopes for a Company planet-find of Class A, and the bonus and the rep-hit that would accompany it, none of the others were eager to subject themselves to possible death, no matter how rare or picturesque the place might be. Hill called for a vote on whether to call off human exploration or not. It worked out six to one against Andy.

"That's it," Hill concluded. "We'll reconnoiter one more week with mobile 'droids on planet. If there are no more bizarre accidents to them, the planet receives a Class D designation: for further exploration only with extreme caution."

The decision make Andy shudder. He'd actually come to anticipate a full thirty-day tour on the planet surface. He'd get more pure T-p silence here than in a so-called thought-proofed room anywhere else. Not to mention deeper sleep. No, it was just too pleasant to give up without a fight. Then too, he had T-p'ed a voice, had communicated with someone, or something, twice. That was his function on the *Dallas* among the crew. He couldn't just brush it off. Especially since that voice had allowed him to save Roy and Patsu's lives. Progress in communication had been achieved. Continued further contact was *imperative*!

Andy began to argue these points. Surely, if he was in contact with a voice that had twice warned him, no harm would likely befall him. And he might discover the source of the T-p emissions. Surely any company team that came in after the *Dallas* would need that kind of information and as much of it as he could provide.

Willow didn't like the idea, and the others seemed neutral, so once again they voted: Should Andy join the 'droids on the planet while the crew returned. Two votes no, five votes yes. Andy was pleased.

The others returned to the *Dallas* and sent back mobile 'droids. Andy continued to go down to the surface daily.

By the sixth day, after he'd covered more than half of the section they had mapped out, Andy was convinced he'd been right. The 'droids, of course, were near impossible to destroy, but they hadn't encountered a single mishap, not even a displaced one, like poppies spewing out powdered drugs in the air. Of course, it was possible that the planet's defense system only reacted to alien life, not to alien machines.

Meanwhile, every afternoon, Andy would relax deeply and communicate a bit more with the T-p voice.

Or was it voices? It was difficult to decide which. He was sometimes reminded of the Swamp Moths of Epsilon Vega, that same feeling of a million voices mixed into one larger, representative voice, all possessing the same thoughts. At other times, the voice, seemed to have a single, even a singular, personality—pesky, yet sweetly frivolous; shy, yet impulsive and bold; deliberately, mischievously unhelpful with anything that could be construed as a fact.

Through T-p, Andy learned names on the planet—the names of certain fruit and vegetables, trees, hills, even lakes. But he never discovered who the voice belonged to, nor where the other sentient beings were—if there were any others. At times, the voice seemed woefully ignorant, in the way a four-year-old human was, so that he had to wonder how mature the voice really was.

His reports each night back on the *Dallas* were as full of detail as he could make them. The others' response was always the same question: "So you made no progress?"

Andy knew what was happening with the remaining six crew members. Having been disappointed, they were already finished with this planet. They were anticipating the next planet-fall, merely waiting until the mobile 'droids were done. With Bim and Howard gone, all kinds of new combinations of Playby and its concomitant relationships were forming and reforming. He'd seen it happen too often before from close up to doubt that they were far more interested in each other than in whatever he might discover. Of them all, only Hill and Willow still even kept speaking to him every night, and he was feeling less and less like one of them, and more and more like—well, not like Bim and Howard so much, but not far off either. Finally Andy asked Hill if he could spend nights on the planet's surface, rather than on board. At first, the others appeared to be insulted; then sad, then angry, then annoyed. Finally they seemed to give up on him altogether. A vote was taken and they all said sure.

As for the planet, Hill and Willow had already agreed that it would receive no higher than a Class D designation, and thus remain off all beaten paths, no matter what Andy or the 'droids came up with.

❖

Giggle, giggle.

—Where are the others?—Andy T-p'ed.

Silence. Then—What means others?—

—You know, more than one. I am one—Andy explained.—Those who died in the Orange Wood, they were *others*.—

It was day seven and Andy was getting nowhere.

—Replaceable—followed by more giggles.—No distinction—

It was astounding to Andy how many fairly ordinary concepts known to a dozen intelligent species that the Company had already encountered were not known by the still elusive voice; children, parents, male, female, good, evil, God. Not a clue. All the voice seemed to know was names. The only actual concepts it seemed able to delineate were "are" and "not are" as well as "care" and "hurt."

—You hurt?—it would ask Andy every day during his daily rest periods. Those and his naps had grown longer and more frequent now that he didn't have the distraction of other crew-mates and the Big Brown Buzz.

—Not hurt—he would reply.

—You care?—it would then ask.

—I care—he would reply.

—I care—the voice would reiterate. Then giggle a bit and vanish.

Perhaps that was why, on day seven, when the mobile 'droids were done with their work, the Company's work on this planet done, Andy decided not to go into the lander with them back to the *Dallas*. Instead he took the skimmer and went to hide in the Peppermint Woods: the densest forest they had found on the planet. All the while, he admitted to himself that he was acting totally irrationally. At first he told himself that it was the principle of the thing, and he was taking a stand. The planet had been misclassified, and he would prove it.

The next day, Hill sent down a lander full of hunter 'droids. But Andy could T-p their simple mechanisms a hundred kilometers away. Not for nothing were T-ps like Andy given high official rank in the Company, given status and power and often great wealth too. Their ability to read minds as well as to elude anyone or anything other than another T-p made them close to invincible. The hunter 'droids returned back to the lander empty-handed.

Andy did keep channels open at times to the *Dallas*, to listen in on the crew, as it voted that night. Willow alone wanted to remain and keep looking for him—even in person if need be. Even Roy, his favorite Playby companion, voted against them staying. But it was evident to all, even Willow, that what had begun on Deneb 3 several months ago had finally worked itself out here, on this planet. T-ps were known to always be the most sensitive and thus the most difficult crew members. More than one had cracked up on board—with disastrous results for all. No one, not even Willow, looked forward to that happening. No sirree. That could get really hazardous to their health.

Furthermore, following the mobile 'droids' full inspection and the ship computer's own fullest analysis, even that Class D designation seemed high for the planet. Every known chemical and mineral on the new Universal Valence Chart did exist somewhere or other upon the little world, true, but all of them in equal quantities, and none sufficient for serious mining. The timber from those billions of trees was all of an ultra-porous, low-pulp quality. The rich-looking foodstuffs that grew so abundantly were lacking in nutrients essential to human life. Although perfectly edible, it wouldn't break down in the human alimentary system—it merely passed through, undigested.

In conclusion, beautiful as the place looked, it was a failure. It might make a good resort planet, possibly a hospital or asylum recuperation spot. But the Company already owned dozens of those, most with far more spectacular settings than this bland little world. The final designation turned out to be Class R: Cost-inefficient to Exploit.

Even if he now wanted to, Andy felt he could *not* now return to the *Dallas*. Not after that vote. Only Willow had cared enough to vote in his favor. She had good qualities, Andy admitted. Among them, loyalty—up to a point. But in the end, the essential superficiality and simple vanity of Willow's mind, which made her a perfect Playby partner and genial travel companion, had—at least for a T-p—resolved itself. He was sure that she too would get over him in no time.

After one more general communication and requests for six hours for Andy to return on board went unanswered, the *Dallas* lifted out of orbit. Its golden glint in the cerulean sky lasted but an instant.

❖

His own supplies had run out, and although Andy had eaten his fill of the fruits and vegetables around him, he felt weaker and more tired every day. He found himself skimming less, exploring far less, sitting more, falling asleep more, feeling a nearly transcendental peace amid the T-p silence, in the cool nights, the warm days. With this new peace, he hardly ever needed to call on the voice anymore for assurances, for company, although occasionally, as he was awakening from his sixth nap of the day, he would T-p the giggles distantly.

One late afternoon, he awakened with the redSun past zenith, the white-blueSun approaching meridian. He'd been sleeping since the redSundown of the previous day. By his timepiece, that had been a sleep of almost twenty-two regular hours. Even so, he had a difficult time clearing his mind and he could barely lift his head. His vision was spotty, his hearing undermined by a series of constant hollow tones thrumming. His stomach felt cavernously empty.

He suddenly realized that he was starving and was going to die.

With what little strength still remained in him, Andy began to cry, sobbing convulsively. He knew that he was being foolish—it would exhaust the last bit of energy left in him. But he was unable to stop himself. His thoughts ran back to his infancy, to the difficulties of being a T-p and the thousands of slights, offenses, insults, and humiliations he'd received over the years in Education and Development, and even later working for the Company. He couldn't forget the pain of being different. No matter how close he came to anyone during Playby, the truth was he'd always been alone. Truly alone.

Giggle, giggle.

At least he'd heard that sound clearly.

—Go away!—he T-ped.

—Away?—

—Go away! You know. Go away from me.—

—Everywhere—it came back to Andy.—No distinction—

—Can't you see I'm starving to death!—

Silence. Then,—You not are?—

—No, I still am. But by tomorrow I'll be *not are*—

—What's tomorrow?—the voice asked.

Andy began to explain about time, then he remembered that the voice didn't know time. Not days, not months, not years.

—*Always are*—the voice said.—No distinction—it giggled.

—I'm hurt!—Andy tried.—I'll be *not are* without—much care—

Another set of misunderstanding T-p exchanges ensued until Andy was completely frustrated, exasperated, and finally before the voice appeared to comprehend him, totally exhausted. Or did it comprehend? He wasn't sure. He was no longer sure he cared what happened to him anymore. He was so tired. He wanted nothing but to fall asleep, but he fought the feeling, believing that once he did sleep, he'd never wake up.

The last thing Andy remembered clearly was what looked like a twig with sharp thorns blown hard against his legs, puncturing his left ankle. He recalled watching his by now much-thinned blood seeping out through the gash and into the surrounding grass and earth. He looked at it objectively, uncaring, really. It didn't hurt. Then Andy went under.

❖

His recovery was slow: it took weeks. When he was finally able to stay awake long enough to see, hear, and think clearly, he realized that he was immobilized. The fingers of both hands and toes of both feet through his thorn-ripped shoes had been transformed somehow into roots that were deeply, safely, comfortingly anchored into the ground, roots through which he now understood he would be fed, clothed, warmed, cared for.

—Who are *you*?—he T-p'ed a question.

—No distinction—the voice replied.

—Then...then...Who am I?—he asked. And even as he formulated the thought, the question seemed utterly academic.

—No distinction—the voice replied.

As he knew it would answer. Then, as he knew it would, it giggled.

—No distinction—Andy repeated.

Andy giggled and giggled and giggled.

Love and the She-Lion

I was told this story at the Windhoek Airport in Namibia several years ago while awaiting a very late connection from Salisbury back to the States. I'd been in Zimbabwe trying to track down some facts on the middle, "lost" African years of a British author whose biography I was planning to write.

The narrator of the tale was a cinematographer named Dale from the Tampa Bay area who'd worked in Namibia as part of a National Geographic Society film team shooting a TV documentary on the Etosha Pan wildlife preserve. Dale was one of those wiry, tense, perpetually tanned women you can spot all over African and South American airport and hotel lobbies, former Vassar and Smith valedictorians who'd discovered that life in the States was too small for their wide aspirations. Despite their formidable appearance, these women are usually great talkers, smart, funny, and confident enough to be able to make instant if temporary friendships with single men traveling alone who make little attempt to hit on them.

Dale and I shared close to two hours of drinks, jokes about the airline's efficiency, and conversation at Windhoek Airport while our plane was being checked out and refueled. She was the very last of her team to be kicked out of Namibia by its then newly installed, comic book Marxist government, a honor she admitted was due entirely to her wiliness, her perseverance, and her desperate desire to get a bit of extra film shot long after the rest of the crew had packed up and shipped out.

This is what Dale told me:

I suppose you've heard a lot of stories about Africa while you were here. Africa is full of weird, awful stories. One especially strange incident happened up around Tsumeb a couple of months ago concerning a woman and a lioness. We were shooting around there and it was one of those stories that makes you stop and think about what it means to yourself, to your life. Especially if you're a woman, and particularly if you're a woman on your own, and by your own choice. There were three women on our shooting crew and we discussed it endlessly, trying to find in it some sign, some significance. Whether the men on the crew talked about it among themselves as much, I don't know, and at the time I didn't think to ask. All of a sudden I feel I have to share it with a man. Not with a man I know well, but with someone who'll be objective about it—if that's at all possible. I'm not sure if I'm completely clear about this, but here goes. I'd met the woman involved only once, on her wedding day. And I just found out a week ago the circumstances that led up to the wedding and to the incident. Partly from her husband, and partly from the local witch doctor. He'd been helpful to the crew while we were scouting around for locations and shooting and it seems that he was in on the story almost from the beginning.

The land around the village of Ohopoho is ancient savanna. Or rather new savanna replacing an ancient one. The farmers still practice slash-and-burn agriculture for the most part, and because of the mild prevailing southerlies, over the centuries, the people there have learned how and when to ring their fires so that land isn't overburned or the soil leached. The local crops are sugar beet, barley, a rough sort of milo wheat, tubers that easily resist the prevalent droughts, tree nuts, and ground nuts. The people also herd cattle, goats, and pigs.

The tribal people aren't rich really, but compared to most of Africa, they're well off, possibly because the Koaoka Veldt is underpopulated. White men have been on that coast since the Portuguese landed there in the fifteenth century. Portuguese, English, German, and Boers have held large tracts of coastland for years. Their coffee and cocoa plantations are extensive and productive and many villagers have enough leisure to sometimes work the plantations for extra pay. As a result, a few towns there—Otavi, Tsumeb, Ohopoho—have large, well-stocked weekly markets.

Even so, the people remain almost untouched by modern conveniences. Few telephones or electricity. Old Land Rovers are the most commonly seen motor vehicle and roads are few, meandering, and often washed away by sudden storms.

The people are healthy and well-fed, and because they've never been conquered by whites, they're rather proud and tenacious of their traditions. A century ago Arab merchants established several trading posts, but while the locals adopted some of their customs and clothing and cooking methods, Islam never took there as it did in other parts of the continent. Neither missionaries nor politicians much affect these people's lives.

The men of the Etosha Pan consider themselves warriors and hunters, although they hunt little and usually only as part of specific initiations and rituals. The bulk of their meat is from livestock.

The women of the area are somewhat more independent than one usually finds in Africa. They inherit matrilineally and even hold minor ceremonial offices. But while they can own property and smaller animals, the women aren't supposed to own cattle. Most marriages, therefore, are important financial mergers, where a female's inherited cattle dowry is mixed into her husband's often far smaller herd, making him a richer man.

This particular woman I want to speak of was the fifth daughter of a prosperous native farmer and herder, and upon his death she received no animals. But at her mother's remarriage to another tribesman soon after, the young woman inherited a second piece of farmland and enough movable property to hire help to farm it. Although she'd been asked to move in with several of her older sisters as co-wife to their husbands, even as a young teenager, she had refused.

She was a beautiful girl and people said that she'd been spoiled from an early age by her aging, near-doddering father—which is rare anywhere in Africa. As a result, her marriage age had come and gone three times. More than a dozen suitors had camped on the edges of her property. None of these marriage offers had been acceptable to her. A clever woman, she'd managed to break down each negotiation at some crucial point—the potential husband had two other wives, he drank too much, he'd never sired a child—leaving each suitor to think that he still might have a chance of winning her. In hopes that the woman would continue to think favorably of his offer, each warrior had returned to his own farm or village, leaving behind a gift of a kid, a calf, a piglet, for her father. Since her father was dead and her mother remarried, in this way the woman managed to collect a small wealth of livestock, and these proved sufficiently fertile that she was soon owner of a small flock of mixed animals. In fact, by these stratagems, at the time she was fifteen, she was the wealthiest single woman in the Etosha.

On market days, she would arrive in Ohopoho with her several boy employees, each laden with produce to sell. Because she was younger and single, her assigned market stall was on the undesirable northernmost end of the women's mart, close to the men's larger stalls. Despite the second-class nature of the location, the woman had taken this particular stall by force the very first time she arrived to sell at the market. It was a spot mostly kept empty to demarcate the men's and women's markets and so her brazen seizure had scandalized her sisters, aunts, and female cousins, who were even more annoyed by the excellent business she did at this key locale from her very first market day.

Seldom did her boys return home with unsold produce, and more often than not, the woman left the market with new bangles she'd purchased at the men's stalls—mostly of beaten copper and brass, but sometimes of silver and even gold. Often she earned enough money to buy another calf or kid. Her special love was for finely woven silk, and she displayed the gaudy rich cloths about her stall and on her body at every opportunity, which only furthered her general allure.

Unlike the other stall-owning women, and because she was unmarried, the woman wore no veil, not even the meaningless diaphanous ones some affected. A silk scarf embroidered with silver sometimes covered her head and shoulders, leaving her face visible to all passersby to lust after her. Equally shocking to her female relations, she offered homemade beer from a large calabash to some of her better male customers, and would herself sip demurely along with them, further inflaming their desire and their fantasies of owning such a remarkable looking and acting—and such a rich—woman.

One would suppose all this was being done to gain her a very wealthy husband, and indeed after market days, young warriors would gnash their teeth and mumble as she stalked off, her new purchases of goods and livestock in tow—back to her farm.

It wasn't a local warrior or farmer, however, who finally captured the fancy of the woman of Ohopoho, but a stranger. His name was

Veato, and he hailed from Porto de Alexandre, just across the border in Angola. Perhaps that might explain the greenish cast to his light eyes and his light pigmentation—the color, they said, of a newly whelped lion cub. So many centuries of white and black intermarried in Porto de Alexandre that no one seemed certain anymore exactly what their own ethnic background was.

Veato worked as a manager on one of the largest cocoa plantations near Tsumeb, and while many Etosha women considered him deformed because of his high color, the woman of Ohopoho was herself fair-skinned and immediately saw him as her equal, and the likely father of her children. Although Veato seldom bought anything at her stall on market days, she always called him over for a taste of beer and plied him with honeyed ground nuts. They would laugh and drink beer in full view of the marketplace.

The woman's aunts and sisters scolded her every chance they got. Wasn't Veato a stranger? And sickly hued? Where were his cattle? His goats? Where was his farm? His grazing land? Who were his sisters and brothers? His aunts and uncles? He was the least fitting husband for such a wealthy woman.

She laughed at their talk, telling them that Veato was better than any warrior they knew. His wealth was greater, although it lay not in cattle and land, but in bank-notes in a hut called a bank in Tsumeb. Besides which, Veato was educated—he held the esteemed magic of words. He could read and understand the signs on a book or newspaper as well as any plantation owner. Her relatives were old-fashioned: If Veato were to become her husband, she would have wealth surpassing that of the chiefs of Otavi and Ohopoho together.

Months later, when two of the boys in the woman's employ returned to their family farms, they told how soon after she and Veato had been seen laughing and drinking beer together, the stranger began appearing at the woman's farm. He would arrive every seven days, the young brothers said, laughing to tell it, as though he were the postman who drove into Tsumeb from Windhoek once a week. From this his detail, the brothers, their families, and soon all of the woman's neighbors came to call Veato "the Postman."

Word travels fast—usually in whispers on market day—and soon no young warrior arrived at the edge of the woman's property with memorized speeches and cattle, or with elderly male relatives intent upon bargaining for her hand.

Equally soon, the fruit of the Postman's deliveries were evident when the woman appeared in Ohopoho on market day. First one, then another boy child was born to her. As indicative of the couple's new status was the fact that Veato seldom came to market day anymore, and when he did, he no longer spent the afternoon at the woman's stall. After a brief greeting, he joined the men gambling in old Bl'oma's stall or looking over cattle for sale or competing in games of sport—running with quoits, leaping, and whirling the bull's pizzle.

Even the woman's relatives had come to accept the odd marriage as the true one, although no ceremony had taken place. Hadn't the woman gone her own way even as a child? Hadn't she as a young girl always hoed yams in her own patch before working the family plot? Hadn't she milked cattle when she was ready, though the poor beasts might be fainting from pain? Her life belonged to her: She had no father, and no brother or uncle had ever been able to get her to obey him.

So it was with some surprise that the witch doctor watched the woman approach his enclosure one morning. Behind her was a boy leading a newly foaled calf in a halter. Doubtless the woman intended it as payment for services to be performed.

I call him a witch doctor, and you probably are imagining some wizened old creature with chunks of bone through his nostrils and ears, garbed in rotting pelts. Not so. He was a young man—the role is hereditary—and among his storehouse of herbs and other homeopathic remedies, he also kept a considerable amount of medical supplies obtained in Windhoek. Nothing too specialized or sophisticated, of course, but as much as any other country doctor might have—analgesics, antibiotics, diuretics, antifungals, and surgical instruments. This aided his medical—and most frequently called upon—practice among the Etosha. His other and more convoluted practice wasn't so much forensic as spiritual. In that respect, he was what we would call a psychologist, except that he not only discovered the causes of depression and schizophrenia and so on, but it was also his job to name the specific spirit harassing his patient, and to somehow heal the broken or distorted link between that spirit and the patient.

The woman's physical health was fine. However, she told him that she was vexed and oppressed, anxious and discontent. Although she and the Postman had now passed more than two years together, he had made no marriage proposal, neither in person, nor by proxy. Nor did he seem about to do so. Indeed, she'd heard talk—much of it envious rumor, she suspected, but some shreds of it bound to be true—that Veato already had a wife in Porto de Alexandre. More than once he'd told her of his wish to return there, and on no occasion did he ever ask her to accompany him.

The woman was proud. She would never ask him to marry her. She would never plead with him. But she was unable to live without the Postman, she told the doctor. She wanted him to be her husband all the time, not one day out of seven. She had borne him two male children. Together they were strong, healthy, handsome, and wealthy. It was time for them to take their place in the community. Yet the Postman felt none of the opprobrium that gnawed at her. He scoffed at her complaints, even jeered at them. The woman had already attempted to win him over with various love potions. The drinks had made him more amorous, but he'd always returned the next morning to the cocoa plantation. What she needed, she told the doctor, was a spirit-binding between them.

The doctor's attempts at marriage counseling fell upon deaf ears. He too had heard the various rumors about Veato having a life back on the coast. But the woman would not heed any of his possible explanations for the couple's difficulties—she was too stubborn.

Having failed at psychology, he switched into his role of spirit-mender.

He sent the woman outside his hut to wait. He quaffed an herbal tea that caused him to enter into a light trance, and he meditated. When he called the woman inside again, he told her that the trouble between her and Veato was a result of their own spirits being at war. The Postman's spirit—that of the great owl—understood that her guiding spirit was too strong. As strong as his own spirit. Furthermore, her own spirit—that of the lioness—was displeased with the woman, who wished to forsake her life as an independent female, provider for herself and her offspring, and instead to act like a woman whose spirit was that of an okapi or a warthog. Somehow or other, the woman must sever the link that existed between herself and the spirit that had so far intuitively guided her life. Sever it, and hope that a new and hopefully more domesticated spirit would enter her life. Once the Postman's spirit recognized this change, his own strong sprit would no longer fight against marriage.

As to how the woman might accomplish this breach, the doctor could not yet say. Her spirit was strong and knowledgeable and it would find the correct course.

The woman paid him with the calf and went home. Many days after that she pondered how to do what had to be done. Sometimes she trembled at her own thoughts. The lioness was a formidable adversary, and although the woman knew in her heart that its spirit had indeed always accompanied her life, she also knew that she must begin to destroy that link.

Lions are not common in the area, but after the rains come to the Etosha Pan, small prides of lions follow herds of plentiful game into what becomes a four-month-long paradise of grass and flowers. The male lions usually keep to the center of the Pan where game is thickest, for they are lazy creatures. But, especially as the wet season ends, lionesses with cubs are known to wander far beyond the grassiest area in search of prey. Over the years, many of the woman's relatives had lost yearlings from their flocks to the hungry marauders. Within weeks, the current dry season would begin: The woman might begin to search for her spirit.

The doctor had told her she would know what to do when the time arrived: All she need do was wait. She waited in a somewhat revived attitude, and as though the Postman already sensed her secret intention, he began to spend more time at her kraal. This fueled her desire for marriage all the more.

The summer, the rainy season, passed over the Etosha Pan longer than in other years, and the woman still waited. Only after three separate complaints had been made public at the market day did she believe that her spirit-link was actually on the prowl. A lioness with two cubs, but no apparent mate, had attacked three times so far in three weeks. From one she'd taken a kid, from another a newborn calf, and from the farm of the woman's youngest aunt, she'd taken a yearling calf. Unafraid of men, the lioness had been interrupted during this last kill by two boys tending the herd. They'd barely escaped with their lives. One boy's shoulder bore claw marks where she'd swatted him away as he tried to save the calf.

The woman of Ohopoho knew her waiting was over. Gathering up her two infants and a pure white kid from her flock, she went to visit this aunt.

The family was surprised to see her but nevertheless feasted the woman and dandled the boy children. The aunt expected to hear news of the Postman's marriage proposal: in vain. Equally hopeless was her curiosity about the milk-white kid. In her heart, the aunt had hoped her niece would leave it as a peace offering. This was one reason why she'd feted the woman so well.

The woman of Ohopoho asked the two herd boys about the lioness that had attacked them. How large was it? How fast? The boys were eager to tell her that it was very large and very fast and very cunning. They also told her a strange fact: the lioness had a single handful of almost black mane across her nape, as though it were partly male and partly female. The animal was a demon, the mauled boy insisted. Because of this unexpected hank of mane, the men on her aunt's farm referred to the beast sometimes as a he-lioness, but more frequently as a she-lion.

They did not expect it to return. Believing it to be something more than a mere creature of the savanna, each farmer in the area expected to lose one of their herd to the she-lion before the drought set in for good. Their spring harvests had been abundant, and their herds had been considerably enriched by many new births. They thought that the world spirit had sent the she-lion to exact tribute from each of them. The next target would be either the woman's first brother's flock—his farm abutted her aunt's—or the small coffee plantation owned by an elderly white woman.

The next morning, the woman left her children in the care of her aunt. She took the kid and walked to a place between the old woman's coffee trees and her brother's pumpkin patch. There, she flattened the brush along a path in the savanna, littering it with kid dung. She tied the kid to a stout tree near a bush of sweet marjoram, so the animal would not attempt to get away. Then, without telling anyone what she had done, the woman went to stay the night at her brother's house.

Her brother had naturally heard of the woman's visit to their aunt and he too welcomed her. He'd also heard that she was traveling with a milk-white kid, but when he asked about it, the woman casually mentioned that while she had napped, the kid had somehow gotten off its halter and away. Secretly, the brother believed the animal still roamed his land. He and his wives thought his sister's lost kid might be compensation for the loss from their own flock they were certain would occur once the she-lion came to their property to feed.

After a generous morning meal, the woman left her brother's kraal and went out to find the kid. She found part of its carcass still attached by a line to the tree where she had left it. The woman shouted in joy, freed now, she believed, from the spirit-link to the she-lion. She returned to her young aunt's farm, took up her infants, and went home without further incident. All the way home through the savanna, she sang.

Less than a week later, the doctor was startled to be revisited by the woman of Ohopoho, more troubled than before. She reminded him of his words to her on the first visits. She told him of her recent actions. Why then, she wanted to know, had the she-lion's spirit remained linked to hers? Indeed, it seemed linked even more closely than before. Hadn't Veato only the day before visited her farm as usual and still not made a marriage proposal? Worse, hadn't Veato told the woman of a new plan to leave his work at the cocoa plantation and to return for good to Porto de Alexandre? All the woman's resolve had broken down then. She'd wept, she'd entreated him. When she begged the Postman to remain with her and their children one more night, he'd grown taciturn and morose. Without answering her, he'd left the hut and the farm.

The doctor had of course heard from others of the marauding she-lion, and he now cautioned the woman. If the creature's spirit was stronger than her own, the sacrifice she'd made to it was probably useless. The woman became desperate. She reasoned that if the offering had merely bound her spirit closer to the she-lion, perhaps she must now do something to harm the she-lion, and *that* would break the link? Once again the doctor warned the woman, suggesting she meditate rather than rush headlong into deeds whose consequences neither of them could foresee. Unpersuaded by his prudence, she returned to her farm.

The woman waited several days, awaiting news of a new attack by the lioness. On market day, Bl'oma dramatically narrated to anyone who would listen the story of his close escape from the she-lion's claws.

No sooner had she heard Bl'oma's tale than the woman closed her market stall, although it was barely midday, and returned home. She took another kid from her flock and went toward Bl'oma's small farm. Once again she tamped down the grass to make a path and once again she laid out dry pellets of the kid's dung upon the path. Once more she tied the kid to a tree in the midst of sweet herbs for it to snack on. This time, however, rather than going away, she remained hidden a short distance away. Hours later, near sunset, the woman was awakened from a nap by the shrill bleating of the kid and the snarling of the she-lion at its kill. She set out on foot to cross the lioness's path. She did this easily enough, and after a short walk in the dry savanna, she found the she-lion's temporary den and inside it the two sleeping lion cubs.

Although the woman hadn't formulated a plan beforehand, she acted in the spot. Seizing one sleeping cub, she ran off with it before it could awaken its sibling or cry out to its mother. She strangled the cub and threw it onto the path she was certain the mother would cross returning to her den from her kill. When the woman carefully edged her way past the place where she'd earlier tied the kid, the still-feeding she-lion belched and rolled over to drowse. It would awaken soon and tear off a leg to carry back to its den. On its way it would encounter its dead cub, and the spirit-link with the woman would be broken.

The Postman's next visit occurred two days later. His frowns were replaced by smiles. He told the woman he had thought much about the course his life ought to take and he had decided he preferred her to his wife in Porto de Alexandre, and he preferred his life in Ohopoho to his life in the Angolan city. He would remain in Etosha with her, but he would continue to work for the plantation owner. The woman and her children would come live with him in his house on the grounds of the plantation. It wasn't so far from her farm that she couldn't go there every few days, if she needed to. He outlined the beauties and conveniences of the house, and he convinced the woman that her happiness with him would be complete. She even agreed with his stipulation that the two of them marry legally—as was required by the plantation owner—in the government building at Tsumeb.

The last detail later provided much merriment to the warriors and relatives in the woman's tribe when they heard of it: You see, the government building at Tsumeb not only houses the county court and administrative offices, but also the post office.

A boy was sent to the woman's brothers' farms with the formal marriage proposal. Carelessly, if secretly relieved, the brothers gave their consent. The first brother, whose farm had been spared loss of livestock due to the woman's sacrifice of a kid, offered to hold a complete tribal ceremony for the couple after the marriage in Tsumeb, acting just as though he himself had received the marriage proposal from Veato and had negotiated with Veato's elder relations in the time-old manner. He set a date for the event.

Overjoyed, the woman sent off the oldest boys in her employ to announce the festivities to her neighbors, aunts, sisters, and cousins. She then dressed in her best clothing to accompany Veato to Tsumeb for the white man's ceremony, leaving her infant children in the care of her other two boy employees, with her niece to care for them arriving at nightfall.

The woman had only been in Tsumeb twice before and she marveled at its roads and buildings, at its bank and automobiles and telephones. But she remained haughty in manner and restrained in her wonder, so that she cut a dignified figure at the Tsumeb courthouse. That's where I met her. My partner and I had been using some out-buildings at the plantation where Veato worked as our base of operations and we'd befriended the groom. We were happy to be official witnesses to the marriage. Delighted too by the extreme beauty of the couple. The woman of Ohopoho, especially, was the handsomest of a handsome people, and she wore her silks and jewelry like a great princess.

After the ceremony, we joined them at a marriage feast held in the town by one of Veato's colleagues and we were favorably impressed by the woman's apparent devotion to the plantation manager and by her ability to gulp down large quantities of the local beer with little outward effect. Many toasts of this liquor were made by all of us in several languages, to the couple's health, their fertility, their wealth and conjugal happiness.

Just as our little party was breaking up, a runner came from the plantation to tell Veato that a lion had been reported on the farm's outskirts. It was unclear whether or not it was the marauding she-lion, but just to be certain, the owner had taken men to hunt it down. Veato was needed back at the main house immediately.

We shook hands with Veato and watched the woman walk off with her husband. He later told us that the two of them returned to the plantation, he to the main house, the woman to his smaller house nearby. Evidently, however, the woman felt discomfort being alone, for in the middle of the night, she gathered up her few things and started off for her farm. Nor was Veato too surprised when he returned to his cottage just before sunrise to find his new wife gone. Not until the tribal ceremony, the "real marriage," would her leaving him be construed as divorce or abandonment. Clearly the woman missed her infants and wanted to be with them.

It's a walk from that coffee plantation to her farm, and the woman probably arrived home near dawn. All must have seemed quiet, with that eerie, delicious silence of pre-sunrise Etosha just before the place erupts into birdcall cacophony.

Given the spiral design of the local kraals, it would have been only after the woman had gotten well inside the enclosure that she would have noticed the door to the sleeping hut open. Given the scare about the lion, she probably first checked the animal pens and, counting, found that none of her flock was missing. When she saw the open door, she must have called into the sleeping hut, and getting no answer, concluded that the two boys she employed had run off during the night. We later found out that her niece had developed some ailment of the stomach and never made the trip at all.

When the woman of Ohopoho entered, all she could have made out in the still dimness of the sleeping hut would have been the bloodied corpses of her two infants, little of them recognizable. She probably didn't have much time to weep over them. The she-lion must have lain in wait. It leapt at her from behind.

The doctor later told us that it surely was the same she-lion who'd been marauding the Etosha, given the strings of long dark hair found clutched in the woman's death-grip fingers. He also told us that during the attack, the woman had found enough strength to somehow manage to turn around, whether to fight off the creature or not, he couldn't say. Claw marks on her breasts and the angle of the lioness's bite through the woman's jugular clearly show that the two must have looked into each other's eyes, if only for a few seconds.

One can only wonder what the woman of Ohopoho thought when she faced herself in that instant.

A Guest in the Heavens

The Age of Silver-Iridium Poetry is vanished, alas. For if only a single one of those geniuses—biological, cyber, or any combination thereof—still existed (no matter what media was being worked in, *that* Poet would be most perfectly suited to perform the task assigned. And not myself, your correspondent/journalist, concerning the impending catastrophe.

In vain did I attempt to over-sway my superior in this matter, explaining that I hardly have the best training as a "Universal Astrophysical Witness."

The bulk of my just completed sixty-seven years of Education & Development, after all, is in the Textual Analysis of Obsolete Classic Physics: Sub-string to Intra-Molecular—with minors in Late Second Matriarchal Bella-Arth Nineteen-Tone Music and in Post-Pha'arg-Era Delphinid Water-Sand-Wind Sculpture.

They argued back that I may lay claim to a full 47 percent of actual human biological genetics, as well as another 26.75 percent of Un-adapted 7th Generation of the Cloned-Cyber-Zoon known as P'al Syzygy. (The balance, like most births, naturally enough, was "newly generated material for maximum effectiveness and endurance.")

This, they asserted, was a high enough degree for me to fit best in observing the upheaval and demise of this tiny system believed by many (59.79033 percent as of the latest poll taken) as the ancient home-world to one of the current Three Species, that is to say Humanity.

To say I have had nothing to do with this non-serious area of the old Orion Spur would be a tautology: Who has? After all, I first saw the light of day in the 182th century, following the Great Reconciliation of "Vir" and "Matri," upon wonderful planet Chrysophase-D, in the Center-Worlds Sag Arm system of Narcissus Terce.

But Janiculus-Chase-onV was insistent. And so here I am, upon this madcap adventure about to approach this nondescript system and its indifferent end.

Oh, Chase-onV was diabolical enough to allow an official witness and observer from another not quite competing organization to ours, the Consumer's Republic of 76ExxonConSeCo66 & Neo-Walmartia, to attend upon this long and rather tedious journey.

Her name, for it is a g. female, is Scroba(CIR-2300), and if she possesses more than 6 percent of human biologicals, I'll be a Perli Berry Bug in heat, in late Autumn, upon Usk (in the immortal words of the Bard—Eis Kell).

Scroba, of course, asserted her gender-ship upon strapping into the Super-Fast that we were assigned (I wouldn't have gone without the latest model, this one has a time-flux scattering mechanism). She complained that the length of shape of her daybed/chair/dais etc. was designed for g. males not g. females and would prove uncomfortable for such a long—seventy-five hours—flight.

I let the Fast Mind respond, of course, and it had 116 possible alterations for the problem out of which she could pick one, many, or all.

When Scroba then complained that the Fast Mind was evidently a *male* mind, it countered by telling her it was originally (twenty thousand years ago, I believe) a female, albeit a highly evolved Andromeda-Galaxy Super-Slime-Mold variety of female.

Scroba got off the chair and the ship reconfigured the bed too quickly for even our augmented eyesight to see more than a blur. Scroba then re-tried it, and sulked that it was "a bit less harsh."

Annoyed that she would have one less Intelligent Being to harass, she promptly had herself injected and fell to sleep. I in turn suggested that the Fast Mind might wish to consider injecting her repeatedly until a half day, Sol. Rad, before our arrival.

This was overruled. "I find her 'cute,'" the ship declared.

"Cute as a Vole-Ratteen popping its head from a Cherm-millet bin," I replied, and the Fast Mind immediately cited the Eis Kell lyric I had referenced, by completing it: "Always deadlier than the Male."

"And she smells funny too," I said. "Neutralize that."

"It's a purposeful scent."

"Its purpose being?" I asked.

"Unclear," the Fast Mind had to admit. "It's called perfume."

"If it's unclear, then neutralize it."

Which the ship did. I mean, who needs extraneous odors for three and three-quarter days, Sol. Rad, anyway?

Scroba was awake, alas, earlier than I'd hoped. I was surrounded by a privacy screen, naturally, but this seemed to make no difference at all, as she stood quite close and made annoying motions that interfered not only with my spatial recognition of the air-screens but also the very coherence of the screen I was working on.

"Fast," said I, "please inform the other passenger of the purpose of a privacy screen," I demanded.

As it began the first of fifteen definitions, Scroba said, "I know what a privacy screen does."

"Then explain why are you gesticulating like a nerve-damaged Diomedean water vole in heat?"

"I'm trying to get your attention."

"You can't have it: I'm occupied. Fast, initiate full material physical privacy screen—instantly!"

She backed away fast when the plasti-metal shot out of the floor and surrounded me.

An hour and thirty-two minutes later, I had a portion of that screen removed.

Scroba was placed at an insta-desk she'd had the ship erect for her and was working at her own air-screens.

"Sixty-two point eleven percent of those insta-polled believe that you have mistreated me," she said.

"I really don't care if ninety-nine percent believe it."

"You can't go against the majority," she insisted.

"Majority of what? Of whom, rather? People you happen to know?"

"I won't stand for your rude behavior," Scroba insisted.

"You were not invited onto this mission by me, and you are free to leave at any time," I added, and had the Fast Mind prepare me a collation.

"You know I couldn't possibly leave."

"You could, possibly. And quite easily," I corrected.

"That would be homicide!"

"Semi-demi-homicide, since you possess such a smidgen of true human biologicals. It would be more like semi-demi-*pseudo*-homicide," I added, pleased with my quip.

At that, she put up her own physical privacy screen.

Not long after that the Fast Mind reported a necessary stop. It had encountered rather far ahead, but still rather evident, an anomaly.

Or rather an actual object, not far off our path.

"Well?" I asked. "What is it?"

"It appears to be part of that solar system we are heading toward."

"So far out?"

"It's been traveling a while. Clearly you understand that particular G-Class has become a red giant. The material intercepted appears to be of rather exact similitude to what had been that solar system's second orbiting world. Lilith, it was called."

"Venus!" Scroba corrected.

"She's correct," I had to admit.

"Apologies. I assumed that mythical names were inter-changeable."

"Names are *never* interchangeable," Scroba warned.

"She's correct again, Fast." Then before Scroba could crow, I said, "So we're headed in the right direction at least."

The ship didn't dignify that with an answer.

"Estimated time of arrival?" I tried.

The readout was a bit earlier than that given to us.

"Would the passengers like to watch a moving diagram explaining the destruction about to come?" the Fast Mind asked. It was clearly annoyed at me too and showed it by lumping us together.

"Do it."

The graphic was dynamic and of course tri-dimensional, as though we were actually within that solar system, albeit at a great distance, from a perspective slightly above the ecliptic and near the moon of the ninth planet. First we were shown what it looked like for most of the system's long life: twelve planets, their satellites and various other planetoids in their appropriately varied orbits. Then the sun turned orange and began expanding, taking the tiny first planet with it. Secondly, it expanded twice as far, became redder, and overtook this second so-called Venus, which—because it had greater mass—actually underwent less of the easy absorption than the first had, indeed more of an explosion; ergo the junk matter we'd come across. We were arriving in time for the sun to overwhelm the third planet, after which, due to its great density, it would absorb so much more material to feed its furnaces that it would march outward rapidly, eating up the smaller fourth and a mid-ring of asteroids, settling to nibble on the gorgeous, gaseous fifth one, which would increase its expansion twentyfold until it shattered the sixth, then flattened out into a flaming disc, quickly eating up the next two, and so raced outward to its cometary cloud level. There it would become so thinned out, it would at last simply fall into itself, molecule after molecule burning each other and themselves until at last there would be a blinding flash and then nothing. Or nearly nothing, as some larger and smaller embers would remain, flickering in and out of the light spectrum for centuries to come.

"Very dramatic," I replied.

"Of course, it could also become what is called nova," the Fast Mind said, and replayed the last few seconds, which collapsed and then wildly expanded.

Scroba pouted and put up her privacy screen again.

Several hours later, the ship awakened me. "We have received a signal."

"There are survivors!" Scroba insisted.

"Where are they hailing from?" I asked.

"A large M-Class world. Gamma of fifteen planets orbiting a good-sized J-Class star, with only a very old name listed in our files: Episilon Eridani."

"Definitely survivors," Scroba insisted.

"How far off our course are they?"

"Not far. This ship can easily detour."

"Bring up the message," I said.

Our air-screens showed human creatures not too different from ourselves in their physicality, albeit smaller, and of course clad almost head to toe.

"They look primitive," I commented. "Are they intelligent?"

Before the ship could answer, we were visibly and audibly being hailed.

"Welcome, visitors. Our world mind is attempting to link up with your ship. Can your ship's mind open a channel?"

"This ship can manage a small and very discrete link," the Fast Mind said only to me, "but only with many precautions and safeguards, naturally."

"Naturally," I agreed. Then said aloud, "Welcome, humans. Yes! Our ship will patch you through more fully."

"I think they're adorable," Scroba said. "Look, some are still neonates." She all but purred. I believe it is already on record that she is a female.

"Are you in need of medical or other such survival materials?" I asked.

"No." It was a handsome, small, fit-looking g. female who responded. "Gratitude. Are you the captain?"

"Captain: a false and once necessary alpha role," the Fast Mind explained the word to me.

They *were* primitive.

"I did sign all requisitions for the mission, if that's what you mean. Yes, so I suppose I am," I added.

"Greetings, human female. My name is Scroba."

"See, they do too have women," we heard the first one say to some others. "Greetings, Scroba, I'm Francine del Abbott. We're all fine here. This is one of the colonies of survivors, as you called us, from the solar system that our world mind says you are headed to. We have everything we require here. But a few of us have a request."

"Go ahead, Francine," Scroba said, relieving me of the strain of talking to them.

"Is it true that your ship is headed to our former solar system?" Francine asked.

"Briefly, yes."

"For documentation purposes only," I added.

"See?" Francine said to the others. "I knew it wasn't being ignored in the Center Worlds." Then to us, "Could we possibly ask you to bring along one or two of us for our own documentation purposes? We're certain you have far faster and safer craft than we have. We couldn't really chance it. In fact, our world mind wasn't a hundred percent certain we'd be safe from it even this far away, if it went nova."

"Ship?" I asked. "What do you say to that question?"

"They'll feel the effects in about six years' time, by which time it will be only…" and here it produced a long string of numerals.

"Unless it goes supernova, which is unlikely, you're totally safe if you remain where you are!" Scroba assured them. She was apparently expert at instant statistical analysis.

"One surviving human," the Fast Mind said, "may join us. We have room for only one, and we will provide all needed equipment for documentation to match theirs."

I passed on the information, which they were also getting directly from their own world mind.

"Our requirements are for a non-attached, more or less disposable member of your group," I read out the Fast's specifications. "Someone young enough to be strong, but old enough to be able to make crucial decisions if needed."

"That's Tony van Jeffery. He's volunteered," Francine said, pointing to the young human, who waved at us.

"He's very attractive," I said. "Which usually means good genetics. Has he left some of his DNA behind, in case we incur a fatal accident?"

"It's all taken care of," Francine assured us with a little smile.

"He's not pregnant, is he?" Scroba was clever enough to ask. The Fast might have been Super, but it's not Super shielded against fine radiation. We of course were safe, having been modified at birth for Fast travel.

"No. Not many of our males are born with Relfian Vivi-parturition Units."

"They are *quite* primitive," was the ship's comment. But I don't believe that was heard by them.

"If her name is Scroba, what's yours?" Francine looked right at me.

"You may call me Syzygy."

"Ziggy?" she asked.

"Close enough! And, Francine? We'll be moving into orbit in a few hours. Please have your volunteer also in high orbit, ready for transfer." I read off their world mind's message to our ship. "His name is Toe-Knee?"

"That's right. Tony," Francine responded.

"Odd name," Scroba commented. "Was he a runner, do you think?"

"In two hours and fifty minutes your time." I signed off. "Fast Mind, will the Toe-knee require anything different? A bed is being prepared and an insta-desk for Toe-knee."

"I'll let Tony know."

"I'm so excited. We're going to be meeting an Earthling. Think of it, Syz, one of the 'originals.'" Scroba was indeed excited.

"If you accept the particular origin theory."

"Of course I accept the origin theory. What? You don't?"

I ignored her. "Fast Mind, were you able to get a full medical scan from their world mind in case this Toe-Knee requires special attention?"

"Indeed. He appears to be ninety-nine point nine-eight percent similar to yourself."

"A brother," Scroba teased.

"A cousin is more like it," the Fast Mind said. "By the way, this ship is modifying our normal bow wind to a wider focus in order to keep other debris from destroyed planets at a minimum. Unless, of course, more samples are needed."

"None. Excellent. Now, Scroba, you interrupted me before, what was it about?"

She looked about as blank as a person could, then said, "I remember. I wanted to know if you had a mate or a pod?"

For *that* she'd interrupted me!

"I'm part of two different pods. Both of whom appear to be trying to initiate some sort of congratulatory message at this time. Why do you ask?"

"Just curious," she said and flounced off.

"She's 'cute,' huh?" I asked the Fast Mind.

"This ship is also excited about meeting a primitive human," it commented. "It wasn't known that any existed."

So of course you, reading this report, may now understand: Given this low level of curiosity and communication among my shipmates, is it any wonder at all what transpired later on?

❖

"'Syzygy' as in a straight line of three or more celestial bodies as seen from a single location?" Tony asked me.

And when I'd assented, he'd smiled prettily, and asked, "And your sister is named Narcissa, right?"

I'd answered, "No, one of my genetic mothers is," and he'd given me a two-fingered gesture, which from his demeanor I understood to be complete approval.

His own surname's middle section, van, like those of Francine and the other survivors—de, del, de la, nach, auf, and of—referred—or so he told us—to particular purebred lineages.

Apparently there had been a not-too-distant period of their history during which Cloned Cyber zoons, like one of my own ancestors, had threatened to overpopulate the entire Terran planetary/satellite/Oort Cloud system, leading to a massive internecine conflict (that I chose not to look too closely into—though the Fast Mind did). But with the eventual result that anyone who was never cloned or never derived from anyone else ever cloned would be able to claim direct lineage and could display that fact right inside their nomenclature: in effect becoming a sort of aristocracy, I assumed, although why that status existed or was deemed so positively neither I nor the Fast Mind could really comprehend.

Tony had arrived in a functional if obsolescent T-pod and had been instantly absorbed through the Fast's side wall, which had rather surprised him, this being a technology not known to them.

In a nod to our usual clothing-less state and the flat, marsupial-like pouches that contain our genitals, Tony had donned nothing but a small, pouch-like garment in a fleshly color worn in the appropriate area, which—rather transparently—contained his genitals. He was almost as tall as Scroba and, as I'd mentioned early, sufficiently attractive so that had he been forced to, he wouldn't look at all out of place in most Center World societies where human physical perfection is so much the norm that anything else is, at the least, glared at.

He turned out to also be personable, knowledgeable, and a quick learner.

He provided the Fast Mind (via converse with ourselves) with a rather sketchy if much highlighted history of how his people had discovered the "unexpected problem" with their little star, the various tests they'd performed, the sudden confirmation of their unhappy finding of its fate so much earlier than had been expected, and the resultant reactions and plans to escape its fury. Those plans, Tony insisted, were long-term, complex, and almost dependent upon who and where one actually was. Some had even opted to remain within the solar system, although at its very fringes, profitably solar-farming chemicals and other living-machines that they said only grew and flourished under the newly intensified solar ray bombardment: They been shipping these off to the Gammans and other survivor colonies for a decade now, and Tony hoped that they would soon ship themselves off to safety too.

His people had begun evacuating over a generation earlier, first to the outer moons, and moonlets, and eventually to nearby systems like Wolf 238, Proxima Centauri, Epsilon Eridani, and other, older Orion Spur backwaters of our Third Ib'r/Matriarchal Republic, utilizing fleets of old Slp.G haulers and ferries. Many of those nearby, non-threatened star systems had been previously thinned if not outright emptied of their younger populations (and in some cases, most of their populations) during the great intermarriage of the Viristic Republic and the Matriarchal Empire's Remnant, which you may recall had opened up so many dynamic new solar systems closer to the Sag A-1, and the Central Worlds.

In most cases, those older Orion Spur worlds' infrastructures were still intact or in need of only a bit of upgrading, Tony told us, and so they were quickly filled with the remaining twenty billion (mostly Human and Delphinid) souls of the Terran solar system. In fact, Tony told us, he might actually be appointed in his absence to return with us to Hesperia in order to claim an ambassadorship for the renewed Eridani planets to once more take an active role in the Republic. The Fast Mind approved of this and put through such a request to the Greater Quinx Council.

Scroba was fascinated, naturally, and even Tony—without our inborn sympathetic senses—was able to gauge her intense personal interest in his person, yet I thought he did an excellent job of keeping both her interest and his own at the properly needed distance.

She did, however, ask a bright question: Why had *he* been chosen to join us, besides the apparent qualities he clearly possessed.

"I believe it's because I don't really remember Earth or in fact anything but one of the smaller Oort Cloud worldlets very far from the center of that system. And that I only recall a bit, as I left it quite early on for Ep. Eri. Five. It's believed that I won't have the same emotional reaction, although I'm not at all certain of that," he said, and we admired him for the expressed doubt.

He then asked if we expected trouble; was that why we'd asked for someone like himself.

The Fast Mind answered, saying it had no idea what to expect, as no one had willfully entered this expanding sun-threatened system before. All of us on board should be able to take control/command if needed.

It then offered him a cocktail that seemed to contain a sedative, as he was soon stretched out on his bed and surrounded by privacy screens.

"Any comments?" I asked Scroba.

"He seems fine. He's barely primitive at all. Ship?"

"This ship agrees. Should you both be incapacitated, I believe this human could aid this ship in returning all of us with safety."

"Then it's agreed that we like him?" I asked. And they agreed.

"Good!" I said, not a little saltily. "Because that's the *first* thing we have all agreed on this trip so far!"

❖

The next few hours were quiet as we headed toward the doomed system. The Fast Mind was busy, naturally enough, as we moved closer, and not merely checking the increased amounts of planetary detritus headed our way, so I was surprised when it contacted me on a closed channel to say, "We are picking up what appears to be an ancient form of distress signal. It's barely binary."

"Can you tell from where?" I asked, quietly so as to not tip off Scroba, who was busy behind her air-screens—I had to suppose greedily looking up details of the human relational life of this early Sol-Terra system.

"Somewhere close to the edge of the Oort Cloud. It appears to be from a vehicle in orbit about a planet."

"What planets are there close to that system's Oort Cloud?"

"According to what was downloaded from the Epsilon Eridani Gamma world mind files, there are three small rocky planets on long, elliptical orbits around that star. It could be any of them."

"Can you read the message?"

"I've attempted to deconstruct it, but it's fairly primitive and I've not found any kind of packets of data within the three repeating so-called ancient 'Arabic' letters."

"Let me know if it happens again."

"There is a string of the same signal, sent out on several pulses. Hopefully somewhere closer to the source...? The downloaded files available to this Fast say that it is a very ancient kind of signal, this S.O.S., and that those Arabic letters merely denote a vehicle in distress."

"So you don't think its one of those commercial chem factories that our guest mentioned," I asked.

"Unlikely, as they would have direct connections with their people already."

"Keep monitoring it," I instructed.

Suddenly Scroba was gesticulating and so I opened up my privacy screen.

"Their history is fascinating. Relegated to this backwater, partly by their own choice, and partly by advanced developments in the Center Worlds that arrived for them so slowly that it made them instantly obsolete, they underwent a social-political history of epicycles. Smaller recognizable cycles with larger cycles," she explained the latter. "It's how the Bella-Arths developed and to some extent also the Delphinids before contact with other species."

"It does explain their somewhat retarded development," the Fast Mind said.

"But it also means every new development is time-tested," Scroba added.

Quite suddenly we received a garbled message in recognizable speech. At first it was just sounds, then the sounds cohered. "...please know that we are at these coordinates, and that we have many women and children with us, in need of rescue."

"It's at least digital," the Fast Mind admitted. "And I've got a fix on its origin."

The tri-dimensional planetary system diagram was put back up onto our air-screens and a spot was pinpointed and flashing. The planetoid was identified as "Quaor" and appeared to be a rocky mantled

M-Class on what seemed to be a decreasing apogee, which meant it was headed back on its orbit back to the ever-expanding sun.

"Open up and answer them," I instructed. "Can you make a link without time delay?"

"This ship has located a small amount of Communication-grade Beryllium 18 inside their vehicle to connect with. So yes, we can speak back and forth in real time."

Scroba was hunched over her air-screen. "Who could they be?" she asked the obvious.

There was an initial ten-minute delay and then we heard the voices again: "Hello! We have contacted you because your signature identifies you as Third Ib'r Republic. Is that true? Or are you Epsilon Eridani Gammans in a Republic vehicle?"

"We are not from your solar system at all. We hail from the Central Worlds. I am from Narcissus Terce. We're are here on a Scientific Mission."

"Thank God," was the reply. "There are approximately sixteen thousand of us. We are on two Slp.G liners, with a few other faster, much smaller, ships. You have our position?"

"We do. We are headed your way," the Fast Mind communicated. "Please identify yourselves."

"You wouldn't have any idea who we are."

"You don't want the Gammans to know you are hailing us for rescue? Is that it?" Scroba asked. "Are you enemies?"

"Not in so many words, no. In fact, they have no idea of our existence. We have lived for the past thirty-five centuries completely isolated from the rest of the Sol-Terran system."

"On that planet that you orbit?"

"No. Quaor appears to have been evacuated a half decade ago. We were on Earth itself. We only arrived here a few weeks ago."

This was news indeed, and now our guest, young Tony van Jeffery, was awake and listening in.

"How is that possible?" Scroba asked.

"Earth is big and, well, there were special circumstances. You'll see and understand when you arrive."

Tony said, "I have no idea who they can be. The Earth, all the planets and moons, in fact every asteroid, was digitally scanned and notarized preparatory for evacuation. They must not have even been on the grid."

I took over. "You have Slp.G liners and they have astral travel capacity. What's the problem? Why can't you just leave?"

"These were old, much-used cruise liners and they appear to have been abandoned in Earth orbit for some years already when we boarded them. Our engineers checked them through quite thoroughly before we took them this far. They seem to have low levels of Beryllium-19 for interstellar voyages. But none of us have ever done star-to-star travel and we're not certain if our vehicles are trip-worthy, or if we have enough fuel to make such a trip. We were hoping one of you might be able to do that."

"Hello. I am this Fast's mind." The ship took over.

"Who are you?"

"It's the ship we are inside of speaking to you," I explained.

"O-kay!" Said very dubiously. "A mechanism?"

"A sentient mechanism, yes."

The Fast Mind took over. "Newcomers, I will be able to check your travel Beryllium signatures from here. Once we arrive at your coordinates, I should be able to rather quickly diagnose the engines and their structural integrity also."

There was silence. Then, "That was your vehicle speaking to us, right?"

"Yes," I said. "But I'm a person." I gave him my name and some of my doctorates.

"Your ship itself is your engineer?" the survivor asked again.

"And our navigator too, yes. It's better at those tasks than we are. Our vehicle is very small," I added. "It only holds three. But it is advanced."

Scroba butted in now, and added, "Our Fast is very nice. It's courteous, and absolutely tolerant and non-judgmental, and it's very smart. It will find a way to help your people."

"Scroba!" I chastised, off link. "Bad idea! What if it can't?"

"Thank God," the survivor repeated. "We've gotten this far on our own. But that has taken most of our inner and outer resources. Frankly, we're pretty exhausted now."

"We're on our way," I repeated. I hoped my sympathy was obvious.

The Fast Mind gave the survivor an approximate time of arrival and then signed off so as to not waste more their small supply of Comm. Beryllium.

We all looked at Tony, who said, "What if they're not who they say they are?"

"Who would they be?" I asked.

"I don't know. Aliens?"

Scroba laughed. "To all of you, *we're* the aliens."

"Well, there must be some reason they don't want the Gamma humans and Delphs to know," he reasoned. "They could be luring us into some kind of trap."

"Toe-knee thinks well," the Fast Mind said. "This ship will follow the most stringent protocols of approach and initial encountering."

"Fine. That's fine." Tony relaxed a bit. "That's all I ask."

"We know all seven intelligent species that exist," I said. "So there *are* no aliens."

"*Seven?* I thought there were only three," Tony said.

"Three currently in existence; actually one more, so four currently in existence. That fourth has left the Galaxy but contacted us shortly before doing so. It told us about those four early species that preceded ours in time, of which its tiny population was the last remainder. They were very helpful. They aided us in locating three more Beryllium 19–bearing dead-stars equal or greater than Hesperia."

"I'd love to know more about that," Tony said.

"I'll send it over to your air-screen," Scroba said, always helpful where this attractive young male was concerned.

"I wonder who those survivors could be?" he mused aloud.

❖

"*Pan Troglodytes,*" the Fast Mind explained. "That is the official scientific name given to this new group of primate survivors from your solar system by your own Gamman world mind."

"They're Chimpanzees?" Tony van Jeffery asked. "It can't be. There haven't been any Chimps on Earth for four thousand years. And certainly none that spoke and used space ships!"

"I think they're perfectly adorable," Scroba said.

"They're wild animals!" Tony said.

"They look extremely domesticated," I replied.

Scroba and the Fast Mind agreed. We were being beamed Vids of the population of the two cruise liners. They were dining in restaurants, watching feature Vids in cinemas, strolling arm in arm along the viewing-decks, and children were playing in little parks and sand boxes.

As we popped back into full non-stellar travel existence only a few hundred yards away from one of their liners, we could actually make out some of their members, suited up for space, working on the outside of one of the liners. They waved to us and we waved back. They all looked rather cheerful, in distinct contradiction to our guest, who was most put out.

"This can't be happening," Tony moaned. "It's impossible."

"Are these not creatures from your planet, Earth?" I asked.

"Yes, of course they are, but—"

"And they are conscious and intelligent and they are survivors and need to be rescued," I said, continuing the inevitably logical statement.

Meanwhile the Fast Mind was close enough to request the Chimp's communications person to establish a link between their vessels and ours.

Cecil, he said his name was, and then said, "We were beginning to get very frightened that no one else would ever come."

"We have an Epsilon Eridani Gamma survivor on board," I told Cecil, "and the young human is quite amazed by your existence and by your presence. We still don't fully understand why it is that you were not included in the general evacuation. It seems a terrible oversight."

"I'll bet he's amazed," Cecil said and began laughing in a most genial manner, shaking his entire body. He regained his composure and it was now clear that he was speaking through some kind of vocal implement either attached at or placed around his throat. "What did he tell you? That we're nothing but wild animals?"

It was our turn to be amazed. "That's precisely what he said."

"We were. Of course humans were too. But that was millions of years ago. We were so more recently than that."

"Four thousand years ago?" I asked.

"Not quite. The truth was that we were evolving in the usual hit-and-miss manner of all Earth-born creatures, and then a large number of us were thrown into direct contact with humans. For a few hundred years our relationship was mostly abusive and we were exploited badly, exhibited, experimented on and with: all kinds of horrors. But then we came into contact with another group of humans who were intent on literally saving us, as we were being exterminated at our source of origin and in our original habitats.

"At the beginning of the [here he used a time term we were not familiar with], one group of humans bought a good-sized piece of land in a relatively inaccessible area of the Earth. They gathered all of us who had been in CSC units scattered about the two continents involved in helping us."

"How were you chosen for this?" Scroba asked. "They must have chosen the most intelligent of your species."

"They actually chose the most abused and exploited of us," Cecil responded. "Chimps who been in scientific programs, on display, or in chemical and pharmaceutical testing. They chose our ancestors out of compassion."

"CSC stands for?"

"Chimpanzee Salvage Cooperative," Cecil said. "Here's Lucia, she'll tell you the rest, I've got to work with your ship now."

Lucia was older, a bit grayer, and elegant.

"We're all been listening in to Cecil and your conversation. Please know that our gratitude is boundless," Lucia said.

"And we are delighted to make your acquaintance," Scroba said for the two of us. "It's a wonderful surprise. What can we do for you, once your liners are star travel–worthy?"

"The children think we are on a long vacation trip. We've not told them we had to leave home forever."

"It's very sad," Scroba said. "And understandable. But if you can provide us with some Vids of the homeland you had to evacuate, I'm pretty sure the Quinx Relocation Committee will be able to find a planet or moon fit to your standards somewhere."

For once, I did not contradict her.

"It's very sad that even fairly evolved humans like our guest cannot accept you," I told Lucia.

"And yet you have no trouble at all?" Lucia said.

"We think you're marvelous. I think your major danger is that of becoming a media sensation in the Center Worlds once they hear about your existence."

"That's a danger we can live with." Lucia chuckled. "Has your guest told you anything about recent Earth history?"

"Unfortunately, yes,"

"Luckily we were well out of all the troubles," she said. "And after a while, we closed down all possible communication links as the humans seemed to become so…barbaric! Our forebears feared for their lives. Cecil was basically correct, however. What he didn't explain was that most of our ancestors were taught the rudiments of language in hand signs and they learned to understand human spoken language to a quite complex degree. They were the top of the Chimpanzee heap, so to speak, to begin with because, ironically, of their human contact. So they were the best genetic material to begin with, which is always an evolutionary advantage.

"When CSC began its first small programs, saving a few score or so of the Chimps at a time, we naturally lived with humans, although they kept at a proper distance from us, so we would build new communities. But when it was decided that the world had become too chaotic for our safety, we were all consolidated into one reservation of some two thousand individuals. Again the Chimps lived near an increasingly smaller set of humans and as those humans died out, members among the Chimps took on the various human leadership roles. In that way they were forced into a kind of hothouse evolution. Some of us became language experts and then teachers of other Chimps. Some became mechanics and then engineers. Some became naturalists and farmers, and eventually even scientists. Within about ten generations, Chimps had achieved basic standards of living equal to humans of the [another time frame unfamiliar to us] era; and it just kept growing from there. When news reached us by our renewed satellite siphoning that the outer world had stabilized, we took a vote, and decided to *not* let the humans know of our existence.

"Groups of our own explorers located marine, land, and even flying vehicles, as well as loads of technical equipment that had been abandoned in several nearby towns and villages during the disorders, and after a while they were all brought back to the CSC. Our cleverer youngsters back-engineered and learned how to use them, and then figured out how to produce more. We advanced the limits of the CSC almost twofold in area, which went unnoticed in that depopulated part of the world, encompassing small factories, etc. Some of those youngsters also began to patrol our perimeter so that any inadvertent human explorers would be returned safely at a distance from us without any knowledge of us. The Chimps used blow guns, shooting from high branches in trees with sedative charges," she explained, "which we'd ironically enough learned from humans who'd first done that in hunting us.

"Of course, the news of the sun's death by expansion, which took only a single generation to sink in, led to another punctuated burst of evolution, and that is how we got our people this far from Earth, pretty much on rubber bands and a prayer, as my mama used to say.

"Now, this Quinx Council of yours…?" Lucia asked.

"It's five thousand five hundred and fifty-five representatives of some fifteen million populated worlds of the Three Species," I began.

"So if they're all that big, and that representative, they sound like they might be okay with just sixteen thousand of us?" Lucia said.

"I cannot officially tell you anything, but it really should not be a problem at all," I said.

Given what they had endured and how they had prospered, I admired her and her people more than I could utter. And Scroba was correct. They would be a media sensation. She and I would have to discuss together along with the Chimp leaders exactly how to best utilize the media and the Quinx Council to get the best possible "contractual deal" for them.

Suddenly Cecil was on-screen with Lucia, and he appeared to be chattering happy.

"We're all fixed," he said to Lucia and us. "Their ship says we're all set. We can go whenever we wish."

"Excellent news."

"Before you do that," I said, "let us discuss how we will proceed. Our ship has forwarded all of our discussion back to our own superior at the University on Diomedes Proxima, which sponsored and supplied this expedition. At this distance it will probably be an hour before we hear back from that person. We're going to recommend that we accompany you on your voyage, just to be certain you have no mishaps, if that meets your approval."

"Thank you," Lucia said. "Let me speak with my peers here and we will get back to you soon. I will recommend your protection to them."

"Fast," I said. "How do we stand?"

"This ship accessed their files completely. Only five percent of their population have an I.Q. higher than 150, yet they've made remarkable adaptations in all areas of the liners, both in engineering and ergonomics. The Beryllium they have is old but pure; it's now reactivated. Their outer structures seem solid. But I agree that as much as possible we accompany them, just in case, as you like to say. And also that we return to the Center Worlds by stages to put less stress on those liners. I'll work out a new navigation chart which does not include Fast travel. It might take as long as ten full days to get us back."

I looked at Scroba, waiting for her complaint.

"That will give us a chance to visit in person and to get to bond with some of them," she said.

"Fine. That bonding and communication is your task."

"Where shall we park them while we complete our work here with the doomed system?"

"Not in the Epsilon Eridani system!" Tony van Jeffreys said. "Actually, people, I'm now as excited as you are by this discovery. But I don't know about the Gamman population as a whole. They're a pretty contentious lot."

As if we hadn't noticed.

"Very wise, Toe-knee." The Fast Mind said what we were all thinking. "You will represent your people well in the council if you can see their faults equal to their achievements."

Tony then went to his air-screen, and in a few minutes, he had a solar system in view. "This is an abandoned system that I'd heard of before. It has only one habitable moon, and that moon has earthlike geography. But it also has distinctive seasons, so they could only stay a few months."

"A stay even that long would not be required," I said.

We all checked into the moonlet.

"It's too close to your people for a permanent colony," Scroba said.

"Definitely," Tony agreed.

"But it will do as a three- or four-day layover," I agreed. "Give the chance for the mothers and children to stretch their limbs, perhaps while we are completing our own mission."

"I will remain with them on that moonlet," Scroba asserted. "Just in case."

Our Fast communicated this welcome news to Cecil.

Then, almost simultaneously, we heard from Lucia and from Janiculus-Chase-onV, my superior.

Lucia said her peers were happy so far with the arrangements, and when she heard about Tony's suggestion for a layover, she was even more pleased. "The children will love being out of the ships for a short while. You see," she confided when we were alone on link again, "some humans can be very kind. The problem is we Chimpanzees don't ever know which ones, nor when."

Janiculus-Chase-onV was smug.

"I said you were the right one for this mission, didn't I, Syzygy? Young as you are, you've made several spectacular discoveries already that are certain to cause comment all over the University system and make your name in Academic circles. Now, tell me, how is your companion working out?"

I held my peace for only a short time. "As it turned out, Superior, Scroba was the perfect companion for this trip," I said. "You were right again."

"It's called instinct, my boy. Follow your instinct. Now get that new species set up for the meanwhile, and then finish your scientific mission. You will all receive Quinx Commendations upon your return. And yes, the Gamman youth looks fine so far. Bring him directly here when you are done."

I was the discoverer of a new species. It only just dawned on me.

"I hope the Fast gets a commendation too?" Scroba said, a recognizable edge in her voice.

"Why not?" Janiculus-Chase-onV said, undaunted. "Of course it will get a commendation. It's part of your team."

"Do you see, Young Toe-Knee," the Fast Mind now asked our guest, "why it will be advantageous to be part of the Third Republic? Tolerance is truly universal."

"Well, the three species and the machine minds *did* once have their problems," Scroba reminded us.

"A minor conflict," the Fast Mind agreed, "a thousand years ago, and now mostly forgotten."

"You people know so much," Tony said, "but I wonder if you know what humans on Earth said and wrote when they witnessed a star like Sol, our birth Sun here, expanding like this will do, and then collapsing on itself and going nova?"

We didn't know.

"It was a Chinese scholar. In our year 1042 anno domini, and he wrote, 'We have a guest in the heavens tonight. He is very brilliant!'"

"And so similarly may some primitive scholar we do not know ourselves, witnessing your Sol-Terra going nova from a distant planet, also write that," I suggested.

"We are ready to begin the layover mission," the Fast Mind said. "Everyone prepare."

Swear Not by the Moon...

It wouldn't have happened that way at all, except that Detective McGraghiu came by that afternoon to pick up a gift his wife was giving her niece. Me and Stella know the McGraghius going on twenty-four years, and after that long I've learned never to ask him about his business and he certainly never asks about mine.

"A hundred dollars!" he fumed as he pulled out the checkbook. "You've got a regular racket going on here, don't you?"

"I don't do charts anymore. Except for friends," I, of course, replied.

"I thought there were computer programs and such like to do all the calculating?" he went on.

"There are. So?"

"Have you tried using one?"

"Eff. Why. Eye. I use three software programs. Classic, Vedic, and the Uranian School. And they're all updated too. At considerable expense, I might add."

As I said before, we know each other over twenty years and I won't back down with him no matter how fancy a policeman he may think he is.

"What's Vedic?"

"Indian Astrology. Jyotish, they call it. They dismiss the use of the precession of the equinoxes. You see, in Astronomy, the solar system..."

"Stop. Okay? I don't need a lesson in it."

"Well, Vedic is a whole new flavoring, so I use it too."

"With curry and coriander."

I ignored that as beneath the two of us.

"I e-mailed Darla the charts and the interpretations today." Darla's his wife. A lovely lady. What she's doing with him…?

McGraghiu signed the check, handed it over, then waited. "That's it? Don't we even get a piece of paper with the fancy colored-pencil circles and all? Christ, it's a racket. In the past at least you got something to hang up on the wall."

"I just said, I e-mailed it…Not you, certainly?"

"Not me," he admitted. "But you know, for girls—and such," he added lamely.

"Sit tight, I'll print it out for you so you can see you've gotten your money's worth. Colored pencils are a little…1974," I added.

I turned and tapped the laptop, fiddled with various printing options. In the other room my multi-laser turned on and got to work.

I handed it to him all printed out—in colored inks, not pencils—for the niece's birth and this year's birthday horoscopes, and he grunted in satisfaction. I also found an old, pebbled, aqua-colored paper folder to slip it into and clasped it shut.

"Well, now this at least looks like it's worth something," McGraghiu mumbled. *Not a hundred dollars*, was the next statement, the one I didn't hear said aloud.

Then we cracked open the strange old brandy someone brought me as a gift a while back and he began speaking about what was on his mind, that case that's just been in all the papers.

I never asked about it. I never do ask. I never probe. And if he ever said I did, he lied. He's got a double constellation with Neptune and Mercury with some Personal Points that's set up for lying when it means nothing important. So he lies about little shit all the time. After a long time you get used to it, in a good friend.

McGraghiu: "The really crappy thing is, he's out there. We know he's out there. But he seems to operate out of such a wide, slow field, we all but forget about him and then he strikes again. And he's so damn methodical that if there's a clue left, it's utter bullshit. So we know he's playing with us…If we could just predict when he would next strike… and you know, at least be a little *ready*! Instead of so goddamned embarrassed all the time."

Me: "Maybe you can. Maybe *I* can," I amended it.

Stupidly, I admit it now.

The trouble was, I'd done a bang-up good job of Darla's niece's chart and birthday update. His wife had oohed and aahed in her e-mail back to me—"Injury via large animals—she had a horse accident last year. Fractured a wrist. And their yacht ran aground in Rararatu—so that's 'the shipwreck!'" I'd felt "hot" doing the interpretations, knowing little or nothing about the young lady to begin with, and then getting so many weird things like those two right on the dot. I was the slave of my own ego. So sue me.

"What do you mean?" McGraghiu asked. "That whorey business you idiots do?"

"Horary!" I corrected. "It sounds like you've been talking with some others in my avocational area of expertise."

"Oh, please," he scoffed.

"Well, what do I know who've you got these days in a station house? Psychics? Table rappers? I'll never step foot in one."

"You wish."

"No. I know. And no, it's not horary either."

"Then what?"

"Well, surely by now you've got an entire *field* of patterns… incidents that happened or nearly happened? Dates? Even times?"

"We've got enough dates and times to choke a horse. So what?" he asked back.

"I might be able to look at them and…"

"Four squads have looked and still are looking, ongoing, and analyzing them. The big boys in Quantico, for Chrissakes, with giant computers. You actually think you're going to find some crucial pattern their humongous Crays and Enivacs working twenty-four hours a day missed?"

So that was when and how McGraghiu dared me.

"You certainly seem frightened enough that I will find some pattern their Big Boys with humongous Crays missed," was what I dared back.

And I added, "I'm sure I could get what I needed out of the newspapers, or even online…If I looked hard enough…If I cared to do so…Which I don't *one bit*."

"C'mon, Mike. I've been slipping in your drool since I walked in the door, you're so hot to hear particulars on this case."

Mac may be born with his Sun in Pigheaded with Stubborn rising, but he's gotten through thirty years in the LAPD, rising slowly and steadily while "the geniuses" have gone down the tubes, ended up in prison or in retirement villages all around him. He's got something on the ball.

"Somebody's nervous," I taunted. "Good thing you weren't outside looking in on this dialogue through those one-way mirrors you've got at the station, or you would have seen how you just all but shredded that left shirt cuff of yours, you were so eager for me to ask about it."

He looked at the messy cuff. Hid it. Then:

"We're not going to actually *bet* on this, are we?" he asked.

"Why not? You've got a birthday coming up. Which one? Hundred and five? Hundred and six?"

"Very funny. Fifty-one, as you well know."

"And so do I. One week later. As you well know."

"So…? A big dinner out?"

"Us and the wives," I finished it for him.

"Deal," he said, without asking what exactly the birthday would cost or entail. "What do I send you?"

"Have your next in line, what's her name, the sexy one, Detective Alvarez? Have her e-mail me and I'll tell her all of what I need."

I knew this would be a provocation. Olga Alvarez had arrived in his office around the same time that a Mars/Cupido midpoint was coming due with Mac's Aries axis. Mucho attraction. And a long-term marriage. Purely occupational, natch. He'd claimed that she would be there for a month and then move on. She was still there, going on year four and some.

"How come she already has your e-mail address?" McGraghiu asked. "You two having an affair behind my back, you and Alvarez?"

"If you were a halfway good one, you'd know we are. Actually, we've got a new kink: We're having a three-way with that pretty new guy you hired in September."

"I wouldn't put it past you."

"Oh, and by the way, your wife's niece's chart showed that her second aunt's husband is running his way toward a heart condition. Running. Not even walking."

McGraghiu said he would make an appointment for a medical checkup sometime—i.e., in the next century.

"Your wife already did. On your day off, next week."

As he scowled and muttered, I rousted him out of the chair and saw him out the door. "Drive safely."

"Why?" He suddenly turned on me.

I smiled. "I'm just fucking with your head, Mac."

Det. McGraghiu uttered something unprintable.

Like I said before, we know each other a long time.

❖

Olga Alvarez had naturally blond hair, a snub nose, and pale blue eyes and looked more or less of East German or Slovakian descent and was unmarried. With that name! Go figure, huh?

She'd sent me the material I'd requested from McGraghiu, neatly organized, and now, two days later, on a Saturday, she arrived in person to discuss it. I immediately put my 90 Degree Uranian wheel in motion and looked for any Moon/Ascendant constellation figures going on. Nothing special showed up, so I figured she just wanted some dope on her boss, who was due in ten minutes from now and who would be joining her for a preliminary consult on whatever I'd found so far on the serial guy.

"What I'd like to know is," she asked, "could you do a chart for someone? Without them knowing? For me?"

"Full one or just how their chart matches your own?"

"How it matches later. Right now I'm just interested in who he is."

"I see. Okay, give me the date and place. You don't have a time? No, I guessed you didn't." Meaning she'd snitched off a personnel record in the office and it was a colleague of hers. "He have a name?"

"Dennis Fisher."

I did a fast natal chart on the basic computer program for noon that day and it came up Sun in Scorpio—no surprise if he was an investigator—Moon solidly in Aquarius. First thing I noticed was Mars and Venus were exactly sextile, their midpoint only a few degrees from his birth Sun—this person really liked himself and took care of himself, and looked good to others. It was also conjunct Neptune. Uh-oh!

"This is a guy, right?" I asked.

"Dennis usually is."

"He seems very attractive. How interested are you in him?"

"How interested is he in me?" she asked back.

"He doesn't do drugs, right?"

"Just the opposite," she said. Confirming he was a cop in her unit. Mac can smell a drug user a mile off. So the Neptune in that pleasure midpoint was not coke and crystal but *glamour.*

"He looks at least bi, more than likely gay." I added, "But not really interested in publishing it."

"Who would publish it in a police precinct?" she asked. "Well, good."

"Good?" I asked.

"Good that I don't make a jerk of myself," she said. "You get anything yet on our serial?"

"Dennis Fisher is the new guy who came into your unit this September?" I asked her re: the chart I'd just done.

"What, Mac tell you *all* our business?"

"Mac already knows about him," I said, remembering the joke I'd made and how he hadn't defended him against my slur. "*Without* doing his chart."

"Fuckin' men's club! Even the gays are in it!" she said. "Some day I'm going to get you guys."

That's when Mac came in—without ringing the bell, as usual.

I had them reconfigure themselves in chairs I have next to side tables around what I like to call my "astro desk," the Lord and Taylor Queen Anne table topped with triple monitors so I can look at three different computerized astrology programs at once.

Mac prompted Olga, "What are you waiting for? Ask!"

She huffed and puffed a few minutes, arranging some papers in her lap, then said, "Everything I read about serials like our boy says they operate on a lunar basis. So I figure that's why you want to see the data. But Quantico has already done charts and charts and more charts and they don't match jack shit on him. No full moons, no new moons. No quarter- or three-quarter moons. Nothing."

"In fact," Det. Alvarez added, "he's not on anything like a monthly or even a moon-based monthly schedule that we can see."

"What if the serial is on the Pill?" I asked.

"What?"

I'd gotten her attention. Mac smiled as though I was softening her up for him.

"Bear with me," I said. "A woman's ovulations take place on a lunar-like schedule. But then she begins taking the pill, say, for a year. What happens to that schedule when she goes off the pill?"

"It's all over the place for the first few months."

Mac asked, "But wouldn't it settle again into a pattern?"

"Not if she quickly went on the pill again for another year and a half," I argued.

Olga: "And when she came off, then it would be way off again."

"And if she went on for two years, then went off again?" I asked.

"Totally different again." Olga then asked, "Are you saying this serial is a woman?" Because everything else reads male."

"What does your departmental profile say, Detective Alvarez?"

"A guy. Sixteen to twenty-four years old. Under six feet, closer to five-six or smaller. Ambidextrous. White or Hispanic. Reads a lot. Meticulous. Questionable hand-eye coordination. Strong rage against middle-aged professional white men."

Mac asked the question she wanted to ask. "Why would a guy be on the pill? He wouldn't, would he?" he answered himself.

"And he wouldn't be ovulating either," she added.

"Back to square one," Mac declared.

"Except he's on a schedule of *some kind*," I confirmed. "And when he goes *off* the schedule, as he must periodically, for some reason or other, then the *other* schedule takes over."

"By the other schedule taking over—you mean the *serial* schedule?" Mac said, understanding me.

"And *that's* when he becomes a serial?" Alvarez asked.

"Not right away, I don't think," I said. "I'd guess it happens only at the very end of what I'd call his 'being free of the pill' period. Maybe just before he goes back on the pill schedule again."

"What if he *knows* he's going on the pill schedule again?" Mac asked. "Like he knows he'll be too sedated to kill. So he does it right away?"

"My sentiments exactly," I said.

"What are the schedules you've noticed?" Det. Alvarez asked.

"All of them I've noted are typical psychiatric calendarial standards for medication, off by maybe a day or two, nothing statistically important. Three months. Six months. Nine months. One was a year and three months. Another a year and nine months. One was even two years and six."

"Meaning?" Alvarez didn't get it yet.

"Meaning that's how long the meds he's taking work, before they *stop* working."

"Oh, shit! That's why Quantico found no pattern," Alvarez said.

"Because it's not a pattern of what's *happening*?" Mac asked for all of us. "But instead a pattern of what's *not* happening."

"Bingo!" I said. "It's a pattern of the pills no longer working."

"*That's all* that you've got?" Mac asked me.

"That's all so far, yeah. But I'm only fooling around a few days with all this."

"You're saying he's a recognized schiz," Det. Alvarez said. "Or paranoid. Or something."

"Don't jump to conclusions," I said. "What we suspect is, he's out on the street and he's usually medicated and so usually normal. But disturbed enough that he's monitored and his meds are changed whenever they're not obviously working. So he's off them at least two weeks for them to fully wash out of his body before he begins to take new ones. And it's in *that* period when he attacks."

"You saw this in the charts?" Det. Alvarez asked.

"I actually saw Neptune and Saturn with Uranus and another point you don't know, called Hades, all activated in some kind of close mambo at every murder he's done. That reads to me like periodic meds and really ugly stuff linked closely."

"Also meaning he can afford to rapidly change meds," Mac added.

"Or someone else can afford it for him," I added.

"That's a million people," Det. Alvarez scoffed. "We got nothing."

"Much less than that. A few thousand or less, locally," Mac said, then agreed. "But it's still too many. We've got *practically* nothing."

They got up to leave, disheartened.

"You've got *a pattern*," I reminded them when they reached the door. "Which twenty guys in an office working for months with computers couldn't find for you. Your *first pattern* in the case. And you've now got a specific sliver of the population. Not everyone. Which you *also* didn't have before."

"He's right," Olga agreed, shrugging at Mac. "It's a break."

"And he's on stronger meds. So I'd hazard that you're safe for a minimum of six months and a week. Oh, and my invoice is in the mail," I added.

"Invoice, maybe. Birthday dinner, no way!" Mac assured me.

❖

They were safe for six months and one week and five days, it turned out, before they found Dr. Sharik Deming. But this time, they'd at least mollified the Powers That Be at One Police Plaza by predicting when the next vic would be found, if not who he would be or by whose hand he would be done in. It was a little, but it was *something*.

Like the others, Dr. Deming had been genitally mutilated and something very particular done with the spare body parts. This was the serial's signature.

Unlike the seven other cases, I happened to be out playing pinochle with Det. McGraghiu when he was called to the scene, and he dragged me along. I protested mightily.

He relied, "You're on the goddamn payroll with all the other kooks and wackos! You're coming along. Who knows what kind of shit you'll uncover."

"I use computers. Slide rules. I'm not a psychic."

He pushed me into the passenger seat of his Crown Vic, slammed the door, which self-locked, and off we went. The apartment building was one of the big old beauties just after Vine becomes Rossmore Avenue, and where working-class, nuts-and-bolts Hollywood segues dramatically into Hancock Park. Twenties or thirties vintage. Big rooms with high ceilings and triple crown moldings. Amazing views. A lobby the size and décor of your average older cinema: classic-era movie star ateliers. Dr. Deming's office was a secondary one, clearly, for at home, maybe even emergency, consultations. Lots of diplomas on the wall. Specializations in Surgery and Ob-Gyn were prominent among them.

Very few medical instruments were around, although whatever was present had been utilized and/or purposely left by Our Favorite Serial.

Who had apparently brought his own hypodermic setup—showing his usual careful selection of the vic, then preparation and preplanning. The needle, as usual, was left for the LAPD to find and was seen to contain a milky fluid, which several people sniffed and guessed at from previous scenes and which Toxicology would later confirm to be just enough of a very strong animal tranquilizer to not knock him out but instead strongly stun him, make him fuzzy as hell, and probably also paralyze him.

"And?" I added, "Also dull the pain?"

"He probably wouldn't have felt that much pain," the on-the-spot M.E. said, "once it kicked in, which looks early on in the evening," reporting this to us as we arrived. The examiner proceeded to give the time and other elements of the death to Det. McGraghiu.

"What?" Mac asked, looking at me.

"You said the serial has rage. Why does he stun them so they don't feel pain?" I asked. "If it was rage, he'd make sure they'd feel every iota of pain! No?"

Det. Alvarez: "I kinda wondered about that myself."

"Take a look at what he does, and you tell me it isn't rage?" Mac said, and dragged me inside.

Now to be honest, up till then, I'd seen maybe three dead bodies in my life, and never on purpose. Two of them old people when I was a kid. And one firefighter I knew. And all of them freaked me out. So you can guess how not eager I was to view this particular "scene."

Meanwhile the place was filled with people, and I found myself thinking that one of the worst aspects of being murdered is the indignity of it: all these folks stomping through your privacy and looking at your privates.

In this case looking was right. It was hard to miss them.

The much-drugged victim had been belted down to his consulting table fully clothed, about a dozen or more times. His trousers and underpants had been carefully pulled down around his ankles, and he was placed upon his back, with his knees up, so his legs were bent up in the middle. None of his other clothing was disturbed, and his hair remained unmussed or might have even been rebrushed; his shirt and tie looked straightened out. This was eerie enough, especially given what had happened to his lower torso. His genitals had been carefully severed, and where they'd been taken out, the area had been sewn up again with surgical thread. It wasn't that neat, but not that messy either, and of course, blood had seeped through the stitching, although that was not the cause of death.

Beneath what would have been the scrotum, a hole had been carved out and sewn around the edges to resemble labia. Again it wasn't that neat, but all of it was clearly enough indicated. And the doctor's genitals, the penis artificially strengthened by some kind of plastic rods the serial had brought along and thrust through its length, along with the loosely tied together testicles, had been placed inside the false labia as in the act of coital penetration. In fact, based on what the M.E. said was traumatic bruising, and what looked very possible, the penis had been used to perform sexual intercourse with the new "vulva"—"Most probably while the victim was still alive."

"And," according to Mac, "given the specific placement of these adjustable consulting table mirrors, all of this would have been purposely visible to the doctor himself, while it was happening."

This last was aimed at me, to prove "rage."

I suppose it was the neatness of the rest of it, the office so spick-and-span, the doctor so unassaulted looking, except for this, of course, wildly awry part of his anatomy, that was so fascinating to me, so that I didn't for a second feel the enormous repulsion and nausea I'd been expecting.

"M.E. says, for sure, he was alive during the rape by his own penis," Mac said. "Isn't that rage enough for you? He was forced to watch it."

"Literally, go fuck yourself," someone else muttered.

I turned to the new voice and guessed it was the new guy in the unit. He was medium sized but athletic, boyishly handsome, with curly brown hair and what women call "smoldering" olive green eyes. I guessed he was an Aquarius Ascendant. So his Scorpio Sun was either 9th or 10th house: very public. That meant his sexuality wouldn't be secret for very long, but instead quite opened up. I remembered that Dennis Fisher was his name.

"And not, Detective Fisher," I added, "'Fuck you!' Right? But instead 'Go fuck *yourself*!' Right?"

"That's what it looks like to me," Det. Fisher agreed.

"People, can I have your opinion of this scene?" I asked, and polled them all about the difference. All of them except Mac, who said nothing, agreed with us. So I asked, "Mac, everyone says it's 'go fuck yourself.'"

Warily, he answered, "Okay. Maybe? What exactly are you getting at here, Mike?"

"Were they all like this?" I asked. "This neat and clean except for down there?"

"I'll show you the photos. But more or less. Sure. The serial's gotten better with suturing as he's moved along. Why?"

"I don't know. But even though we think he's on meds and really disturbed, this just doesn't feel to me like a generalized rage against the medical profession. It's too..." I searched for the word.

"Too specific. Too particular. Too contained," Det. Fisher tried.

"Exactly," I said. "You all feel it? The pathology of it? The downright creepiness of it? This serial is making a point here. A bizarre one. And he has been all the while. He's got an axe to grind with *some* members of the medical professional, and it's all about genitals!"

"Sex reassignment," Dennis Fisher said in a soft voice.

"What are you talking about?" Mac scoffed.

"That's it." I immediately explained, "He's taking a genital male and turning him into a genital female."

"And then showing him what's it's like to *be* a genital female," Dennis added. "By performing sex on him, so he can see it."

"Why doesn't he use his own genitals?" Mac asked.

"Because he's not a male," Det. Alvarez said for all of us.

"Not exactly. Because...he's not a male...*anymore*," I said.

"He doesn't have a *penis anymore*," Det. Fisher said. "Like I said. It's all about sex reassignment."

"I learned those same stitches he used on that fake labia in Home Economics in public school junior high," Det. Alvarez said. "They're basic to hemming, called double-back stitches."

"I never learned that in school," Mac said.

"Only *girls* are taught sewing in city schools," Fisher said. "Let's say he *was* a male," he went on, "at birth. Something was wrong or went wrong and he was sex reassigned as a woman. A girl, rather. A very young girl. By some doctor. Probably when he was an toddler. That's when it happens. But deep down he *knew* he was a male. And now he's showing all of us and the entire world too!"

"You're sure about this?" Mac looked directly at Det. Fisher.

"That's what it feels like to *me*, sir."

"Because that will really narrow it down. We'll find records. We'll find out which sex reassignments are on psych meds. We'll match the periods of drug use. After that, it won't be too hard to locate this perp."

"That's what it feels like to *me*, sir," Det. Fisher repeated.

And in the silence that enused, he was saying so much that Det. Alvarez piped up, "Now that Detective Fisher said it, it feels like that to me too, sir."

I added my own two cents of support to their words.

"Okay. So then we all know what to do," Mac said, and was once again totally in charge. "Alvarez, Fisher. You've got the leads. You know where to go. Now run with them."

Everyone scrambled into motion.

"See!" Mac said as we all left the apartment building an hour later. "My instincts were right. As usual, I *knew* you had to be here."

"I didn't do a thing," I protested.

"Sure you did…See, Mike, it's because you're so goddamn naïve. You opened our eyes to the obvious. And then because you're so fucking hocus pocus, you allowed us to say what we needed to *say*…To ourselves…and then to each other."

"Hey, I always told you I was hot shit. And now the invoice really *is* in the mail," I commented. "And for this, I'll expect a medal too," I added, since both of our birthdays were long past.

He muttered obscenities, of course, and when we got back down to his Crown Vic on the street, we had to call our wives and tell them when we'd be home—so they wouldn't worry.

The Gospel According to Miriam, Daughter of Jebu and Anna, Wife to Johosephat, Mother of Joshua

A nd it came to pass during the second decade of the reign of Caesar Augustus, that a strange new star appeared in the northwest, above the pastures of Gibreon at the edge of the bright new Roman city just begun abuilding near Madgala, at the edge of the Sea called Galilee. After dawn, the star appeared to move toward the village of Nagadar and to stop and hover in the vineyards of Jebu, the virtuous wine maker.

His daughter, the maiden Miriam, outdoors among the morning fields gathering sweet greens and bitter greens for luncheon, was not surprised by the star's appearance, only by its great brightness, flashing light from all its edges as though imitating the noonday sun.

Her mother Anna had spoken of such a sky-crossing star many times before, hushed by her husband should he be near, and thus usually spoken in whispers to her two remaining daughters at home, plain Martha and fair Miriam. Such a star had come to Anna herself once, she told them, near her birth hamlet not far away, many years before.

She told it so: As the girl Anna had watched lo many decades ago, alone in a field, the star had seemed to stop and from within the star's luminescence had stepped two radiant creatures, rainbow colored, smelling like nard and clover, with voices like early June rain, and eyes lucent as with the gibbous moon. They had spoken to Anna then, words she remembered but unclearly, but she was certain that they had sounded like harps, like zithers at their most dulcet.

And now, as she too stood and stared among the frolicking goat kids, Miriam saw this star drop near the stacked ricks of barley and open itself to the air and knew it for what it was. Out of the star stepped two creatures who wafted slowly downward toward her, luminescently dressed, graceful and heavenly, just as her mother had often described.

"Hail, Miriam!" the first one said. "Daughter of Jebu and Anna. Sister of Simione and Tebru and Martha. Graceful are you, as foretold by our Lord, and it is not surprising therefore that many will speak your name with great love in years to come." His tones were dulcimer and honey, as her mother had said.

"Hail, strangers," Miriam replied, versed and well trained and courteous in the ways of hospitality. "Who be you and what may I do to fulfill your wishes?"

"Wishes have we none," said the second, somewhat larger and brighter, garbed as though in palest silver. He looked upon her, Miriam thought, as a man looks upon a maid.

"Strangers though you be, and exceeding beautiful, and bound as I am to hospitality, I must tell you that I am but a virgin, unwed, with no knowledge of mankind, and I cannot fulfill your desires."

"Desires of that kind have we none," they said together. "Look upon us more carefully, Miriam."

Miriam looked more carefully as instructed, and now it seemed to her that the messengers were neither men, as she had first thought, nor women, as she secondly believed. And as she looked further she understood then that these strangers were not like her people who trod upon the ground, but of another, higher, order of beings, wafted by air.

"Our need is but to speak to you, Miriam," the first one said.

"Messengers are we," the second quickly added. "We bring you tidings of great joy!"

"Surely, then, it is my mother, Anna, you seek," she modestly replied, and turned, basket in hand, to go fetch her. "She whom you met before must be whom you seek again."

"Stay." The messengers seemed to be before Miriam, though she'd not a second before turned to walk away from them. "Stay," both repeated. "Sit here by us and hear what we have to say."

As he spoke he waved his hand toward her and she became as though asleep while awake, tranquil while alert, as though by strange enchantment.

The messengers spoke not. Pictures, instead, saw Miriam then before her eyes, moving and flowing, not as in life exactly, nor as in a dream. She recognized her mother Anna, then as a maiden her own age now, meeting with these same strangers who were unchanged in age. She saw how they three encountered, stayed to speak, and how after speaking to Anna, how the messengers touched her belly with a wand of purest silver. As one messenger touched her, the other looked upon a small silver tablet that floated with numbers and words Miriam had never before seen, that flowed with them as a stream flows with water.

Conference between the messengers took place then, and agreement, and once more Anna was touched in the belly with the wand, which this time glowed blue as the Sea of Galilee's waters. Miriam's mother, then still a girl, was told to go unto her house and speak to her mother of the farmer Jebu, whom she favored, and who favored her, and thereto arrange a wedding with the family of Jebu. For greatness now lay within Anna's womb, placed therein by the messenger's wand, to be seeded by Jebu alone, and to be extracted when the time was right.

All this Miriam saw and understood, although the images flowed quickly and before her in the air freely, without wall or floor to back them up as did the images upon tesserae and muralae of the Greeks and Romans in their homes and temples in the cities of white stone that she had once seen. All this Miriam heard and understood, albeit the images were as insubstantial as the smoke from an incensed fire of thyme and rosemary.

"You, Miriam, child," spoke the first messenger aloud, "you yourself were the greatness that your mother Anna bore by the seed of Jebu. And as she bore you, so shall you bear even greater greatness."

Then Miriam anguished, for she was only a maid, the least of her siblings, whom they mocked for how their mother spoiled her and whom they chided for her uselessness in vineyards and fields, by virtue of her slenderness and her grace.

Seeing her distress, the messengers spoke: "Fear not, Miriam. Blessed are thou among your sisters, and blessed will thou be among all the Daughters of Israel."

Then she was touched with the silver wand at her belly, and it glowed golden as the roof of the synagogue at Galilee and she felt calmed by its touch and was not afraid.

"Blessed are thou doubly now, Miriam," said one messenger.

"And blessed now is thy womb," said the second messenger. "For though a virgin, you will bear a child."

"Blessed will this child be, beyond all measure," said the first messenger, "and among all women, will you be honored and revered."

"By this touch," the second messenger said, "is the seed of our Lord implanted into your belly," and he pointed upward, "Our Lord, whose residence is there, is thus given unto you alone, of all womankind."

"Bear and raise this child," said the first messenger, "and be amazed by him, for he will not be as other children, but he will be as the sun dancing among the stars."

Miriam heard them and she was amazed, but also was wrought with sorrow.

"Messengers!" she cried. "Assist me now, for there is nothing I would better wish than to raise the son of a great Lord. But surely the Laws will be against me for being a virgin giving birth. The wicked will mock me and the Pharisees condemn me and stone me as such."

"Fear not, Miriam," said the first messenger. "For in the town of Galilee lives a man to whom we have appeared in dreams. He has agreed to take you in marriage."

"Know then that man is named Johosephat, and he is a carpenter, respected, and withal honored by his neighbors. Two days hence shall he come to your village and ask for your hand in marriage."

"But will this man not then become husband to me at the marriage night, so that I am no longer a virgin?" asked the girl, for such she had heard such from her sisters and their friends.

"Fear not, elderly is he," said the second messenger.

"Elderly. Also unmoved by women's beauty is he," said the first messenger.

"Beloved by mankind is he, and loving mankind alone," said the second messenger.

"Alone, among the Sons of Israel, this Johosephat shall be, helping to raise the son of our Lord in these heavens, exactly as our Lord desires."

"This our Lord has decreed," they said together.

"Long have we waited, long have we sought such a husband and father. None else will suffice if the son of our Lord is to become the man required."

"Then such a man shall be a welcome husband to me," said

Miriam, acquiescing, "as he shall be a welcome father to your Lord's son. But…tell me of your Lord."

"This we cannot do. But we may tell you of the son you are to bear."

"Blessed shall he be among all men," they intoned together.

"And necessary, alas, for mankind has fallen into error and misrule and he is needed to correct them as a schoolmaster corrects a poor student, yet not with a rod, but with his teachings."

"Like his father above in these Heavens, his son shall love mankind."

"He shall become a Rebbe, and preach the love of men for each one another."

"He shall teach that wives are not chattels, that chattels are but meaningless. That peace and love rule the earth."

Then Miriam was filled with great joy.

"But know you, Miriam, that when comes the thirtieth day of the third month of the thirtieth and third year after his birth, that your son shall return to his Lord father." Both pointed heavenward: "For so it has been decreed."

"Fear not that day," said the first messenger, "though it seem terrible!"

"Fear not how the great events then unfold," said the second messenger.

"For they are mysterious. They are the work of our Lord, and of us, his Messengers upon this Earth of yours, and not to be understood yet."

And there was music about them and Miriam felt the love of the great Lord within and without her. And she rejoiced greatly.

So the messengers moved aloft and entered their star and it was gone as though in a twinkling. Miriam returned to her home, with arms full of sweet and bitter greens, and she seemed to her mother much changed.

Two days passed and a visitor arrived, gray bearded, with fine sandals of kid. His name was Johosephat, and he was a carpenter from the town on the sea, as decreed. Miriam's father Jebu and her mother Anna gave him due hospitality, although he was but a cousin's cousin. And all were taken by him immediately, as was Miriam, for he was gentle and given to laughter.

And so were they wed, old and young, and so did all take place as the Messengers from out of the Star had once decreed, and many years later, Miriam told this story to young Andrew, the last and dearest love of the son she had borne for the great Lord of the heavens. Andrew heard her words rapt and together they grieved the loss of her son so recently killed upon a tree, and yet they rejoiced his long presence among them.

Then Miriam succumbed to the lot of all men and women, and Andrew, snowy haired with years, entombed her as befit a notable woman.

Until he too passed on, Andrew could be seen wandering the vineyards of Jebu's descendants, looking to the skies over the fields. Some said he awaited the coming of one more great star.

Absolute Ebony

On a hot and stifling Roman night in the middle of the fifth decade of our century of the Steam Engine, a desultory tête-à-tête between two markedly different Americans was enlivened by a sudden barrage of knocking and shouting several floors below at the level of the Via Ruspoli. The younger-seeming of the two men went to the wide ledge of the window and, peering down, reported that two rough *contadini* were attempting to gain admission to the pensione.

"Leave them, William," his friend replied, with the same torpor and indifference he had displayed during their reunion dinner—fragments of which now littered the uncovered trestle table in the large, gloomy dining chamber. "The housekeeper, good Antonia, will see to them."

"Shall I go, then?" William asked. "Would you like to rest?"

"All I have is rest in this infernal city during this most dreadful summer. No. Stay. Your talk and natural high spirits bring me much comfort."

Although his companion had reason to doubt the exact veracity of these words, an acquaintance that extended some years back to their childhood across the ocean obliged him to remain.

Even before William had set forth upon his European journey, he had known of his friend's various misfortunes and the consequent disordered mental condition they had apparently imparted.

A man in the prime of his life, Michaelis, as he called himself and was so known now, had been an artist of such extraordinary promise that a lifetime of the greatest renown and most elevated rewards had once appeared to be his natural birthright.

As a lad, his talent in draftsmanship and the application of aquarelles had been so precocious as to attract the notice of the venerable Charles Wilson Peale. Under such tutelage, an inherent genius for the plastic arts was both nourished and coordinated. Upon the death of the old master, the young heir to his aesthetic mantle had but one course left open to him: Leaving the young Republic, he set off to conquer Italy, art capital of the world.

Michaelis's arrival in Rome a decade earlier had initially been embroidered with accolades no less ringing than in the land of his birth, as well as with patronage of the highest order. He worked long hours, fulfilling many commissions in the spacious fourth-floor apartments on the Caelian leased by an indigent Contessa who'd been driven by penury to reside with more prudence than style outside the city gates. Nor was the young artist's life one only of labor, no matter that the toil was satisfying and conducive to earning others' admiration.

The handsome and confident youth was early sought out by representatives of the highest cultural circles the capital could offer: not only painters and sculptors, but poets, musicians, and eventually scientists and philosophers of great lore and subtlety and abstruseness. From these intellects, Michaelis had learned the rarefied art of exploring the ideal; and from their examples, he had conceived a new possibility: that of useful relationships between the ideal and his own, entirely material work.

There were lighter matters to counterbalance such sobriety in the young man's life: teas, salons, dinner parties, balls, riding out on the Campagna every fair day; churches with frescoes to be copied and studied, palazzos with paintings to be inspected. Nor was the fair sex absent or indifferent to Michaelis. Several ladies of varying age, rank, and nationality had secretly given their hearts to the dashing artist upon the first or second meeting. In turn, Michaelis had selected his lady from among the four handsome daughters of the Anglican minister, unofficial director of the English-speaking community in the Italian city.

Because the young woman, although apparently sensible and reciprocal in her regard of the artist, was below the age of consent at the time of their first meeting, more than six years would pass before their engagement could be consummated. When at last they did wed, Michaelis's happiness was unsurpassed. He had recently completed the commission of a large mural for the reception chamber of one of the most powerful prelates of the Roman church. His work was never in such favor, in greater demand. His fame and that of his colleagues and circle of friends spanned the Continent. And his Charlotte was the flower of his existence.

Such extreme content was to last but eight months. During a trip to the Campagna, the Signora Michaelis was suddenly taken with a fever. Fragile by constitution, she succumbed within a fortnight.

As was to be expected, Michaelis was utterly distraught. His great disappointment in Charlotte's death caused a melancholia that only deepened long after the natural period of mourning had been protracted. His clerical father-in-law of so short a duration listened with growing anxiety but was able to offer little real balm to the young artist, who set out to lay blame for his romantic misadventure with a liberal trowel, involving not only human but also superhuman personalities. Once the minister had been exposed to Michaelis's more bitter imprecations, he found the artist to be dangerously heretical.

One year passed, then another, and Michaelis found himself still unable to renew his previous connections, or, more important, to return to that labor which had once been the very mainspring of his life. Previously esteemed for his flights of fancy and unforced humor, he was shunned now by friends for the various perorations of gloom he evinced at the least provocation. Former companions fell away, visited infrequently—solely as a duty.

At one time the joy of all who beheld it because of its bright, noble evocation of youth and hopefulness, Michaelis's painting too underwent a transformation consonant with his much altered sensibility. He began to espouse a new theory of art: that color itself was an aberration of the senses, a snare, and an illusion. He declared that all colors ought to be resolved into a more coherent system. Studying earlier theoreticians of chromatics, Michaelis found that half-truths and errors constituted the greater part of their writings. Finally, and by some never adequately explicated chain of reasoning, he declared that only by a subtle, yet complete, mixture of the chromatic scale would color be true both to the mind and to the senses.

When he picked up his brushes and palette again, at last, his tints began to darken, his hues became scarcely distinguishable from each other; reds diminished to deep indigoes, brilliant cobalts became muddied midnight navies. His skills were as evident as before—indeed intensified, more discriminating colleagues attested. But few sitters wanted portraits so dark, so evidently color-saturated that a brace of candelabra were needed to illuminate even the penumbral foreground, and where details of feature and attitude were as transitory to the viewer's eye as a taper's flicker in a dungeon.

Baffled patrons soon began to eschew his studio. Patronage dwindled. Michaelis's once brilliant renown was distorted into that of an eccentric, or worse: a fraud. That his new work was mocked and scorned only confirmed his private belief that he had discovered the long-hidden truth of art. He applied himself with renewed vigor to elaborating the darkening of his palette, the complex obscurity of his vision. Bitterness and poverty soon seeped into and throughout his existence. Voluntary seclusion, loneliness, and desolation of any joy in human activity coarsened his courtesy. Mistrust, misanthropy, and a growing sense of the growing enmity about him soon silenced him.

Thus had William found his friend, and thus Michaelis remained throughout his visit, despite all efforts to rouse him and elevate his spirits by the recollection of shared youthful joys and follies. Nor was William persuasive in suggesting alternative courses of action to a future even Michaelis himself now could foresee as one of deepening decline. The American pleaded for his friend to return with him to the less somber environs of their mother commonwealth, and to the more wholesome memories and occupations the voyage home would surely entail. But the painter could not entertain the idea of leaving the locale of his greatest happiness—and of his most utter devastation.

Sadly, William acquiesced, again scanning the haggard appearance of his friend, which once had bloomed so vigorously, as though he too were an artist and wished to memorize each cruelly imposed new distortion of feature for a future portraiture.

Michaelis's continued silence and his companion's own resultant silence became suddenly intolerable. William had just stood back from the table to signal his intention to depart, when there was a knocking on the apartment doors, which, while less clattering than that earlier heard, had a more portentous resonance due to the echoing of the high-ceilinged rooms.

His host bade William stay a minute more while he answered the summons. From the outer corridor, William heard the housekeeper's rapid sputter of Italian, followed by his friend's morose accents in that same tongue, soon intertwined with another lighter voice, speaking in a dialect of the language.

Michaelis reentered the room with an astonishing alteration of demeanor, and energetically gesturing, he ushered inside the two grimy *contadini* William had early seen without. They gazed about them with hesitancy and awe at the apartment's size and elegance, for even in his squalor, the artist remained a great man. The artist, meanwhile, cleared half the table and asked the men to set their parcel down and open it.

When the moldy cloths had been flaked off and the peasants served flagons of wine, Michaelis touched and fondled a rough stone-like object, the size and shape of a three-pound loaf of freshly baked bread.

William was as perplexed by his friend's sudden transformation of mood—hectic, ruddy, enthusiastic—as he was by the object itself.

Taking up a small mallet such as marble-carvers use, the artist inserted an iron wedge into a hairline crack that ran along the top of the stony loaf and began to gently tap at it, all the while talking excitedly to his compatriot.

"These men, William, are from the countryside near L'Aquila in the Abruzzan Apennines where lie the deepest natural anthracite pits in the entire peninsula—in all Europe, it is rumored.

"If they speak truly, then I have at last found the pigment I have been searching for these past three years; the inevitable, yet almost ideal result of my studies and experiments; the base color I shall have ground and then mixed to make a linseed oil to complete my most perfect masterpiece—there, that large shrouded canvas you beheld earlier and questioned me about, and which I would not show you nor any man, and which has lain incomplete awaiting this final color.

"If these men speak truly, William, we have before us what I have dreamed of, what I have required to prove my theory. I will be at last vindicated, within the fortnight, when the new salon of Rome opens and my painting walks off with the greatest acclaim."

Michaelis tapped a final soft blow upon the wedge and the stone gave off a sound soft as a sigh before it fell apart onto the surrounding cloths. Within it, the size of a man's fist—of a man's heart—lay a mass so black, so dense that the *contadini* and William too were forced to gasp and draw back from it.

Michaelis stared, merely emitting a guttural murmur. "Ah, my beauty!"

William was unable to draw his eyes from the dark mineral on the table. Its blackness was so intense it seemed to recede from his vision, drawing his sight deeper within itself.

"What in the Creator's name is it?"

"Only a fine chunk of anthracite now. But when it is made into a pigment, William, then it will be Absolute Ebony!"

William repeated those last two words to himself, with growing uneasiness.

"All colors composed of light in our world mix to pure white," Michaelis explained. "Goethe proved that. But all colors composed of earthly material mix to form black. Therefore I have painted a masterpiece in black so comprehensive as to make Rembrandt's darkest works seem like summer fripperies. We must see how the coal pulverizes. Good as its hue is, it must powder correctly or it will mix poorly and be worthless to me."

So saying, he scraped one side of the wedge against the lump until a fine powder descended. This the artist held up on one finger, inspecting it by candlelight with great care and eventual satisfaction.

"It will do," the artist said, then sat down and sipped more wine, once more becoming pensive.

William believed the arrival of the *contadini* with the coal represented a turning point in his friend's life. He had never doubted Michaelis's skill or ingenuity, but he sensed disaster impending from this latest event. In applying to an all-black painting a pigment blacker still, the artist would surely seal his fate in Rome. His canvas would be completed, true, hung at the salon, but surely it would be scoffed at, made the butt of jokes and lampoons. Michaelis would be utterly crushed. Then William's arguments for a return to his homeland would fall upon more open ears, since that might be the artist's only remaining alternative. Forced to consider his error, like the virtuous and true man William knew Michaelis to be, the artist would undoubtedly return to a more moderately developed philosophy, to a life of light and color.

Yet the coal itself was strangely disturbing, and William was forced to busy himself in order to avoid having his eyes continually drawn to it. He paid the peasant out of his own purse and, finding the housekeeper, sent her to fetch Castelgni, the pigment maker, explaining that Signor Michaelis had urgent need of him, and he must be roused out of sleep.

The artist did not move from his seat. He sat on, regarding the coal with a concentrated attention, as though he foresaw more than vindication in its depth, as though he could envisage an entirely new universe potential within its dark heart.

So entranced was the artist, William had to at last shake him out of his reverie so he might take his leave.

Passing out the front door of the building, William was greeted by the pigment maker, nervously, hurriedly ascending the wide, dim stairway to Michaelis's studio.

❖

After the pigment maker had scraped a chip off the lump of coal, he ground it to a fine point, then swept the powder into an old bronze dish aged with many previous mixings. Water was sprinkled in, the binder added—a concoction Castelgni had learned from his father, his father from his, going back, it was said, to the days and to the very studio of the great Veronese himself. When he had done, Castelgni called Michaelis, who meanwhile had been busying himself uncovering what seemed to the old Roman guildsman to be a large, obscure canvas.

"How does the color look, old man?"

"Nerissimo!" the mixer replied. "Blacker than any black before it."

Indeed, the flat dish, coated with but a quarter inch of the new pigment, seemed to hold more than a pint of it, as though it had suddenly dropped open to the size of a large flagon, as though ordinary laws of depth and foreshortening no longer held true in its presence.

"Chip and mix all of it! But carefully, mind you," Michaelis warned, "I'll need all of it. Bring it as soon as you're done."

He wrapped up the remainder of the coal, carefully sealing it back within its mantle of rock.

"As soon as you're done, you understand? No matter the hour. Leave the dishful. I must test it."

When Castelgni had gone, the artist picked up the dish, looked once more into its depths, and brought it to the palette board that had been set up facing the uncovered painting.

Not even the Roman night was dim enough for the subtleties of darkness he had already committed to the canvas. The studio's arras were drawn doubly. Two dim candles in wall sconces were foreshadowed by painted black baffles. Within this rare obscurity stood Michaelis's new painting: the summation of his life's work, unlike any work conceived of before.

It was a life-sized painting of Michaelis himself, clad in the masquerade of a Spanish Grandee of a previous era. In the painting, he half turned from the observer, as though he had been walking away and, suddenly called, had turned back to face his caller—a most difficult view to achieve, even were it done with a live model. For it to be a self-portrait was amazing, especially as Michaelis's care and technical skills ensured that the portrait would be a compendium of every refinement of proportion and perspective.

But the unusual angle of the subject had another, more crucial purpose: to provide more than half the entire space of the canvas to one single area—which he would fill in with the new pigment—the area of a full-length cape that Michaelis wore. It fell heavily from his broad shoulders, plummeted leadenly, and swung slightly at the tops of his boots to effect a sudden movement, as though by the exorbitant force of gravity.

This area had been long prepared for the new color. For months he had covered it with a base coat of his own perfecting, designed to totally wed pigment to canvas. Once that had dried, the artist had painted over the area with Lamp Black, the darkest hue available to artists. To others, that might appear to be the end of the matter. However, Michaelis had looked upon the Lamp Black with an emotion close to pain, knowing as he did how far from his ideal the Lamp Black proved to be. Yet after it too had dried and he had tediously scraped the entire area of the painted cape, he was pleased to discover how well his base had held. The razor point he wielded was so thin it almost sliced the canvas at moments, the area now to be repainted was so fine that should a person stand behind the canvas he or she might almost be discerned through the area; and yet it was black, front and back, fully primed for the final application.

Michaelis decided upon yet another refinement—a caprice. He would let remain a thin border of the Lamp Black, no more than half an inch, to outline the cape, to bring into relief the new pigment, and then—as a further act of bravura—he'd also paint in various undulating lines of Lamp Black to suggest the vertically flowing hints of the cape's folds. Though Lamp Black themselves, against the new black, they might appear almost silver.

He dipped a brush into the dish of the newly made pigment, careful not to miscalculate his touch because of the curious effect of extra depth. Emerging with the utter dab of darkness on the fine cat-whisker hair of his brush, he lifted it to the canvas.

The pigment almost sprang onto the portrait of its own accord. Only a faint inkish stain remained on the bristles. It was fully, instantly absorbed onto the prepared canvas, standing out against the other blacks like a speck of eternity.

Quickly, greedily, Michaelis dipped his brush and applied more of the pigment, broadening the spot, adding more, then more still, and then all of it, until the dish was merely blemished and once again possessed its natural flatness, and the new pigment, to the size of a man's hand, covered the upper right-hand corner of the outlined cape.

"Nerissimo!" Michaelis whispered, repeating Castelgni's words. "Blacker than any black ever before."

The artist pulled up a bench and sat staring at the canvas, pondering his work, admiring the new color until the hours of night were obliterated. When finally—in answer to his housekeeper's knocking—he at last left the studio chamber, he was astonished to discover that it was some time past sunrise.

At dusk, the pigment maker arrived, accompanied by an apprentice who helped carry a large covered vat. When Michaelis had the lid prized up, he thrilled seeing the intense depths of the black pigment they had labored to produce. As he'd been promised, it mixed beautifully.

The guildsman apologized for their tardiness. His wife, the old man said, would not allow the block of coal into her house. The superstitious old woman had lighted candles and had muttered litanies all day. Castelgni had been forced to beg work space in the atelier of a fellow craftsman to complete the grinding and mixing.

Upon hearing this, the simple-minded young apprentice, already frightened by the intense blackness of the pigment, whined and pleaded for them to depart.

"But it was a very easy pigment to make," the phlegmatic old man said with a smile, ignoring his younger's pleas. "Almost as though it was eager to become paint for the Signor."

❖

"It is said that the great Frans Hals knew twenty-seven different shades of black, and when to use each of them for perfect effect. Rembrandt himself provided twenty-nine different shades of black for the hats and doublets and backgrounds, to differentiate each of the doctors in his mass portrait, *The Anatomy Lesson*. The Chinese have an entire school of ink painting where no colors are admitted. Their gradations range from grays so indistinct as to seem the mere smudge of a virgin's finger upon the petal of a white chrysanthemum, to that deepest of blacks, which is used to write but one word in their curious visual language—that signifying the eternal restlessness given to those who seek to usurp the throne of heaven. Their shades of black number thirty.

"Already I have discovered one more shade than they. Intimate to me as to those Mandarins are these various tints and black hues with iron oxide bases and the merest hint of scarlet which seems to me to be the true color of bloodlust in battle and the fever of pestilence. Other tints of black with browns and green hinted at are luxurious, as though embedded in velvet plush. Some blacks are the colors of certain practices of Roman courtesans whispered in my ears by masked women during lewd street celebrations, while other shades speak of quiet diplomacies, of saddened courtesies, of the final noble words spoken by highborn men and women meeting their ends by treachery and the executioner's block. Other blacks still are almost charming: One with a hint of blue indigo is as tart as a Parisian soubrette. Yet others are somber as widow's weeds, heavy as the unheard curses of decades-old prisoners in airless dungeons. I have acquainted myself with these varieties of despair and in turn invented new hues to reflect those new despondencies I myself have experienced.

"A pure Lamp Black from Liverpool is so black that in bright light it glitters almost silver white. But there! That only proves my point. What I've wanted, what I searched for was a different kind of pigment, one that would not reflect outwardly, by prismatics, but inwardly, by secret refinements upon nature itself."

Michaelis ceased to speak and fell into a brooding silence. William could do nothing but sigh.

"Will you begin tonight?" he at last asked the painter.

"The very minute you leave. And I will work on until it is done."

"Then good night. Tomorrow morning I ride for Pisa and thence on to Venice. But I will be returned before the exhibit is to open its doors. Promise me that day to return with me to America."

"After the exhibit, sweet friend, I will no longer need to go anywhere," Michaelis said. "I will have arrived."

❖

It was in the earliest hours of morning, the following day, when Michaelis applied the last dregs of the ebon pigment to the final uncovered square inch of canvas. As with every previous brushstroke, the paint seemed to leap off the brush onto the canvas, as though rejoining that portion of itself divided in the act of application.

During the exhausting labor, the artist had scarcely glanced at the canvas before him, or if he had it was only to ensure that the pigment lay evenly alongside the Lamp Black outline he had devised for its entire perimeter.

Now, finished, he stood back to inspect his self-portrait, and instantly felt a catch in the back of his throat. It was precisely as he had fore-visioned it: the figure in is usual attitude against its dim background, his face half hidden by the gleaming Lamp Black domino he lifted with one black gloved hand, the shadows, the thirty other individual shades of black he had used for the costume, shading of silver blacks crosshatched to suggest the sheen of satin, golden blacks delicately embossed for the silken expanses of his doublet and pantaloons, blue blacks and indigo blacks in whorls and minuscule circles to intimate the textures of a throat ruffle, of shirt cuffs bursting from each dark sleeve, browner blacks in careful streaks for details of facial hair, and for the highlights of the broad-brimmed hat he wore, all wrought so ingeniously as to offer a palette as rich and complex as the brightest chromatics of David and Delacroix, his esteemed contemporaries.

And even if one were so myopic as to misapprehend these many dark subtleties, dominating the portrait was the new pigment, the immense utter blackness of the cape.

Looking at it, Michaelis felt as though he were seeing through a portal into an entirely new dimension—one intrinsically opposed to any ever seen by man before. Where the Lamp Black edging ended and the new paint began, so sharp a delineation occurred that it seemed to signal that another reality existed.

The dark cape curved inward by some curious property of the pigment, drawing his vision inward, spiraling counterclockwise deeper and deeper within, until Michaelis felt unable to fix himself to any stable underpinnings of floor or walls or ceiling, nearly weightless. Suddenly afraid that he would fall into the blackness of the cape, he pulled himself away from the canvas and carefully sat himself down in an armchair at a fair distance from the easel.

That precaution failed little to dispel his initial impression. From a dozen feet further back in the room, his sense that the newly painted area was both more and yet less than a flat surface was much intensified. As though he had assisted in representing the abysses of the heavens themselves, a starless heaven, somehow pulsing alive with the very negation of matter.

A further curious side effect of the new pigment was that the large, gloomy studio itself seemed smaller, almost intimate, especially at that end of the chamber where the canvas was placed. One might infer that light itself could no longer exert its periodic powers or proportions wherever existed that utter lack of light.

It was a bitter triumph, this ultra-black painting, yet it *was* a triumph Michaelis experienced. So entranced was he with his creation that he sat hours in front of it before falling asleep on the rough studio cot.

When he awoke from his extended yet signally un-refreshing sleep, the day outside his window was damp, gray, and airless. He was still fatigued, chilled by the sudden wetness that seemed to hold the city in thrall all that day. He passed the afternoon and evening enraptured by his masterpiece, discovering within its maw of absolute black echoes of all the suffering and unhappiness he had so long felt.

That moment he was able to draw himself away from the canvas, particularly from the yawning chasm of the cape, he was filled with a vague sense of unease and restlessness. He picked at his solitary dinner, distractedly began and then put down unread a half dozen volumes of poetry and philosophy he'd had been wont to turn to previously as balm for even his most melancholy hours. That night, as he began to slip into slumber, he thought he heard the distant approach of flood waters rising.

The consequent days were spent by Michaelis in an attempt to overcome a sense of exhaustion that strangely persisted. His housekeeper said she hoped he wasn't ill, but as he could find no specific symptoms to complain of, the doctor that was sent for could do nothing for the artist, and went off again baffled, prescribing bed rest.

Michaelis took advantage of this new regimen to actively avoid all contact with others. In fact, he had begun to find the presence of others intolerable to his sensitivities. He asked that his food be set outside his apartment door, where, often enough, Antonia would happen upon it, hours later, scarcely touched. He moved from sleep to waking through far easier transitions than ever before and a great deal more frequently during a single revolution of the hours. Soon it became difficult for him to fully separate these states of consciousness with his prior conviction.

Instead, he began to inhabit an intermediate state, and in this he would find himself gazing out a window for hours, or—more frequently—leaning against the studio doorjamb, his work chamber grown tiny to his eyes, except for the portrait, looming immensely, its awesome depths flickering and breeding odd presentiments.

He began hearing soft sounds that seemed to derive from somewhere behind, and then upon closer inspection, somewhere *within* the canvas, sounds like those he had first taken to be rising waters, as though some liquid medium of great viscosity had been stirred somehow to life from a vast distance. The movement appeared to be caused in a quiet, yet dark, viscous pond, insistently, tediously lapping against the edge of the canvas.

He began to have inexplicable fantasies, sleeping or awake, of a small, misshapen creature—black as the blackness of the cape—who hid within the pigment, and who softly whimpered its dreadful, its unfulfillable need.

Once that was heard, the delicate lapping noises ceased. But the whimpering continued, sometimes for hours, at times barely audible, at other times so loud he could not hear himself think. Nor could he escape it. He found he was unable to step beyond an invisible yet still defined radius around the canvas without experiencing an unspecified although all-encompassing panic, and actually physical pain in the form of a megrim headache. At times, he fancied the whimpering noise so near that it was within his very veins and arteries. He dared not nick himself shaving, or his life's blood would pour out of him not humanly crimson, but absolutely black too.

❖

The childlike whimpering was approaching the door of his bedchamber. Although he slept and dreamt and knew he both slept and dreamt, still it slowly advanced through the precisely described dimensions and details of his bedchamber, black and small, almost viscous itself, moving toward the edge of his bed. A fearful thing! He turned away, but could not awaken. It came to the bed's edge and slowly, viscously, clambered onto the bed linen, the whimpering subsided now into a soft panting, not so much respiration as the inverse of breathing. Still unable to awaken or move away, he huddled further away from it, within himself, dreading its approach, curling his body like an infant, to avoid it. The maddening sound was in his ear now; the creature from within the chasm that was his self-portrait stretched itself next to him, slowly, with infinitely minute pressure leaned its viscous form against his shrinking, dreading back, legs, and neck, as a freezing child might timidly approach a sleeping stranger for warmth. It caused him to tremble, then shiver, then shake so violently with its sense of living blackness and nothingness come to life and its sapping of all warmth and life and color from him that he did at last awaken, with a start. He leapt from the bed and rushed out of the room.

He found in a cupboard a flagon of brandy and drank a cupful, to warm and steady himself. Its half century of bottled spirits helped a bit to dispel the more immediate palpitations from the terrible nightmare, and he wrapped himself in his outdoors cloak and more deliberately sipped another cupful of the old brandy until his hand no longer trembled about the chalice and his breath no longer frosted the cold metal edge. Yet he dared not fall asleep again, but passed the remaining hours before dawn huddled in the dining room chair, peering into the studio doorway left half-ajar, and, at times, out the window awaiting the first warming ray of the morning sun.

The nightmare had shaken him out of his previous week of

lethargy. He bathed and dressed rapidly, and even before Antonia could come to him, he went down to the ground floor for the first time since the pigment had arrived and asked leave to breakfast at the common table set daily for her family and for several other pensioners.

After so long and so complete an absence, he was congratulated upon his recovery, as evidenced by the new prodigousness of his appetite.

Cheered, he gathered up a wide-brimmed hat against the hot Roman sun and decided upon a long morning walk. Antonia was free to clean and air out his apartments, a task she'd long anticipated after weeks of being denied her housekeeping there.

Michaelis returned past noon. Already most of the Roman citizenry had escaped the debilitating heat of the outdoors for cooler, afternoon siestas. The artist felt renewed by his walk, his fears of the night dispelled by the benign morning sunlight. He had just settled himself at his table and had begun reading his weekly *Corriere*, attempting to catch up on news of the town, and he was anticipating the coming evening's dinner with William, who was expected back, when Antonia appeared before him, her various implements of trade in hand and an arch expression upon her kindly face.

"You have worked very hard, Signore. Too much work, it is poor for your health. When you first appeared at our table downstairs, we were persuaded you were some baleful spirit."

Michaelis murmured the appropriate response.

"Never have I met such a persevering artist," she said, shaking one finger as though scolding him for his industry. "Why, you even paint in your sleep!"

"How do you mean?"

"Come look!" she said, leading him to the bedchamber. "*Ecco!* What did I say! *Ecco!* There! Those spots of black resisted all my efforts to remove them."

At the far side of the bed from where Michaelis usually lay down, two spots of the new pigment lay upon the floorboards. The artist wondered if he had been so distracted during the last stage of his work on the canvas that, unawares, he had tracked them into his bedchamber. He dismissed Antonia, assuring her he would ask the pigment maker for a solvent to remove them.

After she had gone, however, Michaelis returned to the side of the bed to more closely inspect the spots. This near, they took on a more defined appearance: one was a mere half inch or so of black smudge, the indistinct shape of a semicircle. But as he looked more closely, it suddenly struck him that the other black mark could be nothing other than the pad and first three toes of a small foot: large and clear, the very impression that would be made by a small child with paint on its feet as it leaned to climb onto the bed.

❖

"I was certain the painting would be done by now," William protested. "You look as though you've worked on it without a minute of sleep since I've been away."

"Only one more night of work. Then I am done," the artist replied, not unaware of his friend's vigorous health, almost a censure to his own haggard appearance.

"Do you still mean to display it?" William asked, looking toward the studio where the painting remained covered. "The salon opens tomorrow."

"It will be done."

William was yet to be appeased. "We were to celebrate its completion tonight. And also my return. We were to dine out. I have already accepted an invitation to a fete for us both, at the Marchesa de B———'s."

"You must go to that alone. Tomorrow night, after the exhibit, we will celebrate, you and I. Have a bit more patience with an old friend, I beg you."

"Tomorrow night for certain, then," William agreed brightly. "You'll have no way out, I assure you. I feel duty bound to see you done with this canvas. Its last stages of labor have taken a terrible toll on you, I fear."

Although exhausted and sad, Michaelis was calm, which William misperceived as the serenity of near completion rather than the resignation it in truth signified.

"Let me only step into this pharmacy," the artist said, "I am promised a draught to sustain me during the last hours of labor."

William left his friend at the herbalist shop. Michaelis received his prescription and ponderously took his way home.

Arrived, he mixed the potent stimulants the pharmacist had prepared into a flagon of strong, hot espresso and, sighing, he brought the cup with him into the studio.

Two large canisters sat before the shrouded portrait, delivered by his orders, via the pigment maker and his apprentice. Michaelis pried up their lids, then drank the potion he'd received, along with the first of a half dozen espressos he would continue to consume in the coming hours.

A great initial effort was required for him to dip a paintbrush into the vat before him, and even greater effort to lift the brush to the area of the canvas where the Absolute Ebony had only just dried. but Michaelis made his nerves iron to his task. Only his heart was a waste of icy emptiness the moment he applied the brush to the canvas and began the destruction of his masterpiece by applying over it the purest, thickest, whitest Zinc White to ever come from Castelgni's workshop.

Perhaps it was because of the precautions he had taken before beginning the task—the dozens of candelabra with the brightest tapers illuminating the chamber as though the grandest party were in progress—perhaps for other, unknown reasons, but he had already emptied one large canister of the bright new pigment onto the canvas and had begun dipping into the second when he began to sense a sort of pulsing from the remaining black pigment that formed the cape.

He worked faster, dipping the brush more rapidly, applying the white in great swaths over larger areas of black.

He became aware of the lapping sound, at first so quiet he merely sensed it: at the tips of his hair, on the very surface of his cheeks. It went on, growing ever stronger, louder, until Michaelis could hear no other sound and worked feverishly now, with greater dispatch to cover the remaining areas of the terrible black. Several times he felt the brush he was using almost twisted out of his hands by some force from within the canvas.

When only a square foot or so of the original pigment remained, he switched over to another, larger, rougher brush. That's when the whimpering started up. Like the lapping sound before it, it began scarcely audible, but as the artist dipped his brush and raised it with yet more Zinc White to the canvas, it became louder, growing to a crescendo of piteous, fierce moaning so encompassing he was certain the everyone in the surrounding dozen streets and houses must be able to hear it.

He filled his ears with wax melting off the many candles around him, and, temporarily protected from the terrible sound, he worked on yet more feverishly.

Now only a few inches or so remained of the black. But when he dipped his brush into the canister of white, it came up dry. The pigment was gone, used up. He frantically scraped enough from the sides of the canisters to cover a minuscule section of the canvas, cursing, kicking over empty buckets.

The large canvas began to belly outward, as though attempting to reject the application of the white, as though whatever existed within it was pushing through, to get out—and at him.

Michaelis ignored its buffeting as best he could, shuddering all the while, yet for all that concentrating all of his distracted attention to devise how he might cover that last spot of black. His heart beat wildly with the memory of last night's visitor, and of the footprint he had seen, and the whimpering that now pierced through the wax stuffed in his ears, as though the sound derived not from without, but from within his very brain.

Not a thimble full of white remained. It was four o'clock of the morning: impossible to secure more pigment. How could he cover it all?

Michaelis almost went mad then. He sensed a power within that tiny remaining spot of black pigment that had to be obliterated lest it annihilate all else. The canvas continued to shudder from top to bottom, sometimes vertically, other times diagonally, as though to shake off the new paint. It would. It would, he knew, unless he managed to cover every last bit of the infernal hue.

As though by inspiration, he suddenly recalled his own supplies, not looked into for the past several years since he had turned to darker colors. Ah, and there in the small cupboard it was—not a great deal, but still clean, clear, unsullied, an almost full tube of ancient Zinc White he had used for children's dresses and maidens' hands. Deafened by now, near to maddened by the piercing whining from within that still screeched on, he worked to extract the pigment into a dish. Looking up, he saw the canvas blowing in and out as though it were the topmost sail of a clipper ship under a typhoon's gale.

He managed to get enough white pigment mixed with water and binder, rapidly stirring until he supposed it thick enough to completely coat the last bit of black.

He dipped his thickest brush into the paint, swirled it to soak up every atom of the liquid. But as he lifted the brush from the palette dish to the spot, the billowing canvas went utterly flat. From the remaining portion of Absolute Ebony the color seemed to emerge completely, as though the black had taken on full life. Before Michaelis's unbelieving eyes, the pigment grew forward, forming itself into the grotesquely black lineaments of a small, unnaturally proportioned, three-fingered hand reaching out for him.

He clenched his teeth to stifle an utterance of terror, then dabbed the brush with the Zinc White at those fingers, covering them with lines, blotches, streaks of white. As he did, the hand pulled back; simultaneously, a shriek emerged from the canvas so high-pitched, so fraught with fear and pain as to send him reeling backward.

The scream ended as suddenly. When his head had ceased to ache from the sound, he once more approached the canvas. All was silent, the whimpering gone, the surface still and flat. Quickly, ruthlessly, he painted over that last spot; then, calmer, he inspected the canvas and returned that brush of Zinc White over every possibility of insufficient pigment, no matter how thread-thin any possible crevice, until he was satisfied that not a single iota of the awful black pigment remained.

Exhausted, Michaelis slowly, arduously, dragged himself out of his studio and swooned onto his bed.

❖

"Arouse yourself, dear friend. It's past four o'clock in the afternoon."

Michaelis sat up in bed and looked about him as though he had awakened in a strange land.

"Have a cup of this *caffe latte*," William pleaded. "It will help you awaken." He sat in a chair near the bed, holding out an earthenware cup. Late-afternoon daylight played over the floorboards through the open curtains of the window.

"The exhibit has been open since midday," William went on. "But now you must rouse yourself and have a bit to eat before we go."

The artist sipped the almost insipid liquid, coming slowly more awake, as though from some long dream.

At once he started. "The portrait! It still must be brought to the salon."

"On that you may rest assured, my friend. It is already accomplished."

"But...!"

"Accomplished. Carted to the salon. This morning, when I called on you, I found you sound asleep, fully dressed, wearing the paint-daubed wear you now sport. You had wax in your ears, I supposed so as to not be disturbed by noise during your well-earned rest. I called for Castelgni and his man, and they carted it off."

"Did you see it?"

"Alas, no. It was already covered over when the two brought it out, for its own protection, I presume. Meanwhile I tried unsuccessfully to awaken you."

William insisted that food be taken at a local *trattoria* nearby the salon, a place much attended by artists of various nationalities, at one time during his palmier days, Michaelis's favorite haunt.

Several times durng the course of their meal, the artist was recognized by colleagues and acquaintances, and though he greeted each, he held no converse with them.

But as their sweet *Zuppa Inglese* was served, Riegler, the noted art critic and prestigious historian, came to their table and requested discourse.

"I have seen your self-portrait on exhibit," he said, taking Michaelis's hand in a warm clasp. "Allow me to be the first to congratulate you and to acclaim it a masterpiece."

Seeing Riegler not repulsed by the formerly misanthropic artist, others now approached more closely. All had either already seen the portrait or just heard of it from others. All were filled with congratulations and that unrestrained heartfelt pleasure that true artists feel in a deserving colleague's triumph over their shared and recalcitrant material and even more elusive muse. French Champagne was ordered by Reigler. Toasts were proposed to Michaelis and his work. The dinner became a fete.

Soon the party spilled out into the piazza, and from there, it moved toward the salon with ever-increasing festivity.

Michaelis had barely stepped over the threshold of the salon when a man who for the past three years had mocked him to all who would listen stepped forward to embrace the artist.

"You have been awarded the *Palma d'Oro*, the highest honor Rome can bestow upon a work of art."

A cheer rose from the crowd. Others in the salon, hearing of Michaelis's arrival, rushed to greet him.

The President of the Society of Arts himself arrived and pinned the medal consisting of a golden palm-tree to Michaelis's jacket front and launched into a speech of flowery laudation and excessive length.

The artist heard and witnessed all this with a scarcely hidden sneer and with no great enthusiasm. What did these fools mean? The painting was a failure. A mere whisper of a possibility of what he had once intended—what he had idealized, what he had achieved if only briefly, and oh so perilously. Could these idiots not understand what he had done? What he had been forced to *undo* by his own hand? Would they never understand the depths of darkness which he had plumbed, first in his imagination, then—when the pigment was actually produced—in his art, in his life? If his undoing was the cause of so much honor, what would they have thought to see the painting as he had planned it, as he had first painted it?

The president was at last done speaking. Applause was followed by more congratulation, more toasts, and by the drinking of more Champagne. Michaelis was asked to speak too, and he demurred. But William, who among all the others the artist truly believed was delighted in his friend's good fortune—persuaded him to attempt it. So the artist spoke, quietly, sadly, of his travails, of his search for new modes of expression, of his experimentation with new and old forms and themes and techniques, of how the ideal he had envisioned would live on, although the finished work was compromised and would always be a failure, a mere cipher of that ideal.

"Enough modesty. Let us see this marvel!" the President declared. "We have installed it at one end of the great salon, with no others nearby, for all would doubtless suffer by comparison."

"The others are mere exercises by comparison," Michaelis heard his former enemy declare.

Nor was he the only man to utter such sentiments as the crowd, Michaelis in its midst, flowed into the great salon, past one fine painting after another, each one ignored or subjected to abuse and invective from the onlookers.

When they had gathered and opened a space around the painter and his portrait, it was William who read out the inscription: "Self-Portrait in Absolute Ebony."

"Amazing, isn't it?" Reigler demanded of his companion.

"Astounding!" several agreed.

"Utter genius!" oner man declared. "Who would have dreamed of outlining the cape in Lamp Black?"

"And the cape itself…remarkable!"

"Of course, of course! The cape! The cape!"

The President was speaking into Michaelis's ear during the hubbub.

"When the canvas was first brought in, we feared it had been damaged during the carting. Two tiny spots of white in the lower center of the cape seemed to mar the edge of the cape. Fortunately, within seconds, they were gone. They vanished as we looked on."

Michaelis did not appear to hear the words. Instead he seemed entranced, his eyes completely filled by what he beheld: the portrait, exactly as he had finished it a week and a half before, with the cape painted in Absolute Ebony.

"Why, I feel as though I could put my hand right into the pigment, there at the cape." Riegler reached toward it.

"No!" Michaelis shouted. "Don't touch it!"

"He meant it no harm," William said.

"Don't touch the canvas," Michaelis repeated more softly, but with as much anxiety in his voice. "Don't go too near it. Not ever! Not if you care for your sanity."

"As though it were a window cut into some other dimension," he could hear another man saying. "One of utter blackness, naturally."

"Why, even the room appears smaller at this end," yet another viewer observed. "As though it were made smaller by the portrait."

"There's never been a painting like it," several agreed.

Michaelis turned away, grasping William's arm.

"We must go," he whispered.

"Go? Where?"

"To Boston. Tonight, immediately. The first packet that sails."

"But surely you're jesting. after a triumph like…" Then, seeing his friend's face, he changed his words to say, "The packet doesn't leave until tomorrow afternoon."

"I must gather a few necessities tonight. Now. You will help me," the artist said, quietly, drawing William away from the others, still gathered in wonder about the portrait.

"I'm delighted, of course, to help you leave," William said, "since that was the purpose of my mission to you here in Rome. But why such haste? We were to celebrate tonight, surely? And to leave Rome now, at the height of your sucess?"

William had to repeat his question, then repeat it again.

Although Michaelis stared at him from only inches away, he could not hear his countryman's words. All he could hear was a soft, viscous lapping sound, then the awful familiarity of a barely audible whimpering that spoke of an unfillable abyss that would reach out slowly, inexorably, and draw him in, deep into the maw of absolute ebony.

Room Nine

The hotel was prepossessing enough in that red-brick overstuffed Victorian manner. If, that is, one discounted its somewhat confined appearance sandwiched between a round-cornered, recently erected, multistory strip of shopfronts and an enormous concrete slab car park undergoing what seemed to be perpetual reconstruction.

He'd entered that latter labyrinth to leave off the hire car, secured inexpensively if incorrectly at the vast, impersonal Midlands airport where he'd alit from a cramped aisle seat in an economy aircraft after an eleven-hour-and-forty-minute flight.

The period since then had been distinguished by his attempts to follow printed-out Internet directions so irregular that a logician would conclude the country's road plan to be at best provisional: Street names, when actually posted, had a curious habit of altering without warning, from one corner to another. Numbering, naturally enough, observed the same Lewis Carroll process, retrogressing from, say, 398 to 12 with stunning amorality.

Still one more confounding element was the suddenness, extent, depth, and finally the interminability of a low-lying mist that set in and hovered between the rental vehicle's bonnet and the streetlighting's upper metal. That a cloudless, starry, black night rose all above those lights provided the further impression that he somehow was motoring through a particularly uninspired museum diorama, perhaps one titled "Mediocre British Manufacturing City of Certain Age and Decreptitude."

Nevertheless, once he was within the warmth and relative newness of the hotel's most external lobby, his three oversized pieces of luggage almost completely in hand by then, he paused.

The typical foyer gave almost immediately on the right to an atypically attenuated gallery of a bar, with uneven tiled floor and an unpolished timberland of painted-black spindly tables and chairs of the cheapest assortment. Opposing them was the by no means contemporary, utterly undistinguished, long-uncleaned, dark wood stand-up bar, its uppermost regions plastered about with blazing company adverts, all of it redolent of beer, whiskey, and wine.

The second he peered in, a fusillade of lascivious, mixed-gender laughter erupted from out of an unseen section of the public room, so he quickly withdrew, only to focus abruptly upon a figure seated nearby in a straight-back rattan chair, a figure so ubiquitous and unmoving that at first he'd deemed it part of the background.

An elderly fellow, Mid-Eastern, Parsi perhaps, given the ethnic-appearing hat shaped somewhat like a bottle cap, dust speckled of course, wrinkled by antiquity and immutable usage. Beneath what might be a very old and dingy gray lambswool coat, the stick-like teak-colored personage seemed to sport tiny mementoes of his unspecified homeland in the shabby edges of a once-bronze-toned, silver-thread-embroidered vest and an achromatic shirt and collar of exotic fabric, all indubitably hoary and begrimed. His narrow head was so sculptured and noble in that UNESCO poster mode, his face so grim and unmoving and unquestionably toothless, and the old thing was muttering something in such a low consistent voice, that he could not possibly be understood unless one moved directly beside what was certain to be his noxious exhalation.

So he turned instead to the hotel desk, such as it was, a timid affair, squashed into one end of the aforementioned bar and separated from it by only the merest of particle boards. An effulgent violet cloth notebook, like that an eight-year-old girl would use as a photo scrapbook, lay ajar as the hotel register.

He knew this, as it was immediately thrust toward him by an amber-skinned, all but kohl-eyed youth, effeminately pretty in a graphic novel way, wearing a matching if more metallic, purple *blouson*, who never once ceased speaking quietly—he presumed amorously—into a mobile phone held against one ear as the clerk juggled a melange of items.

In the light of the hung-high competing monitor screens above—one an unchanging perspective of the front steps, the other a television tuned to a silent talking heads information show—the young hotelkeep's skin and especially his improbably tinted (hennaed?) hair cast off glints of apple green, lilac, and mauve.

After a sufficient amount of time evading the letter thrust, rethrust, and repositioned for greatest effect upon the registration desk, the young *houri* on the mobile phone excused himself from his all-important caller to ask if he wanted to check in.

"The university booked for me," he responded. "It's paid for in advance."

Despite these facts, he still must show his passport as well as a "valid credit card," which he found slightly galling and undoubtedly an abuse. Funds were tight enough as it was: He didn't need to have to constantly monitor some bank company trying to clear off frivolous charges being made from this desk.

"Room thirteen. You enter past the bar," he was instructed, with a fluid wave in the general direction of where the laughter had squirted out at him before.

The key dropped in front of him, he all signed in, he still waited, as the unending barely audible mobile phone chatter went on. The heaviness of his bags had been obvious enough when he entered to require assistance. He waited until he had to actually interrupt the interminable conversation yet again: "Someone to help me up. The bags are so…"

Prettily unmotivated, the lad oozed from behind the desk and went directly for the smallest and lightest bag, which our friend, seeing his intent, quickly took up himself, forcing the youth to irritatedly lift another, heavier piece of the remaining two.

The lad pranced ahead through the bar, hips closely encased in boisterously bleached denims, swaying provocatively through the nearby doorway. Leading the way, he ignored the table of revelers—two middle-aged salesman with whiskey-wrinkled countenances, and an oddly unlined tart, once pretty and young, still dressed and coiffed in the style of Julie Christie in her high days of the Seventies.

He was guided through the quite long bar, where he was certain the trio were staring at him, ready to comment the second he was out of sight, through a doorway and up two sets of steps, down a stair. There a key attached to a plastic ring was flung into his hand, his third bag was released with a thud onto the wooden floor, and the young Middle Easterner was gone as entirely as though he'd never been there.

A struggle with the key ensued, while he remarked to himself how unseemly warm it was in the hallway. At the same time as the door finally opened to a small and dingy room, he turned to the nearby central heating grill and splayed his hand to test the temperature. Nonexistent, he discovered. Cool. Wherever the heat was coming from, and it was now almost chokingly warm in the narrow hallway, it wasn't from that grate.

A step into the room confirmed two unpleasant facts: The room was even more stifling than the corridor, and one reason might have been that whatever windows it possessed—two of them, single-paned, head high above the narrow single bed—opened not onto the street, but onto yet another hallway.

When he stepped out of the room a minute later to see exactly where they did open onto, he was surprised to walk directly into a wall. No ingress in that direction. And none in the other direction either, as that gave way to a stairway with tiny windowpanes.

He stood only a few seconds reflecting. He'd been hired for an indeterminate amount of time by the university. He hadn't expected grand accommodations. But this ghastly room, small, dingy, and worse, with no possible ventilation, was an abhorrence. He couldn't stay in it a single night, never mind weeks, possibly months, of nights.

Unwilling to drag his luggage back down again, he left them in the room, locked it, and went back down the stairs and past the bar—and the Dickensian-looking trio—to the front desk, where unsurpisingly the exotic youth was primping into a small mirror folded out onto the desk while still nattering into his mobile.

"That room won't do at all. It's hot in there. Too hot. And that room has no windows onto the street for ventilation. I'm certain you weren't told to put me into such poor accommodations."

The kohl-encircled eyes rose briefly from their adoring perusal of themselves, and the young hotel-keep turned to the back wall of the registration area where he himself could see dozens of hooks patterned onto a board of tiny squares—with only one single pink-plastic-ringed key hanging. The clerk lifted the key delicately—or was it distastefully?—off its hook and swung it mesmerically before his eyes. "Room nine is the only other room available."

He grasped at the key. "I'll take a look."

"You enter past the bar," the clerk said, indifferently returned to poring over the fold-up mirror in search of any overlooked fatal flaw.

Past the trio of loungers and bar again, up the two landings, past room thirteen, around another corner where a closed door stood two feet off the ground, locked, and completely unexplained, and from there on to another, one step down dropped, corridor and to a single door reading "9."

Even though the hallway had been stifling, the room itself was cool. Its single tiny mullioned window looked out onto an air shaft between the hotel and a blank concrete wall of the large car park where he'd earlier left the hired Vauxhall. The room was ridiculously tiny. Smaller than the not-very-large bathroom in his flat at home. There was barely room for a single cot of a bed, at the feet of which the window began, with one tiny space barely adequate to place his largest bag. Opposite that loomed a built-in closet, with it seemed enough shelves and hanger space to hold his meager wardrobe. Between that and the corridor door, nearly hidden, lurked a minuscule desk and chair.

One had to move the chair to open the closet. One had to close the closet door and move the chair to open the bathroom door. That too was tiny. A small, ugly, once dusky-pink painted room, its height greater than any other dimension, with a light brown tiled shower built in under an overhang, so it resembled nothing so much as a dark glass coffin, next to a sink barely large enough to place a sponge flat into, and opposite, a dullish pink toilet. But like the room itself, the bathroom was blissfully cool, even though windowless.

"It's small but it will do until something larger comes up," he told the uncaring desk clerk some five minutes later, after yet another trek around corridors and down stairs and again past the unsavory triumvirate at the bar, by now, he was sure, quite sick of seeing him. "At least it's cool, and opens to the outside."

"Room nine," the clerk said, altering his registration book, then turned unconcernedly back to the unending fascination of his complexion.

"But as I'm staying for a time, I'll need a larger room," he insisted, he was certain unlistened to and unheeded.

The old ethnic fellow was muttering more loudly as he passed, so he turned to see the old stick of a thing who was now almost vibrating with a kind of inner excitement.

"What is it, old-timer? What's got your motor going?" he asked, he thought kindly enough, taking notice when no one else about seemed to.

And listened to the fossil mutter words that he would later—from hearing them so daily—make out to be "Something not quite right, you know!"

"More than something," he would respond to the same uttered mantra daily in the weeks to come. "More than just some one thing is not quite right around here!"

❖

Called into Dr. Blethworthy's office, he sat, regarding the report he'd made, which faced away from him and toward the American Studies department head, standing, facing a window that gave onto one of the university's less insalubrious commons. His chief for the past three weeks, Edwin Blethworthy was a tall, well-built fellow, even a rather handsome fellow, despite his high color, who dressed himself and in general spoke and acted with the casual impudence of someone of equal rank in, say, Wisconsin or Nebraska. Upon them first meeting, Blethworthy had made some half-joking remark about the length, extent, and even the "substantial depths" of his own personal American experiences as a cultural exchange student, summer student, then assistant professor in "the States." All of it totaling, as far as he could make out, but a few years at most; yet more than sufficient to make Blethworthy rather a personage at the university here. One with powers and perquisites either he or one of his minions were always bringing forth whenever the merest suspicion of a hint of criticism was in the slightest danger of arising.

"Let us review," Blethworthy now spoke into the window panes he faced, "your task here, young sir, these past few weeks."

"My task, as I understood it, was to read the text being used for the final year of American Studies courses, and to compare it to a newer text covering the same material which it has been suggested might replace it."

"And then?" Blethworthy urged.

"And then to evaluate the one over the other based on various criteria... Isn't that precisely what I've done...here?" He lightly tapped the report on the desk. "I thought that's exactly what I'd done," he concluded.

Blethworthy covered his handsome face with one large, fluid hand, then spun around and seemingly in a single movement placed his body in his chair across the wide desk, where among other papers and books, the report in its pale blue plastic cover now glittered, a touch cruelly.

"What you've done, young sir," and here one of Blethworthy's large, masculine, yet somehow extremely elastic hands shot out and covered his own hands laid on the desktop in a light, slightly caressing grasp, "is...excellent! If...altogether...preliminary."

"How could it be...preliminary? I covered every chapter and..."

"Preliminary...since you could hardly be expected to do all that work, all that judging, all that reading, all that thinking, not to mention all that evaluation in a mere three weeks and one day."

"Yet I did," he protested.

"You did so...preliminarily," Blethworthy corrected, caressing his hand with such fervor that he became somewhat uncomfortable and wondered if he dared slip out of the grasp. "It's a three-fortnight task. At the least. Four fortnights makes more sense to me, before you could possibly have all the material in hand."

Eight weeks? Eight weeks on such a simple task? Blethworthy had to be kidding. He'd done it in three, three and a half weeks already at a half dozen universities already. Not these texts precisely, of course, but others awfully similar, since they were all awfully similar. He had evaluated American Studies courses in Reykjavik, in Mayaguez, in Riyadh, in Bangalore, in Darwin, even in Vancouver. The material was, one must face it, limited. The "takes" that textbook authors adapted were a mixture of the couth and un, of the trenchant and the bland, of the factual and the speculative. One, for example, might spend pages decrying the folly of "The Vietnam Adventure." Another barely mention it in the context of the "The Counterculture Wars" or "The Sixties Rebellion."

No matter. He knew the material seldom varied, as the authors' attitudes toward the material by now could be filed away into a mere handful of approaches, all needing to be toned down, of course, made more generalized, to be worthy of conclusive text.

He'd been hired by the university here, by Blethworthy himself as it turned out, based on all that previous work, all those evaluations he'd done, all over the world. What was all this now, suddenly, about the work being preliminary?

"You wish me to take it back," he asked, and watched the blandly handsome features for a hint. They softened, the cool blue eyes gleamed, the upper cheek creased. "You wish me to take it back and spend five more weeks evaluating the material?" he asked, just to make certain that indeed was what Blethworthy required.

"To get it exactly right," Blethworthy agreed instantly. "You see, that's not so hard, is it? Not so hard to work at it a bit more. The salary, I dare remind you, is not 'by the job' as it is 'by the time spent,' you know... And that," after a brief respite, Blethworthy's hands had found his and were once more caressing them, "that couldn't possibly be construed, even by the most pessimistic, as a discouragement, now, could it?"

"No. No, of course not," he had to admit. That he needed the money badly was certain. That double the amount he'd signed on for would be late Brahms to his mother's ears back in the States, he knew for certain, almost managing to pay his brother's extensive medical bills for the period. "Except," he was forced to say, "well, except... there is one matter that is discouraging. Quite awfully so."

"My poor young sir," the blond-haired hands now all but did a dance atop his own, "what ever could that be?"

He winced having to say it, knowing it was far from the first time he had said it, right here, and into that blandly handsome face, "The accommodations! I'm afraid they remain unaltered from the first day I arrived here and..."

The big hands released their captives, the big body retreated, the handsome face closed against him, turning inward.

"Ah, but you already have heard how utterly out of my hands that situation is?" Blethworthy mewled.

"I have indeed. But it doesn't in the least solve the problem."

"The problem being a small space." Blethworthy had listened—at least once.

"A monk's cell is larger," he confirmed. "And considerably warmer."

"But this isn't 'the States,' you must know, with its endless prairies and deserts of space, nor its unstinting central heating!" Blethworthy repeated words he'd uttered at least twice before.

"The hotel has central heating," he argued. "The corridors are hellishly warm, day and night. It's my room alone that remains icily cold no matter the weather or the central heating." And before he could be stopped, "And even that monstrousness I can put up with. I have put up with, all these weeks. But the bathroom…the bathroom is… impossibly icy. And the shower. Well, it's simply unusable. There's some kind of film, not quite mold, not quite fungus, but—and it can't be scrubbed off. I've tried. Bought a local scouring product and scrubbed and scrubbed. To no avail. Once only have I showered in it, and the water began warm enough only to become quickly arctic. While the shower tiles were all but alive with some growth, who knows what exactly…! Never again. I swear it."

By now Blethworthy was staring closely at him.

"I'm not an expert, but," sniffing, "you aren't of particularly high odor, you know."

"Probably because I've been using other people's showers. Well, one other person. A young woman down the hall. It's not what you think!" he quickly corrected, as the blond-furred hands had crept forward onto the desk again, approaching his own. "We meet over breakfast downstairs most mornings. I was upset and I confessed my problem and she's never actually in the rooms when I use the shower, naturally, and I clean it down properly, afterward."

"And so you see, you've solved the prob—"

"Except that solution won't do any longer," he quickly interrupted. "As the young lady's been forced by circumstances I don't…well, anyway, she's been forced to leave the hotel. And no," he headed the dean off at the other path, "I've not yet met anyone else with whom I can share my problem or whom I've come to know well enough to possibly even ask—"

"Nonsense!" Blethworthy's hands now did sidle over and take his own in a loose, warm grasp, and for a second, he wondered if there was a shower bath here, behind the big office, one he could come use whenever he wanted. Until Blethworthy said, "I've just the place for you. It's mid-distance between here and your domicile. Always spick-and-span clean. Large, empty at certain hours, and with scads of blistering hot water and soap."

He waited for the other shoe to drop.

"My club! Or rather," Blethworthy corrected, "my former team's clubhouse." He suddenly stood and was at a cabinet tray, turned, and cast some keys upon a heavy metal ring onto the desktop midway between the unsatisfactory report and his lap.

He could make out two door keys and a thinner locker key attached to a metal tag carved to represent a soccer ball.

"In truth, I still belong." Belthworthy swaggered a bit. "They hung up jersey number fourteen for good, you understand. So I'll simply ring the grounds manager and tell them to expect you in my place. It's only busy around practice time and game time, of course. So most late mornings no one uses the place at all. You can stop, take as long as you wish in the large shower bath, and arrive here sparkling clean and lovely, as you always are."

He picked up the keys and admitted that they in fact did solve the problem, or at least the shower problem, if nothing else. So he said, yes, okay, he'd stay, he'd do more work, he'd reevaluate the manuscript yet again, and at greater length and depth, yes, he could even bear the cold little monk's cell for that longer period of time.

"That's a big fellow." Blethworthy raced to where he'd just stood up and grasped him in what he could clearly now feel was a former winning amateur athlete's grip around the middle, all but lifting him off the ground, and planting an official kiss on his cheek. "You're so needed! I just knew I could count on you doing the right thing!"

Cregnell listened to him relating the gist if not the details of that meeting, strangely unmoved by it all, a few hours later. His interlocutor had one ear tilted away, as usual, aimed toward the corner aluminum food service bins where other scholastics tended to gather and murmur news and gossip that he couldn't make out but that he was sure Cregnell could pick up, given his extra-sensitive hearing.

"It's transparently clear, then!" Cregnell placed a slice of pineapple from the salad bar at the widest possible angle to his lips. "The Great

Bleth intends for you to approve of the replacement text and discard the one in use."

"No, he doesn't."

"Of course he does! That's what he's telling you by making you redo it and paying you handsomely for your effort."

"But why would he want to do that? It's no better than the text already in use."

"No matter. He personally knows two of the four authors of the new volume. By getting their text approved, he washes their hands. Next time they find some way or someone to help wash his."

It was such a cynical statement that he simply sat there, unbelieving.

Cregnell jumped into the silence. "He's clearly got you seduced with his big blond head and footballer's body!"

"Men do not interest me in that manner," he said quietly, so as to not seem to protest too much. He strongly suspected they interested Cregnell in that, and in other manners too.

"Not to mention those big blond-haired hands. I believe he puts some kind of elixir on them to encourage that specific hair to grow. Possibly, he even tints it to blond it up more than would be natural." Cregnell seemed blasé enough about his outrageous statement.

"He's done nothing in the least to lead me to conclude that he wishes to seduce me."

"You certainly resemble enough that Irish tosh he went gaga over." Cregnell snapped up his pear triangles like a happy alligator. "The one who was here last season. What was his name? Agathorn?"

"That's a character from Tolkien. A deposed prince. I'm almost sure of it."

"A. G. A. Thorn. The Cowley specialist. The Great Bleth seduced the bejesus out of him."

"Excuse me if I don't fully credit your account of Dr. Blethworthy seducing younger men he works with. Has he ever made anything even resembling a pass at yourself?"

"He doesn't have to. He knows I'd fall to my knees at his feet, eyes closed, mouth a…"

"It's your fantasy entirely, then. It…is…not…reality."

"That's what Agathorn said to me at this very table. And look at him now!"

"How can I? He's not here at college."

"What did I tell you? Seduced and abandoned!" Cregnell assured him, holding up an index finger as though pointing out the moral.

"Isn't that Jocelyn Cardew?" he observed of one of the younger women who'd just entered the dining hall. He found her pretty and nice, and, hoping to end this profitless conversation, he zealously waved her over.

"It's not going to help," Cregnell said. "Being all la-di-da and making up to the girls like you do."

"I happen to like girls. I like them a great deal."

"Excessively, perhaps?" Cregnell suggested, blotting his lips with a napkin as though he'd just applied lip gloss.

"Not excessively!...Suf-fic-iently."

"Well, that's too bad, then, for them. And for you too. As," and here he whispered furiously, "Bleth's got you by the short hairs already."

"Miss Cardew!" He greeted her. "And is that Mamselle LaFoyant? Please join us! Won't you?"

❖

He'd been alone so completely in the weeks that had passed while here in the huge pale green tiled shower or steam room that he had to shake his ears free of possibly interfering water to realize he was actually hearing voices. Meaning someone else was here at the club besides himself. Just beyond the showers, undressing, he postulated, at the triple row of stand-up lockers. Not quite conversing, he thought, over the loud whoosh of his heavenly warm shower, so much as playing around, as young lads tended to do. So he ignored them. Especially when their voices took them around the tiled wall to another queue of showers which were suddenly turned on deafeningly, almost but again not totally drowning out their voices.

If the showers were heavenly hot, his hotel room, despite the change of seasons, remained glacial. No wonder he all but leapt to come here daily, sometimes twice daily, to warm up, to and from his study cubicle at the university.

Blethworthy had only stopped him once in the weeks since their talk, during a chance encounter at a local pub frequented by the staff, to confirm that "matters were working out as promised." They were so much so working out here at the club that he couldn't bring himself to remind his superior that his room still needed looking into.

Certainly his mother appreciated the protracted checks arriving back in Indiana. She'd even gotten Robert to shakily endorse a tasteful thank you card, doubtless one she'd herself picked out, as his brother, though nearly thirty now, tended to favor artwork emblematic with cuddly bears and large-eared elves.

Therefore he would make do, as he said he would. Eke out things, really, he reminded himself, since sending home such a large ratio of earnings allowed little for forays into public houses here, even for an occasional half pint, never mind restaurants or "cinema dates" with any of the younger women, including La Cardew and Mlle. LaFoyant, whom he now daily stopped and chatted up.

Still, matters could have been worse; coming to the club, he could use the toilets at leisure, avoiding his room's polar, daily cleaned yet somehow everlastingly loathsome lav—except for lightning-fast whizzes.

Right now spotless, warmed to the core once again, relaxed, he shut off his showerhead and grabbed for a bulkily soft club towel to wrap around his middle. Steam saturated the large chamber, and he exited onto the floor into yet more billows of it, groping his way back to the borrowed locker, until the mist seemed to abruptly clear, enough for him to stop and look and see…

Not five feet away in the other large shower, in which oddly there was almost no steam at all, but instead, quite clearly, two young men he'd never seen before, who had to be athletes given their musculature, rocking together front to back, wrestling perhaps, making peculiar grunts like horses or… He realized precisely what they were actually engaged in the very second that the larger and redder-haired fellow, who was clutched behind the other, turned, and without for an instant losing his stroke, noticed him watching; noticed and scowled.

Shamed to the roots of his hair as though it were he, not they, who'd been witnessed in full *flagrante*, he fled that face and those rocking bodies, fled to his locker, where he changed into his street clothes as quickly as humanly possible, flinging on clothing and footwear any old way, as though it burned his skin, not bothering to properly dry his hair, driving the metal door shut just as he heard their commingled voices rise to a unanimous, not quite human pitch, indicative of shared passion. He thrust the sopping towels onto the floor and raced out of the bottom-level rooms up and out into the clean seamlessness of a chill late morning.

He didn't stop rushing until he felt the hot burn of a stitch in his side. Then he stopped, gasped in pain, watched by strangers, gesturing them off—he was okay, okay.

Later that day, he almost related to his lunch companion, Cregnell again, what he'd witnessed in the club's changing room, then decided he'd actually derive greater amusement withholding it, since that was exactly the sort of drivel Cregnell craved to hear. Making that decision he ate on, feeling a certain superiority.

That sensation, alas, didn't last. Returning to his chamber that night, while standing on a street corner, he couldn't help but notice the entire side of a passing omnibus, as it waited for a traffic light, was plastered across its lower half with an advert for the local football team. And there, pictured flying into the bright yellow air behind a head-struck soccer ball, was the very fellow he'd seen cohabiting in the shower. "The Derrick's Going to Do You Right!" the ad read.

"Isn't that Derek Stransom the dreamiest ever," he heard behind him and turned to see two pretty coeds ogling the poster. Turning back to the bus, he was startled to think he saw Stransom's eyes following him as the vehicle took off.

In the days that ensued, he encountered The Derrick more often than he could ever desire. He'd been told that no one from the club used the showers during the morning, yet there were young men there all the time now, four mornings in a row. Unable to tell in all the steam who was who, and wanting to avoid the particular pair he'd stumbled upon, he withdrew from the field altogether. Until those around him made it clear that he needed to clean himself.

He decided to try going during lunch break, even though it meant a bit of a run to and fro. The club was blissfully unoccupied, and he indulged himself in both a shower and steaming. Only when he was all dressed again, exiting the still-fogged-up room, headed up the ramp, did three players descend toward him. Though he slid obliquely to one wall to let them pass, one was Derek Stransom, who recognized him, who threw out a long arm to grip his shoulder hard briefly, intoning darkly, "Got my eyes on you!" Making the other players turn toward him with scowls as he cowered against the wall. They moved on as one, and down at the locker room, he heard Derek say something he couldn't quite make out and heard them all laugh.

Derek was there again next lunchtime, alone this time, a towel wrapped low about his hips as he daintily shaved tiny areas on his face in the floor-to-ceiling mirror.

Before he could turn away, he'd been spotted.

"Don't go yet!" Stransom said in an almost inviting tone of voice. Without turning away from his perusal of his face, he added, "We've got a little talk, you and me."

"Who, me?" he asked.

"That's right. Club member, are you?"

"No. I'm using Professor Blethworthy's membership."

"That's all right, then." Stransom seemed conciliated.

He sidled over to the locker, opened it, and began to cautiously undress, ready to make a dash at any suggestion of trouble. He'd gotten down to his tunic when the player was suddenly before him, towel off his midriff and up around his shoulders. Derek stood erect, large, and it was bobbing up and down all on its own.

He fell back, consternated, against the locker, wishing he could to fit into it entirely.

"Now, I know we're not going to ever say a word of what we oversaw."

The thing bobbed and grew as it bobbed. He couldn't stop looking at it, but dragged his eyes up to the menacing face, the huge arms and shoulders capable of so much harm.

"I don't actually know what you're talking about." He managed to stutter out what he hoped would be appeasing words.

"You're a damned liar. But that's all right. I just wanted to show you what you've got to look forward to," it bobbed and grew, bobbed and grew, "in case you change your mind. From me and from a half dozen of my closest mates. And that will just be the beginning, understand," he added, making a fist the size of his head by way of illustration.

He was able at last to look away, murmuring in the smallest voice, "Never. Not a word. Ever."

"That's the boy!" The rock fist dropped onto his shoulder in an abrupt, sinew-burning grip.

When at last the hand was gone and Stransom was walking away, his perfectly square buttocks pistoning up and down like a machine of annealed flesh, he mewled, "I needn't come here anymore! If that's what you wish. Not ever?"

Stransom either didn't hear or didn't wish, as the athlete vanished silently into the steam billows of the shower.

He quickly dressed again and dashed out. Periodically during the day at school he would find himself shaking all over. When Cregnell came upon him having a late cup of tea, he wondered how archly the Assistant Prof. would react to the threat of being beaten and gang-raped by a rugger team, but thought it prudent not to reveal an iota of his distress.

He did return to the club, slowly, every three days, each at differing times, so as to avoid detection, and each time found himself blissfully alone; except one time when there was a boys' team at the club, none over the age of ten.

So it was that slowly, he began to be less afraid of the rugby champion and his threat.

❖

Pauline LaFoyant had said yes. Or as much as had said yes, which was good enough for him. This evening in the garden at the Applewhite Arms American Studies department party they'd found themselves alone, wandering. She'd come closer, they'd kissed, he'd been enveloped in a lacework frisson and their kisses had deepened and continued. He'd "taken liberties" with her soft upper body until the two of them had nearly coalesced into one, with her at last pulling away for breath, which he had to admit, he was in need of too. With none of their compeers anywhere near, they'd once more coalesced for an even longer time, and when they'd been forced to break away by the arrival of others in the lantern-dimmed garden, he whispered, "I must see you again…alone." And she, thoughtfully, had responded, "Jocelyn won't be home tonight. You know where we live?"

Did he ever. But they mustn't be seen going there together, of course, she said. And Jocelyn might still be home a few minutes before she left, so he'd need to stand out on the street where Pauline would signal him with a window shade, and of course, he needed to make certain to bring with him "protection," didn't he? All tiny little travails, silly small obstacles, easily leapt over.

Which was why, however, he found himself racing up the entrance to his hotel at eleven thirty of a Saturday night, then stopping dead at the sheer population, noise, and depth of some kind of party being thrown at the hotel bar, a completely unprecedented thing, which seemed to even include the mumbling old Asiatic, on his stiff chair just inside the bar, who was decorated with the green and silver colors of whatever team or group it was celebrating.

He'd been threading with difficulty through the crowd, being forced to say hello, to "make nice" to this one and that, including the three grotesques who always sat at their table—now newly festooned in some team's colors—when he realized with a bump why he knew those colors so well. They were from Blethworthy's football club. A closer glimpse at the festivity-makers made it clear that one or more of them were team members.

"...off to Madrid! I tell you! A first for our boys! Then on to take those Juventus wogs and the World Cup itself!" Someone instructed him so he understood that the team he showered with had risen to the very top of their nationals and was headed out. Good for them, he felt, with a bit of shared pride, and even downed the dregs of a half pint an overcosmetized brunette offered him to toast them.

But he had other matters to attend to now. Pauline LaFoyant, to be precise. He was trying to remember where he'd hidden the condoms he'd packed so many months ago. He'd have to crack at least one out of its packet to see they were still lubricated. Maybe even give himself a fast sponge bath, highlighting areas soon to be exposed.

At last he got through the crush and onto the back stairway. More partygoers loitering there and on the first landing, he had to sidle around several, until he could get free to the next floor.

Just as he did, a hand shot out and grabbed his foot from below. "Hey there!" He turned to a young face he didn't recall. "Aren't you him? That toff of Derek's?"

"Who? What?" Fear shot up the back of his head, as he pretended not to understand. Then he faked cheer. "Congratulations, fellows. You're the best! Knew you could take the nationals." He managed to shake off the hand by reaching down to shake it. "Sorry to leave. Nature calls."

He sprinted up the stairs, thinking is he following, is he following me? Stopping, to try to hear, above the renewed noise from downstairs as the door opened into the bar whether he could hear anyone following. Yes. No. Who knew? And now nature did call.

No revelers this high up or this far away from the bar. No one in the hallways. So he dashed to his door and struggled with the key. Inside, it was, as always, Baffin Island, and he threw off his jacket and kicked off his shoes on the icy floor and rushed into the lav with its Moons of Uranus frigidity, where he relieved himself and began to run what he hoped, dreamed, would be the merest speck of non-frozen water to bathe his face and genitals in—who knew what she'd think to touch, being French—and heavens be, he managed it, got water to come out of the H which if not really hot then at least was more than tepidly warm.

Of course it all got very damp and cold immediately after, given the milieu. Him more or less clean, he felt dankish. Must change his undershorts.

He was back in his room in the midst of that, humming to himself, when there was a rapping at the door.

No one had ever once in the months he'd been here rapped on the door. He looked through the peephole provided, but it was almost frosted over with age and wear: All he could make out was a rather distorted face. The rapping resumed with more force.

"I know you're in there." The sound came through clearly. And the voice now seemed familiar. He peered again through the frosted porthole, trying to see if was at all possible if—

"We know where you live now," the voice repeated, and even though it was somewhat slurred, he knew now it was indeed, and the porthole confirmed it distortedly, Derek Stransom.

"We know you're in there. Robbie saw you go in just now. Didn't you, Rob?"

Words of assent followed, joined by the sound of yet another, then another person. There were at least four of them. Maybe five.

"What do you want?" he began to ask. Just then a body slammed against the door. "What is it you want?" he repeated in a more strained voice. Another body slammed against the door, which took it poorly.

"What do we want?" was yelled into the crack between the door and the molding. "Don't you read the adverts all over town, you bad little toff? What do they read, boys?" There was an inarticulate shouting.

Then "That's right! The Derrick's Going to Do You Right!—And his boyboys too!" This was illustrated with another slam against the door, then another.

Fear filled his head. He leapt to the bed to the window. It opened, barely enough for him to squeeze his body through. But there was no landing, not even a shelf for a foot. At least not for another forty feet down. And what he'd land on would be the concrete lip of a side roof of the car park. No.

Two more slams against the door shook the timbers of the room. He could see the door frame splitting. If there were five of them out there, drunk and enraged, they'd have the door down in a few minutes. Gathering up all of his strength, he managed to pry the bed away from the side wall and semi-wedge it against the door, which was now being slammed into so regularly and with such shouting and cheers from the other side that it would clearly go in a minute. He threw suitcases upon the bed against the door, just as a section of door frame ripped loose on one side and a shoulder smashed through the wood of the door.

"The Derrick's Going to Do You Right Good!" two of them shouted, and arms reached in, tossing the suitcases aside, ripping down the door to unwedge the bed.

He retreated into the frozen bathroom. Locked the door, had the sense to wedge one last piece of luggage under the door handle. But they'd gotten into the room now and were shouting, headed here, and this flimsy door was already under barrage.

There was no explanation for why he suddenly turned and opened the shower bath door, a door he'd not opened in months. In his mind the place had been so disgusting that he couldn't even think of it. There was no real reason why he opened it, except that in his extreme panic, it beckoned him, glowing cleanly, healthily, pink and wholesome for the very first time.

He peeked in, curious, as the assault continued on the bathroom door, which couldn't last even as long as the room door. They still chanted with glee: "The Derrick's Going to Do You Right Good! And We Are Too!" and he looked at himself in the shower glass's sea wave reflection, thin, wearing only one little under-brief, utterly set for the taking. As the party raged on, as the revels in the street outside continued for Their Boys, he would be assaulted, raped again and again, harder and harder, beaten and pummeled all the while, with no one to hear his screams, until there would be no life left in him. He didn't understand how this had come to this, only that it had. He had no choice.

He stepped into the shower bath and it wasn't gross and splotchy, loathsome and awful. Instead, it was rather sparkling. To block out the noise and chanting, the fearful sounds he could no longer hear, he reached up and turned on the faucet's H. And it came out warm. Not tepid. But warm. He held himself against one side of the shower, waiting for it to turn cold. But it didn't. It got warmer, and a steam even developed around his feet. That was when he thought, well, might as well, and removed his undershorts and stepped under the showerhead.

It was warm. Luxuriously warm. And the soap was soft, so he tossed his underwear out the shower door, and settled into the shower box, indulging himself in the first warm shower he'd ever had in the wretched little frozen rooms.

They must have crashed through the bathroom door just in the nick to have his shorts flung at them. Because they came at the shower stall enraged.

And the most curious thing happened. The shower seemed to simply seal up. It was like fresh warm putty rushing out of the walls and sealing off the door, from the sides, then top, then bottom of the door, as they pounded on it. It began doing cross stripes of sealer all across the door, on the frosted glass ceiling, each stall side, as their shadows dimmed the outside light, and he no longer felt in any away afraid that they would get in, but instead, safe, utterly safe. After a while they seemed to give up, to go away, and he showered until he was happy, and warm, if utterly exhausted, so he sank down slowly into the caressing waters of the shower bath, which received him tenderly and rocked him like a blanket-lined bassinet into the supplest, gentlest slumber he'd ever imagined. All safe now. Free from harm.

Detective Sergeant Gryce hated this sort of thing. Hated the poorly or badly explained crime. The criminal not there. The victim plain as day and wrong, off, daft in some way as this one was, fetal, smiling, holding the curled-up face cloth to his face like a baby with a blankie, drowned in his own shower bath in mere inches of water, and who was to say how or why it even had collected there when it should have flowed out, while the football party went mad outside and downstairs, and room doors were torn off and luggage strewn about by perpetrators unknown. It wouldn't do. Looked bad in reports, Looked worse in his mind and memory. Hated it. Simply hated it.

"That police tape is up there for a reason!" he lectured the kohl-eyed Wog Ponce behind the desk. "You understand. Once we're done here, all that shower must be torn out and replaced. It won't do to have shower baths that can't drain properly. And when repaired it shall be inspected."

The dark-skinned Nancy pouted his understanding.

Detective Sergeant Gryce looked about one last time at this dump of hotel and just then noticed the wizened old brown creature on his chair, vibrating like a mechanical top, trying to get his attention.

"Yes, old-timer!" Going up to him. "What is it you want to tell the police?"

He got nearer and heard the thin old voice pronounce, "There's something not quite right."

"Something not quite right?" Detective Sergeant Gryce asked. "Something not quite right about what?"

"Something not quite right about Room Nine," the voice barely whispered.

Detective Sergeant Gryce stood up. "Thanks, old fellow. I'll heed that advice. Jermell! Douad! Take over! I'm done with this scene!"

One Way Out

Bay threw down the apple core and stomped it into the soft loam until only a little mound of dirt was left. The bells from a distant steeple—the highest point of a tiny village nestled in the New England hills—were just striking twelve. It was Sunday. That would mean even less traffic than usual, less chance of truckers and easy pick-ups, especially as this wasn't a highway, only a double-lane country road.

He tightened the straps of the knapsack over his shoulders and loped off the ridge back down onto the road. He tried to adjust his mind and body for a long afternoon walk, trying to stay off the frayed edge of the macadam and on the dirt as much as possible, to make the trek easier on his feet.

After ten minutes or so, he still hadn't seen a car. Everyone must be at home, having dinner. The dark gray of the road shot away from under his feet down a long incline, rising up to another ridge half a mile away where it hid from sight, then rose straight up to another ridge, rising and dipping, again and again, into the spine of hills—like a ribbon grabbed by the wind.

Bay was just bracing his legs for the long incline when a rush of air and force slashed past him. Swop, swop, it went, knocking him to the ground amid a flurry of dust and small pebbles.

Whatever it was, it had been too fast for him to catch sight of it going by. He picked himself up, brushed off his denims, looked back in the direction he had come from, muttered a few curses, then started off again. Then he noticed something.

Ahead, like mechanical insects rapidly climbing down the side of a wall, two small, very fast vehicles were moving toward him along the ribbon of road. They fell out of sight behind a lower ridge for a second, and as they did, two identical vehicles appeared at the top of the road beginning the drop down toward him.

They were coming so fast that as he refocused from one pair to another, they seemed to change places. Then he saw the effect was being caused by a third pair of identical vehicles, which had now appeared at the very topmost point of the road he could make out.

They flashed so brightly in the noontime sun that Bay could scarcely see them coming at him. He could make out that they were low, squarish, and painted a metallic green. But what was so odd after seeing no cars at all was that these seemed so regular, systematic—each one side by side, covering both lanes of the road, the second and third pairs exactly as far away from each other, exactly as distant from the first pair, as though they were in formation. Bay was reminded of a slot-car set he'd once owned and played with as a kid.

Then a pair of vehicles was upon him. Then passing him. As they went, they made the same sound: swop, swop.

That left no doubt. An earlier pair must have knocked him down. This time he was braced. Even so, he could barely stay on his feet in the dust and blast of their passing.

He followed their squat, retreating figures down the road, only a double blur by now, in all the dust they lifted, following them like little cyclones. How fast were they going? Over 100, maybe 150 miles per hour? Maybe more?

He couldn't help feeling there was something more than a little odd about the vehicles. He braced himself on overhanging shelf of rock and shaded his eyes, trying to catch a better look at the next pair as they passed. When they did, he was even more unnerved by what he could discern.

They were indeed unlike any other vehicles he had ever seen: low, flat boxes, angled toward some indefinable apex three-quarters along their length. No lights he could make out, front or back. No chrome or any other kind of decoration. And no glass—and therefore no way for him to see inside them—if, that is, they even had an inside. He had thought at first they were painted a metallic green, and in truth, seeing them closer, that was still the closest he could come in describing their color and material to himself. But it wasn't metal, not really. And it wasn't green either. At least not any green he'd ever seen. More shimmering, like the bodies of some of those Japanese beetles that liked to chew on rosebuds. The material was an unknown substance, refracting light in a way he'd never seen any material do, with a color that seemed to both shimmer and absorb light. Worse, as the vehicles had lifted slightly going over the ridge of road, they had lifted slightly off the road—going 150, 180 miles per hour, any vehicle would do so—and they had no wheels!

Bay was thinking whether he had noticed any military base in the area on the filling station map he carried with him. No. None. Could this instead be a testing ground for an automobile company? These could be experimental cars? No?

The last pair finally shot past him, interrupting his thoughts, and making that dull swop, swop sound again. He turned to see if any more were coming. No, none. Then he turned to watch the last pair speed off in the direction of their predecessors, and he was amazed to see that they were instead slowing down, and then almost stopping, before swerving off the road and onto a pasture very close to the same ridge where he'd spent the night.

All the curiosity and vague discomfort he'd felt came to a head. He had to see what these vehicles were. He turned around and ran back toward the stopped vehicles.

It was only a few minutes back to the crags that he had left shortly before overhanging the open meadows. But in the short while, the occupants of the vehicle had gotten out and transformed the area.

What had been a dry grass pasture now seemed to be a cleared area of some hundred feet in radius, roughly circular. Dark-clothed, helmeted figures moved about stiffly, if quickly, carrying strange objects. Two figures bent into the now-opened backs or fronts (he wasn't certain) of the vehicles parked at the circle's edge.

Two other figures were setting up a hollow-looking platform exactly in the center of the circle. From a long-snouted tool one of them wielded, a pressurized liquid shot out onto the ground and hardened into a concrete-like substance the instant it touched the dirt and grass.

As they worked, the first pair of figures edged a canister-like object out of one vehicle and onto the ground. Although Bay was concentrating on the object and the figures, he could see inside the vehicles now, and they were artificially lighted, half-pink, half-yellow, blinking on and off.

The canister must have been extremely heavy or very fragile, as the figures carrying it moved very slowly, in exaggeratedly mechanical, yet dainty steps. At length, they got the canister into the center of the cleared circle and sank it slowly into the cement material. Another shower from the spray tool covered the canister completely so it was no longer visible.

The four figures then retreated to beyond the edge of the circle and one of them pulled a little hand-sized cartridge out of a deep pocket in his form-fitting suit. He adjusted one or two buttons on the little panel, and the trod-down grass began springing up again in the clearing, so quickly and so completely that even from his bird's-eye perch Bay could scarcely make out the exact location of the platform and sunken canister.

The entire operation had taken perhaps eight minutes. All of it had been completely hidden from any possible view by the ridge of rock from the top of which Bay watched them. Even had there been a traffic jam on the road to see it, no one would have. And where the canister had been sunk, it now looked like nothing at all happened.

That was when Bay began to feel a tingling along the back of his neck. He'd had that feeling once or twice before in his life. Once when he was being followed down the dark, deserted street of a Midwestern city by a stranger who kept falling out of view whenever Bay turned to check up on him; another time when he had heard prowling, heavy steps outside a tent he had pitched in the Green River Mountains of Utah. Both times before it had meant danger, and now he knew it meant that whatever was in that canister was about to go off, and go off big. Without stopping to ask why or how, Bay knew something momentous had been sunk in that meadow. He had to get away fast! Now!

He almost stumbled running down the ridge onto the roadway when he remembered he had taken off his backpack and left it on the rock. Leave it! he thought. Go! he thought. Then: No! I have to have it! I have to get away fast! In a car! That thing's going to go off any minute now. I need a car to get away from it. The backpack will get me a ride.

He was tying on the pack when he reached the road again. No cars, and those two which had been here had vanished totally. He started to walk as fast as he could, following the direction he'd begun in before.

Why this way? This is where the vehicles had come from. They might have laid a whole chain of these things. They might be laying down more at this moment, behind him. He had to go north. North.

There had to be a northern crossover ahead. He must get to it. But first he needed a lift. Still no cars. Damn. He felt a little calmer now as he strode along the road, knowing he at least had a direction now, a way out. The thin hot trickle was still burning a network into the back of his neck and his shoulders, and he was beginning to feel a sharp little pain in his side from his exertion. He was sure the first was adrenaline rising, and the extrasensory fear of whatever was going to happen.

If it was, just supposing it was what he thought it was, what could its radius be? Two miles? Five? What had been the radius of the last test? Five miles, no? Or was that only the radius of total destruction? And if so, what was the radius of the firestorms? Another five or ten miles?

He turned to look behind him. No cars. As he turned back, one coming toward him passed by—but it sped on as it neared him and he scarcely had the chance to flag it down anyway, he was so intent on walking hard and getting away, straining to keep up a fast pace, yet stay in control, to keep himself from simply running ahead blindly, breaking away totally. No. He had to stay in control. To let go meant to invite the end. Survival lay only in holding on. Holding on.

And still the burning of his nerve ends. It seemed stronger the further he got away from the canister. Still no cars.

Then there was one coming up behind him. Dark and sleek. Bay almost fell as he stumbled to a stop and thrust his arm dangerously out over the edge of the road.

The driver saw him and made a great show of screeching to a halt, braking so fiercely that half the car was under Bay's outstretched hand when it came to a full stop. One of those little German coupes that looked like metal race cars he'd played with as a child.

He ducked down to open the passenger side door.

"Haven't asked you yet!" a voice said.

Bay removed his hand from the door handle. Oh, God, no! Not a joker! Not now!

"Sorry!" he said. "C'n I have a lift?"

"Sure." The passenger side lock snapped open.

Bay got in, closed the door, was encased in the pervasive odor of leather and new car. The man faced ahead. Nothing but profile. Why wasn't he starting the car?

"Where you headed?"

"North!" he said with a determination that surprised him.

"This way's west."

"There's a crossover a few miles up. I'll get off there," Bay said, thinking, Let's go!

"No need to. I'm going north there myself."

A joker. Great. Finally, he threw it into gear. Bay was still doing up his seat belt shoulder straps when the car took off.

At least the backpack was loose. He swung it onto the floor and sat back watching the rounded V-shaped hood lap up the dark macadam.

"Nice car," he said.

"It's all right."

Thank God he's not in the mood for company, Bay thought. Imagine having a conversation about the weather now. It might just slow him down. Drive faster!

"You seemed to be in a bit of hurry there," the driver said nonchalantly: "As though you were running from someone."

Did he know? Could he know? Could he be connected up with those pairs of vehicles? Could he be their scout? Or not, rather their cleanup man. Here to get rid of any possible witnesses?

Bay said nothing.

"Of course," the driver went on, "there seemed to be no one and nothing to run away from where I picked you up. Right? Just a coupla nothing farms in the distance." He laughed and Bay looked at him. His own age. Good-looking in a city-slick way, like his car. Heavy, straight, almost blue-black hair. Sultry eyelids over dark eyes. Tanned. Spoiled-looking. But otherwise all right. Like a hundred others.

"Nothing farms and a coupla cows, eh?" He laughed again.

Even if the driver didn't know about the canister, he still might be off. Christ! Just what I need now!

Before Bay knew it, they'd reached the crossing and the driver flicked the wheel left and spun across the other lane right onto the crossroad. "No!" Bay shouted. "That's wrong! We're going south." He almost jumped out of his seat.

"What?" the driver said, and cupped one hand to his ear, as if he were hard of hearing. Bay began frantically repeating and explaining that they were going the wrong way. But the car was already in the middle of a U-turn, then across the road again.

"You seem a mite nervous, friend," the driver said, with a little smile.

"Maybe."

"A smidgen stressed, I'd say."

"A smidgen."

"Doubtless on account of those nothing farms and coupla cows." He laughed.

Bay all but collapsed back into the bucket seat. But he felt little relief. This guy was a jerk and a joker, and who knew, maybe he was insane too. And the burning fear from the knowledge that Bay was still within range of the canister was getting worse now, pricking every nerve of his skin.

How the hell had he gotten into such a situation anyway?

How had he? He was trying to recall and coming up blank. Well, no, not entirely blank. He knew he was hitching east. He remembered that yesterday he'd caught a ride out of Albany and into Kingston, New York. There he recalled he'd eaten a hamburger and malt shake at a roadside Friendly's, had ridden with a car through the Berkshire Mountains, and had been dropped off in small town called South Egremont. He'd been picked up there by a truck driver, literate guy who talked about the fact that Herman Melville and Nathaniel Hawthorne and all kinds of nineteenth-century writers had lived in the area, if not regularly then part-time, during the summer. Bay had ridden along with the guy, who was looking for an ear to listen to his chatter, and he'd finally allowed himself to be dropped off not far from where he'd spent the night. And before yesterday? Well, that wasn't quite so clear to him. He'd traveled, he believed. Hitchhiked through mountains, plains, around cities, past deserts, all of it blurred and kind of vague now, unimportant, not all that detailed.

Bay was feeling certain that whatever was inside the canister would go off soon. Why and who had set it were no longer real questions. He knew that being there and witnessing it being sunk into the ground had somehow forged a link to it, a connection, and that might be why he carried the knowledge of it within him, as though both it and now he were a time bomb, literally running out of time.

"How far do you think we are?" Bay asked, trying to sound casual.

"From where?"

"I don't know, say from Boston? Or say how about from where you picked me up?"

"About hundred and fifty from Boston. Sixteen and a half from where I picked you up," he tapped a dial sunk into the leather plush of the dashboard, "according to Mr. Odometer here."

"Is that all?" Bay asked.

"What do you mean?" The driver sounded slightly offended. "That's pretty good."

"For going sixty-five miles per hour," Bay agreed. "I thought this car went a lot faster."

"I'm in no hurry," the driver said.

"Speedometer reads, what is it? One forty? Or are those just numbers painted on?"

"It'll do one forty. These roads are lousy. You want me to rip up the underside, just so you can have a joy-ride?" Already the speedometer had tilted up to 70 mph.

"Car like this was probably built to cruise at a hundred or more," Bay said, very wise-guy. Speedometer now read 75.

"I sometime cruise it around a hundred. On good roads." The speedometer was nearing 80 now.

"German, right?" Bay said. "Tested on the autobahn?"

"That's right." Closer to 85 now.

"Which has no top speed, am I correct?" Bay asked.

"It's a perfect road, that autobahn." He was close to 88 now.

"I was told that these high-performance vehicles, if you don't really open them up every once in a while, their oil lines clog up."

90 now. "Is that right?"

"That's what I heard," Bay said. The car was pushing 95 now and the car seemed to be slipping along the road. It was taking the dips so fast it was getting Bay a little queasy. The landscape began shooting by, trees going flick, flick, flick, so fast they began to bunch and blur as they reached 95. Alongside ran a stream that seemed to appear and vanish, reappear and snap and curl along past, like kids shaking a dark rope along the ground, playing snake.

Up to 100 miles per hour now.

Bay's nerves were on fire. He could hardly keep still in his seat for the twitching. Soon. Soon. Any minute now. He had to brace himself. prepare himself. Looking at the odometer he saw that they'd managed another ten miles, up to what, twenty-seven, maybe thirty by now, but would that be far enough? He'd have to get out of the car when it happened. Throw himself out clear. That would be suicide at this speed. Better get the guy to stop and find cover. Where? Cover where?

There! The stream, down in the water. The water would protect him, keep him from being badly burned. But how?

"Stop!" Bay shouted, and grabbed at the wheel. "Stop. I get off here."

"What the hell?" The car sped on as they wrestled for control.

"Stop! Stop! You've got to stop!"

"Get your hands off the wheel." He'd already slowed down to 70.

"Okay, but you've got to stop here. Now!"

"You're nuts. There's nothing here."

"Stop now! Here!" Bay tried opening the door.

"Sit down. You'll be killed!"

The car braked and swerved to a halt, twanging and spinning around two-thirds of a circle.

Before it was even fully stopped, Bay felt an agony all over his body. He threw his door open, flung himself out, and ran to the side of the road and thrust a hand into the water. Only a few feet deep, then brackish mud. But it would have to do.

Behind him he heard the driver muttering to close the damn car.

Bay grabbed up two hollow reeds and broke them off at both edges. He put one end into his mouth and breathed. Then he slid, back first, into the stream, face sideways, hearing the car rev up and take off as he got underwater and felt the sludge against the bare parts of his legs and neck, trying to stay calm as he immersed himself and slowly began to turn over sideways, to get his face as far away from the air as possible while keeping the air coming in.

The tubes worked; even bent like this, they let him breathe. He opened his eyes, but the stream was totally muddied now and he closed them instantly to not get any silt into his eyes. The agony was gone. He felt totally calm. Very calm. This was the right thing to do. Yes, exactly right. How did he think of it? Was it instinct? Some life-preserving instinct?

Abruptly, he twitched all over, as though he were having a brief epileptic spasm, from every nerve and muscle, from every cell of his body. Even facing mostly down, and with his eyes closed, his sight was flooded with a whiteness, a light that surpassed any white he'd ever known or thought to know, a white that explored depths and subtleties of sheer white light he'd never suspected even existed, a white that grabbed at every inch of him, illuminated his entire body from without. It seemed to grow in intensity, to throb, and as it did, the sludge around him seemed to grow tepid, then warm, then hot. And still the white blared on, even whiter if possible, brain-hurting white, a thousand brass instruments all playing white. He could feel the water and sludge receding from around his head and hands. Then the reeds in his mouth were hot, useless, since he couldn't breathe anymore, and he spat them out, dropped them and turned over, directly onto his face, finding an empty space there and filling his lungs from dark, quickly drying pockets of dank around him, while the universe continued to go white, white, white, seemingly forever.

A giant pulse slung along the land, seemingly lifting his body inches even within the mud. He held on for dear life. Then it was gone, after having flung itself right through his insides.

The white became yellow, then orange, then red, then dark red, then a deep, flickering magenta.

But the twitching was over, and the pain, and the fear. The hair on the back of his head no longer felt on fire. The sludge around his face had begun to boil and bubble, but now it subsided. When he was able to lift his head a few inches and use his hands to pry open his crusted-over eyes, he could see the stream bed around him was dried to aridity, desert dried, and like that dried and crusted all over his face and hands.

Cautiously he rolled over onto his back. Cautiously he tried to breathe. The air was oven-warm. Acrid, with the smell of burning. Breathable. He took a few more breaths. They hurt his nasal cavities and his throat. He swallowed once or twice and it was better. The air was cooling rapidly. That was better. He tried to sit up, had to use his hands to help himself. He flicked the crusted dirt off his hands and picked the dried crust off his face.

The sky around him was pink. Pink and purple and orange, but mostly pink, a deep roseate, Valentine's Day pink. Everything lining the stream bed was black. He knelt and then managed to stand. The land around him was totally blackened. Road and meadow all the same color, the only difference being that the road was partly melted, buckled in places. In the distance, across flat charred fields, he could see a grove of pine trees burning like a huge torch. The air was still warm. But the worst was over.

Shakily, he reached his feet, checking for breaks, fractures, bruises, and finding none, he stood up on his feet. His knees felt weak. Instantly, he began to retch, and then vomited chunks of his apple into the thick cracked bed of what had once been a stream. He immediately felt lighter and stronger, wiped his mouth, stood up straight. He lumbered out of the stream bed, afraid to touch anything, and stumbled forward along the half-melted, disfigured road.

Everywhere were fires. Showers of ashes descended all around him like rain. God knew from what. But he was all right. He had gotten through it.

He walked on, just looking. Then, around a bend in the road, through trunks of trees in flames, he made out the dull metal shine of a car. It was stopped dead in the middle of the road, as if its driver had just stopped a minute to take a leak on the side of the road and would be back any second.

As he got nearer, Bay saw there was no glass.

Even closer, most of the outside of the car—sheet metal, bumpers, fenders, roof—seemed intact, but as though heated and simultaneously pounded by a hundred thousand tiny hammers. Then he saw that it was the same car that had picked him up before, and he made out the back of the man's head, erect, sunk into the backrest.

And if weren't for the millions of gently trembling shards of glass splinters covering his head like a delicate lace helmet, and the red trickles that stained their edges, the driver would have looked as if he were alive—merely staring ahead, a little surprised.

Even the seats and floor and dashboard were rimed with glass shards. But the dashboard dials were still lighted, and the motor was still idling in neutral. The driver must have been suddenly blinded by the light, and by reflex stopped the car. Then the blast and the glass hit him, and who knew, but probably the fire too that had dappled the sheet metal, seared the leather inside the car, and his flesh and skin too, until they were all the same mottled half-brown, half-bright-pink color.

Bay opened the car driver's door, swept a drift of glass shards off the metal with his foot, then gently pulled at the corpse from behind, until the body fell over onto the road. The smell of burnt flesh was stronger. Sweetly awful like a charred loin of pork.

He cleared the front seat, reached the glove compartment where he found a piece of chamois to help him do the job better, and used that to wrap around the still hot, partly fused steering wheel. Would it work? It turned normally. There was still dangerous-looking glass left in the windshield and side vents. He knocked them out.

When he was done, Bay sat in the driver's seat wondering for a minute whether instinct would tell him what to do next. He gunned the engine. It worked. It whined, but it worked.

"I'll go north," he said, aloud. "North."

He moved the lever from park into drive and the car whined, then leapt forward.

❖

Two hours later he ran out of gas.

He'd been surprised, even a little alarmed that there were so few cars on the road. Where had everyone gone to? Were they all dead? In hiding? Where? The further away he drove, the less there seemed to be damage, even signs of what happened. But everything seemed abandoned. Everything meaning the few clapboard roadside diners and brick gas stations he'd passed. If he'd only thought to stop and get gas...

He left the car on the shoulder of the highway and began walking, again north—always north. Every once in a while, Bay would turn around and look behind, seeing the sky still pink, with clouds of ashes falling in the distance, and one area to the southeast—could it be Boston?—bright red and orange, as though the air itself were consumed by flames.

He reached a weathered wood-shake house off the side of the

road, behind a picket fence and gate. Several sedans and a pickup truck were parked on the grassy side road. There had to be someone inside. Maybe they had gasoline. Or would be able to drive him to the next gas station.

Aside from the blown-in windows all about, the house didn't seem at all damaged. The front door swung open. Bay called "hello," and when he received no response, he walked in.

It seemed deserted. The kitchen had been in use recently: Food was half-cooked in pots on the big double range—two cups of coffee were set out on an old table, untasted. Bay called out again. Still no answer. He half-absently picked up a coffee cup.

Would it be all right to drink it? Would it be radioactive?

He went to the sink instead, an old-fashioned metal pump and basin, and pumped himself out a glass of water. It was cool, slightly mineral, but good. He had another glassful.

Was that a sound behind that door? Voices? Or one voice maybe droning on?

"Hello," he called out to whoever would be on the other side of the door. "Anyone there? My car ran out of gas down the road!"

No answer. But the droning seemed to go on.

Bay went to the door and tried its handle. It opened. He carefully turned the knob and stepped aside, not knowing what to expect to come charging out at him.

A steep, well-lighted stairway, leading up.

As he ascended, the hard, cracked old voice he'd first heard became clearer. Bay thought he heard the words, "And behold! There came up out of the river seven well-favored kine," followed by a pause and what seemed to be the shuffling of several pairs of shoes upon bare wood.

At the top of the stairs, he found himself in a long corridor with closed doors, and on the floor itself, a worn, multicolored knitted oval rug, looking like a faded rainbow.

One door was ajar. Beyond it, the old voice took up again. Bay approached and slowly pushed open the door wide enough to look in.

His first impression was a room filled with people: men, women, children, old folks, all sitting or standing behind wooden dining room chairs or leaning against the side of the room where, because of the angle of the light all but blinding him, all Bay could make out was the shadowed figure of what was an elderly man.

Bay stepped into the room silently. The old man was still in obscurity, although now Bay could make out a dark leather-bound, frayed-edge book, open on a lectern in front of the man, and in full view.

"So Pharaoh slept and dreamed a second time," the old voice went on, toneless. Neither the reader nor anyone else in the room turned to look at Bay.

The old man paused again, and there was a murmur from the assembled group. One little boy, no longer able to hold back his curiosity, peeked back at Bay from behind the protection of a woman's shoulder. As Bay noticed him, the lad darted back into hiding, then timidly edged back into sight.

Half of the child's pale blond hair was gone. The remaining scalp, a purple splotch with large brown blisters and smaller broken-pus pink sores, looked as though he'd been raked from the crown of his head down over the single closed, congealed eye and red-black chin with an acetylene torch. It took Bay a great effort to look away from the boy and to fix his sight upon the worn natural grain of the wood floor.

"And behold! Seven ears of corn came upon one stalk," the old man read on, "fat and good."

Everyone murmured their approval. Bay looked at the boy again. But now he was hidden by the bulk of the woman, his mother perhaps, who turned out of profile toward Bay. She too was burned and mispigmented, as though a swath of intense fire had been whipped across her face and torso.

Bay backed up against the door he'd come in through, holding tightly to the dry wooden molding behind, spreading his feet apart for support as he surveyed the others in the room.

Everyone else he saw was blasted, burned, discolored, bleeding, or suppurating.

"And behold! Seven thin ears of corn, blasted by the east wind, sprung up after the others," the old man intoned, voice as dry as the planking Bay gripped so hard it was beginning to flake off under his fingernails.

A woman closest to Bay, her arms crossed over her cotton-print housedress, turned to him as though first noticing him. Purple splotches mantled all but a tiny central triangle of her face. Her lips were charred lines. Her teeth almost glowed green as she smiled. Only a few clumps of glossy auburn hair still flowed, held in place by a blackened hair-band.

Bay had to look down at the floor again, but he also couldn't stop himself from looking up again, now at one, then at another of the listeners, all of them quietly, attentively, listening to the man reading, monstrously ignoring what happened to them.

"And the seven thin ears of corn devoured the seven fat and full ones."

The people seemed animated by these words, moving about unsettled in their seats, gesturing, and in doing so revealing new facets of their horror. One scabrous-faced man with only a projected bone of nose left leaned over to whisper into the blasted shell of what should have been another's ear.

Bay shut his eyes, fighting down what was in front of him, declaring he wouldn't open his eyes.

He was out in the corridor now.

"And it came to pass in the morning," the old man went on, "that Pharaoh's spirit was greatly troubled by what he'd beheld in his sleep."

Bay shut the door, held it shut, knowing they could jump up from their chairs and smash it open on him. His skin felt as though every pore were bursting with poisonous filth and infection.

When nothing happened, and the voice went on droning behind the door, Bay fled, leaping down the stairs, stumbling over his own feet to get down, almost tearing the stairway's bottom door off its hinges as he careened out, fleeing the house onto the roadway, running.

When he stopped running, his body aching with the sudden exertion, he was far from the house. No one had followed him. Ahead, over rolling country, he couldn't see any other hamlet within sight. What was the difference if the people there would be as mutilated and as oddly unconcerned with their fate as this group?

Past a stand of trees on the road, he came upon a local bread delivery van parked. No driver, the key still in the ignition. Had this driver been struck by the blinding glare, burned to the bones of his skull, and staggered off, maimed, into the high grass, or worse, back into that house?

When Bay turned the van's key, the tank light on the dashboard showed half-full. Should he siphon it off? Or just take the van?

Before he could really make up his mind, his hands had done it for him. The ignition was switched on and he'd thrown the clutch. All around him, he smelled fresh bread. He reached for a loaf of pumpernickel, tore the plastic wrapper off and ate three pieces, gulping them down. He threw the van into gear and took off.

He hadn't realized how hungry he was. He ate the entire loaf of bread as he drove.

The van couldn't go anywhere near as fast as the sports coupe had gone, but it was taking him north all the same. He couldn't help but think that there were going to be more bombs, more trouble, and that he'd be safer the further north he got.

He'd reached the deep humps of the Green Mountains when he realized that the buzzing he'd been semi-hearing ever since he'd gotten into the van must be coming from the radio. The driver must have left it on when he'd stopped.

Bay tried tuning it. For a few minutes all he got was cracking and popping. Universal static. Then he managed to capture a voice, distant, faint, high-pitched.

"...to report to their local distribute...eleven oh seven two four... all battalions followed by codes J as in Jester, H as in Happy, R as in Rebel, S as in Standing..."

Then it was gone, no matter how much he turned the dial to tune it.

He continued to fumble at the radio, having to lean across the side of the high dashboard to do so. Finally, he reached another clear station,

"...ime Minister and the British Parliament declared full neutrality in the startling, total conflict between the government of the United Sta..." Then it too drifted. Bay kept on trying to tune it back in, and after some time received "... participating member of the Geneva Convention, the Commonwealth of Canada has opened all borders to evacuees from the States. Emergency centers, food depots, and shelter are being offered to all..." Then it was gone again.

So that was it, full nuclear attack on a massive scale. But Canada was neutral. There was food, shelter, safety there. He'd been right all along to head north. Bay pressed down the gas pedal as far as it would go, then tried to retune the radio.

After fifteen minutes of nothing but hisses and words isolated in radio-drift, Bay pressed one of the buttons on the front of the set that had the word "emergency" marked on it, thinking that's a weird thing to have, but then again maybe it would provide a direct line between the bread van driver and his home base. For a long while, nothing happened but more static. He turned it down a bit lower, but left the radio on at the emergency bandwidth, in case it might catch some signal. He drove on, thinking.

He'd been close, but lucky. Too close, and very lucky. If he'd still been in Albany, or already reached Boston...any city, really, it would have been all over for him. That was one certainty. And he had been lucky to be this close to Canada too. He could visualize hordes of evacuees from the cities trying to reach Canada over hundreds of miles of melted and disfigured thoroughfares. Horrible. It was a lot easier for him. Only another hour or two and he would cross the border. That was the value of hanging loose, traveling light, being on your own. Nothing, no one, to hold you back. Always in the right spot when you needed to be for survival. Survival.

He paused once on the top of a high ridge of mountains the road ascended to, and got out to look back, feeling like Lot in the Old Testament, seeing the destruction behind him. The skies south were still orange, fading to pink. The sun itself seemed to be contained, almost cradled, within a flaming new corona, one that rose from the earth. A flock of birds were rushing north over the mountains. They knew. They knew where it would be safe. He got back in the van and started off again.

There was more static on the radio station. He raised the volume and tried catching the station. That static was unnerving, almost dizzying. There were voices behind it, he was sure of that, although he couldn't make them out clearly or hear what they were saying. Two men talking. He turned the volume higher.

What was really odd was that it didn't sound like news, emergency news. But more like a private conversation he was overhearing. Had he somehow picked up two ham radio operators conversing? And if so, why were they so damned calm?

He now shut both van windows to cut off the wind current sound and turned the radio volume up higher.

"So far," he heard very clearly, "the case exactly parallels our projected graph of reaction." Then it was very clear. "Quite extraordinary. Almost classic." The voice was so calm it was annoying. Didn't they know what had happened?

"And you're quite certain," the second, somewhat less confident voice asked, "that the sudden communication will not be too much of a shock? I mean, given the intensity of the application?"

"That shock," the first voice responded, "is precisely what we want. You see, by cutting the possibilities down to only two—one a total nightmare—the patient will invariably opt for the other choice— reality, compromised though it may be. He should do so voluntarily. Even willingly. The knowledge that there is a choice, when there wasn't any chance of that moments before, should override any shock from the communication itself."

Static returned over the radio, and puzzled by what he was hearing and wanting to hear more, Bay fiddled with the dial. He got back onto the channel again, but now it was merely silent, no talking at all, so he left it there and continued to drive, divided now between the bizarre and bizarrely serene dialogue he'd somehow overhead, and what he could see out the windshield: the country completely destroyed, about to submit to an invasion by…by who?

"Bay! Can you hear me?"

He almost jumped out of the car seat. Then he realized that the voice came from the radio. It sounded like one of the two men who'd been talking. The man said:

"Bay! This is Dr. Joralemon. Can you hear me?"

What the hell was going on?

"Dr. Elbert is here with me too. You remember Dr. Elbert, don't you, Bay? If you can hear us and understand me, and if for some reason you can't answer, then shake your head from left to right. Do you understand? Left to right, slowly."

Bay did as he was told.

"Very good!" Enthusiasm and a little relief too in the voice. "Now, Bay, do you remember who I am? Dr. Joralemon. If you remember me, shake your head again."

The name wasn't familiar. The voice was. Or was it?

"Bay? Did you hear what I just said?"

This time Bay did nod from left to right, thinking, what the hell am I doing that for? Where are these voices coming from? The radio? He opened the window and flipped the back mirror all over the road behind to see if anyone was following him. No. No one there. Nothing but forest now, sparse, mountainous forest.

"Now, Bay, do you remember Dr. Elbert?"

"Bay?" The other voice came on. "This is Jim Elbert. I'm your doctor. Or at least I was. Do you hear me?"

Yes, yes, Jim, Bay thought. "Jim," Bay said. "How can I hear you through the radio? It doesn't look like a short-wave."

"Bay," Elbert's voice interrupted his own. "If you remember who I am, then shake your head as you did before. I see that you're trying to talk, but I can't hear you."

Bay nodded vigorously. What the hell was Elbert doing on the radio? Where was he? And how had he managed to locate Bay?

"Do you remember me, Bay?" It was the other voice. The one that called himself Dr. Joralemon. And now Bay did recall the voice. But not the way he recalled Elbert, which was pleasant, like a friend, like growing up and playing stickball and going around driving together as a teenager. That's how he remembered Jim Elbert. But not how he remembered Dr. Joralemon.

Dr. Joralemon repeated his question, and Bay heard rooms in his voice, rooms and doors. Far-away rooms in pastel colors. Venetian blinds half-closed all the time. The constant, insistent murmur of someone's muffled groans and sobs.

Bay nodded much more slowly in answer.

"Good," Joralemon said.

"Bay?" It was Jim Elbert again. "Now that we've made contact and communicated, you must understand that what I'm going to tell you is the truth. I've never lied to you before and I'm not lying now. Do you understand that? Do you believe me? Do you have any reason not to believe me?"

No, Bay thought, I don't have any reason to not believe you, Jim. He nodded, then reversed the motion of his nodding.

"All right, I'm taking that to mean we're okay," Elbert said. "Now, listen, some twelve hours ago, you underwent a brand-new approach that's been developed in cerebral surgery. It's only indicated in the most hopeful of…well, to be honest, of extreme cases. Dr. Joralemon invented the procedure. He calls it Trans-Morphing. It's a sort of active interference into the dreaming state. A kind of probe."

"So far," Joralemon interrupted, "We've had close to one hundred percent effectiveness with Trans-Morphing."

"What it does, Bay," Elbert went on, "I mean what it is actually is a combination of a psychotropic drug that operates within the cerebral cortex at a precisely specific given area, and with it a series of carefully calibrated electrical shocks to the brain. Its purpose is to channel your fears and anxieties into one major fear and anxiety. Sort of like dumping it all into one box. And that process builds up and builds up into an experience you fully believe you are having. Generally, and from what our previous cases have said, this is a tremendously catastrophic experience."

Bay heard the words and understood them well enough. He just didn't really understand what Elbert was getting at.

"What I'm saying," Elbert went on, "is that whatever you are doing and wherever you think you are, it's not so. You're actually in a semi-comatose state, close to a somewhat overstimulated R.E.M. sleep. You may think you're awake. But you're not."

Bay gripped the steering wheel. Sleeping? Who was he kidding?! The trees were whizzing by on either side of the van, clumps of Scotch and blue pine at a time. Still no vehicles behind him, but the air was scented with pine. Of course, he'd not seen a car or truck in a while. Still, he hit the dashboard hard, and it impacted his hand, making it throb. That was real enough.

"That's right, Bay," Jim Elbert continued. "Semi-comatose but sleeping. Dreaming. Everything that you believe has happened to you, and it must have been a humdinger, given how your EKG and EECs reacted, all that actually happened while you were asleep and dreaming."

"We realize that it's not an ordinary dream." Joralemon put his two cents in. "That's how this new drug works. It doesn't attempt to approximate reality with silly symbols and inane inaccuracies the way most dreams work. Its effect is to make it seem real, intensely, unbearably real."

"You must realize, Bay," Jim Elbert now said in the defensive tone of voice that Bay knew so well, "that this was a desperation measure, Bay. At first I was against using it. But your increasing catatonia, your growing lack of any affect at all…well, I let Dr. Joralemon persuade me to accept that it was the only route left for us."

"Do you understand us, Bay?" Joralemon asked.

Understand what, Bay thought, total folly? A stupid joke in bad taste?

"Bay?" Elbert was talking again. "Can you still hear us?"

He half nodded.

"I know this may be difficult to believe," Joralemon said, "because it was so concentrated in its effect, so every aspect of it, every detailed impression seemed completely real and accurate to life."

"In effect," Elbert said. "It was another, a parallel, reality."

"An alternate parallel reality," Joralemon corrected. "Do you understand?"

Bay didn't, no. Whoever these jokers were, they were clearly off their rockers. He looked up to see if there was a helicopter chasing him. Looked out the windows. No. Nothing there. But how did they stay in contact with him? How could they be tracking him? The radio alone wasn't the answer. By satellite? Maybe the combo. Maybe if he shut off the radio. Maybe that had a tracking device in it that allowed their satellite beam to locate him.

"Fine," Joralemon said, all hale and hearty. "We're guessing that it's a pretty horrible alternate reality you're experiencing there, Bay. But everything is going to be all right now. You don't have to fear, you don't have to run anymore. You've experienced a catastrophic alternate reality. You've faced up to the very worst that you believe you ever could have faced—and you've survived, haven't you? Yes, Bay, that was the most extreme, the furthest that you could possibly go in the direction that you've been headed in all these past months. But now you're going to come back and you're going to be all right."

"We're going to help you come back," Elbert put in.

"Right," Joralemon said, with that smug, arrogant edge back in his voice. "Because you see, Bay, you don't really have that much of a choice. Do you? If you don't come back with us, then you'll have to continue living in that nightmare reality you've constructed. True, you're over the worst, the climax has come and gone, but given that, what can you truly expect to follow: a catalogue of horrors one worse than another. That's the logical extrapolation of the monumental trauma you've just gone though."

"Now, Bay," Elbert put in, "to get you out of that alternate reality and back with us, all you really need do is break through the sleep paralysis the drug has induced. To do that, all you have to do is move your right hand. It's not going to be easy, but you've got to do it, Bay."

Bay drove lefty. His right hand lay idle by his side.

"Okay, Bay," Elbert was at his most professional now. "Move your right hand so it lifts up."

Who were these guys anyway? Bay wondered. And why were they trying to stop him from going north? Could they be the enemy? The same people who'd planted the bombs? Destroyed so much? Killed so many? Almost killed him?

Bay decided to string them along for a while. He had to be getting close to the Canadian border. He'd been driving so long. He moved his hand off the car seat.

"Great, Bay! Now move your hand over to where your heart is. Can you do that?'

I can, quite easily, Bay thought and did so.

"Terrific! Now you ought to be touching a pocket. Can you feel it there?"

Of course, there was a pocket in his flannel shirt. Big deal.

"There's something very important in that pocket, Bay. We'd like you to reach inside and take it out of the pocket. Can you do that?"

Bay reached into the pocket, felt around, and touched something small, smooth, and flat. He pulled it out. A Plasticine packet of something. How did that get there? What in hell was that stuff in the packet?

The road he was driving on suddenly began to angle downward, dipping now and again, but clearly descending out of the mountains he'd been driving through for so long. This might be the last stretch before he reached the border.

"Open up that packet, Bay!" Elbert commanded.

He did. Inside were two small pellets, shaped like pink barrels.

"Good," Elbert said. "We want you to take those pills."

"At first," Joralemon came on now, "after you've taken the pills, you'll appear to fall asleep. But that's only to you, where you are now. What will really happen is that you will wake up. Do you understand that, Bay?"

Sure, sure, Bay thought, and black is white. Whatever these pellets were, how had they gotten into his pocket? He hadn't put them there. Had somebody else? While he was sleeping last time, maybe? And if the pellets actually were exactly what this guy who sounded like his buddy Jim said they were, what would that really mean? That he was asleep in some hospital? Some asylum? Follow the logic, Bay. That's what he was telling you. In some nut house, probably strapped down. No sir.

"Can you understand, Bay?"

He nodded.

"Fine. So just pop those pills into your mouth. Both at once."

Bay rolled the pellets in his fingers.

"Is there some problem, Bay?" Joralemon asked.

"It's going to be all right, Bay," the guy who sounded like Jim Elbert said.

Bay kept rolling them in the fingers of one hand.

"Is it," the Jim-one asked, "that you aren't in a position to take them in your alternate reality?"

Bingo. He nodded.

"Let's see. You're walking or driving or something? Is that it?"

Double bingo.

"And you're afraid to take them and go to sleep while you're engaged in that particular activity?"

What do you think, mister?

"Because then you'll go sleep and fall or crash or something?"

They could be poison, right? Arsenic? Cyanide? Planted by those guys with the quiet cars without wheels, the faceless guys? While he slept?

"I'm assuring you, Bay," the Joralemon-one went on, sounding terrifically sincere, "that it's going to be fine. Pull to the side of the road, or go sit down if you need to. Then take the pills."

"I'm also assuring you, Bay," the Elbert-faker added. God, he was good. "In a day or two you'll be well enough to get up and walk around, maybe leave the facility a day later. You'll be proud of yourself. You won't be afraid anymore, Bay. Think of that. Not afraid of anything!"

Afraid? He wasn't afraid.

Afraid? And far-away rooms. Walls painted odd shades of green and blue and canary yellow. Walls converging, tilting at odd angles, then falling in on him. And no matter how much he screamed, no one ever came to help him. No one, except for sometimes a quick glance, lying words, another syringe-full. Murmurs of soft crying all about him, insistent, constant, interminable. Maybe even his own sobs and groans, heard as though rooms away, through locked doors and very far away.

"Now, Bay," Joralemon was being a Dutch uncle, "we've got great confidence in you. Great faith in you. That's why you were selected for the procedure over other possibilities, other patients who…"

"Is there a reason you can't take the pills?" Elbert's pretender asked.

Bay nodded. Of course there was a reason. He had to reach Canada. He'd be at the border any minute now. He'd just passed a small sign saying, "Customs and Immigration—Slow Down Now. Stop Ahead." Of course, there might be other cars and trucks there already, before him. He vaguely remembered several roads converging on this spot. So there would be others ahead of him, others closer to safety than he was. There might even be a longish wait. The road dropped more sharply now. He must be close.

"Whatever the reason is that you can't take the pills, whatever it is that you may be doing," one of the two was saying now, trying not to sound panicky, "you have to stop, Bay. Stop and take the pills! These pellets are the antidote to the pill he gave you. Do you understand?"

"Bay? No one wants to hurt you!"

Pastel rooms and medical smells. Shadows squatting and burbling. Grotesqueries in the guise of humans burbling and muttering and occasionally the ear-hurting screams cutting through it all. Shadows vomiting, screaming, colliding. And always, the distant sobbing and moaning.

"Please, Bay. I'm begging you now. Take the pills and wake up!"

"You have to take the pills, Bay!"

But Bay wasn't nodding or anything like it. Ahead, along the road, he could see the highway rise slightly, and two other roads converged, and their center was a kind of wooden log cabin, with windows and dormers, belonging to the Canadian Mounted Police.

"Bay! Bay! We're going to have to come in and get you if you don't take the pills."

"I don't know, Elbert. I've never injected the antidote before. We simply don't have any idea what that will do. Or where exactly it will leave him."

"You mean it won't bring him out of this?"

"I don't know. It's never been used. We've never had anyone opt for the alternate reality before."

"Inject it!"

"I'm going to need authorization for that."

"I'm giving you authorization. Inject it! Do it!"

No, you don't, Bay thought. As the van coasted down the road to the border crossing, he lifted his right foot off the gas pedal and kicked the radio as hard as he could, so hard, it crumpled in the middle, the voices jumbled then turned to static, then died completely.

There weren't any cars there. Just a Mountie waving at Bay, urging him on.

Bay waved back out the window, laughing out loud. In his hand were the pink pellets. He threw them out the car window, clear into the woods. Then he slowed down at the station, stopping inches from the big, healthy-looking Mountie.

"Welcome!" the Mountie said, smiling at Bay.

He would be safe in Canada.

THE PERFECT SETTING

After having lived more than half a century I am certain of the value of very little in this world. But of one thing I am quite certain: We cannot easily sustain the loss of a gifted artist. Especially one as beautiful and charming as Ottilie Chase.

Perhaps that will explain why I could not rest after her death, and why I felt constrained despite what seemed impossible circumstances to investigate the events leading *to* her death. And, further, to learn enough to be able to expose the motive *behind* her death. This search was to take me to some odd places indeed, and to one spot in particular which lingers in my thoughts, refusing to settle into oblivion. Even more disturbing was what I learned about Ottilie Chase herself: that special talent which infused her later work, almost determined its content, through a process I still cannot explain, and which I believe must fall into the realm of the inexplicable. But I'm getting ahead of myself.

❖

I hadn't heard from Ottilie in five years when I received the postcard inviting me to the opening of an exhibition of her new paintings. Ever since the purchase of two of her works by the Cleveland Art Museum not long ago, Ottilie—always something of a perfectionist—had become an even more exacting artist.

Her choice of medium somewhat dictated that. She had abandoned oils, experimented briefly with acrylics, flirted with printmaking. But her final decade's work—the paintings of hers that will be collected long in the future—were in the difficult art of egg-tempera. Of necessity, her work was slow, but the possibilities of atmospheric expression were that much more heightened. Her sulky, often eerie, landscapes seemed the work of some still unknown late nineteenth-century Luminist master.

But there was something else beyond her technique—extraordinary as that was. Each painting added an enigmatic, new, yet also familiar locale to viewers' own store of memorized places. As though you had lived there a month during some astonishingly uneventful and thus poorly recalled vacation. Sections of vast granite escarpments fronted by solid green; utterly vacant meadows; blistering, bereft, sunlit shorelines; littered giant boulders, as though tossed by a titan's hand; deep twisting forest paths through shadowed pine-needled carpets—you'd been there before somehow, and you stood in front of each painting racking your memory for where, when exactly.

None of these places were identified on the canvas, which made their amazingly detailed, utterly faithful rendering even more bizarre. However, invariably, a date and time were painted in over Ottilie's signature: usually a very precise time. Not the date it had been painted. Not the date it was hung to be viewed. Nor, in fact, any date that made any immediate sense. Many of the times listed predated Ottilie herself, having taken place months and years before she was even born. And more than half of them predated the period during which she painted. Adding to the mystification, Ottilie never once attempted to explain those dates. She did say that they came to her as she worked. I naturally always assumed that Ottilie insisted upon this so she might add a sense of mystery, because otherwise she was the least mysterious of beautiful women I'd ever known. But that theory still didn't account for the distinct sense of discomfort, uneasiness I felt looking at her landscapes. Nor was I the only person with that reaction.

An art gallery opening of a new exhibit is a bright, noisy affair. So many people chatting, re-encountering, so many ice cubes clinking in glasses, one scarcely sees the works on display. Ottilie Chase's own vernissages were more sober affairs. People gathered to look and whispered in small groups. Other viewers stood a long time musing before a single canvas, often with a slight frown on their brows. Others paced, almost as though avoiding the actual display of work, then would suddenly stop to catch a peripheral glance at one painting before moving restlessly on.

I always understood why. I wouldn't have been at all amazed to stumble upon a landscape by Ottilie that I would utterly recognize, completely recall. And I was certain it would be the recognition of some place I never again wanted to see, a memory I wanted obliterated.

This might help explain why I waited until the last moment to go to the exhibition, titled, by the way, "Imaginary Landscapes, Series Three." Having put off contacting Ottilie until the day of the vernissage, when I did call her, it was to ask if she minded terribly that I would arrive late, probably not until the closing minutes of the evening. She didn't at all mind, she said, so brightly that to assuage my own guilt, I asked her to join me for dinner afterward. To my surprise, she accepted.

Even so, I dithered that evening over details of dress even more than usual. Then I couldn't find a taxi on Riverside Drive for another fifteen minutes. I didn't arrive at the gallery at nine twenty, as I'd promised Ottilie, but after ten. It was still lighted up, although I suppose that entire area of upper Madison Avenue filled with galleries and high-end boutiques remains lighted up till midnight, open or not.

The downstairs glass door led directly up a flight of dimly lighted industrially carpeted stairs. At the first-floor landing I found the gallery door locked. Or at least I assumed it was locked when I first tried the handle. One thing was clear, the opening event was already long over.

Ottilie might still be inside. Alone, at night, with the downstairs door unlocked, she had no doubt sensibly locked herself in the gallery to wait for me. I knocked on the door twice. No response. I thought of going back down and outside to find a pay phone to tell her that it was me knocking. Then I knocked again, and in irritation called out my name and wrestled with the door handle, this time with some effort. It seemed to suddenly click and fall open. Indistinct azure light filtered through what looked to be otherwise darkened rooms. My immediate thought was that it might have actually been locked, if poorly, or faultily so, and that Ottilie had not waited for me.

Even so, I called out her name. Then I recalled a cigarette lighter I'd held for a friend on an earlier occasion which had ended up still inside one pocket of the coat I'd put on that night. I flicked it and it worked. I located the wall light switch. Both the lights and the ventilation went on as one, blinding me and deafening me for an instant. I stood in the first of three rooms and could partly see into the other two, which were totally bare save for the hung paintings. Then I noticed something completely out of place: In the most distant room, a pair of legs stretched out on the carpet, one high heel snapped off.

I remember gasping out some partial sentence before rushing forward to fully see what I already feared—Ottilie Chase's body, twisted into a half-sitting, half-sprawled position. Her face was a mottled blue, contorted almost beyond identification by the spasmodic fatal pain of the Prussic acid that spilled out of the a wineglass fallen from her hand onto the carpet several feet away. Black stains on the skin of her lower lip, one bared shoulder, and her left wrist were as though charcoal burned paths where the poisoned drink had splashed, probably in the instant she'd discovered its perfidy and too late flung it away.

More frightening, however, were the reddened whites of her open eyes, angled up at a landscape she had grasped in a futile attempt at steadying her collapse. Or as though in those last moments before her vision had been burned away along with her existence, she must once more gaze upon her work.

❖

I did all those banal things one does when one first sees a friend horribly dead. I fell to my knees, staring in disbelief that she actually was deceased. I finally got up the courage to take her un-charred wrist in my own hand to prove to myself that indeed there was no pulse. I stood up, then felt a wave of nausea, ran to find the lavatory, spilled out what little food remained undigested in me from lunch, then sat down, took deep breaths; then, still not in the least bit calm, I dialed for the police.

In the minutes before they arrived, I calmed enough to bring myself to get up and go look at Ottilie again. For the first time I noticed the subject of the landscape askew in her grotesquely ultimate grasp: a landscape of unearthly beauty.

It depicted two dark, forested shorelines surrounding the clear, unruffled water of a sheltered bay at twilight. To one side, riding low in the tide, lay an island, and asymmetrically placed upon it, a copse of trees shaped into a deep green dome. The sun had already set behind the opposite shore. The outline of pine trees was most defined at the painting's right side. The sky was a quiet majesty of grays shot through with husky violets and magentas.

Besides what it portrayed, this three- by five-foot tempera possessed in every square inch that ineffable Chasian quality—it was a masterpiece of haunting remembrance which I couldn't for the life of me precisely remember.

Little wonder she had gone to it last. As though to tell me— might she still have remembered in her last moments that I was still to arrive?—take this painting of all of them. This is my best.

But as I heard the police sirens pull up outside the building and saw the scarlet glare of their rooftops reflected outside the gallery windows, I also had another impression, that the index finger of Ottilie's outstretched hand pointed—pointed straight at that eerie little island in the painting, as though it somehow would explain her death.

That moment, I vowed to purchase the landscape, no matter the cost. I also vowed to find out what Ottilie had meant by that final gesture.

❖

To my surprise, the police scarcely questioned me. I suppose my shock at Ottilie's death and at having to find her dead was still quite apparent. To my further surprise, however, it seemed to me that they were barely intent on investigating her death at all.

True, photos were taken of the death scene. Chalk marks were laid down upon the carpet and on the wall, outlining her position and that of several objects—the wineglass, one of her shoes, the broken heel of the other. The gallery was closed the following day, and later in the afternoon, three of us—Auburn Anders, the gallery owner, Susan Vight, his assistant, and myself—were collectively questioned at the gallery, although it struck me, in the most perfunctory manner.

Did Ottilie Chase have any enemies? Detective Compson asked.

None that any of us knew of.

Had she any close friends?

Again no. And of close friends, none besides ourselves.

Any family?

I recalled that her mother lived in Portland, Oregon, but I was, I admitted, unsure whether or not she was still alive.

Any recent relationships with men?

Not since a year ago, Susan Vight informed us, when Ottilie had stopped seeing Anthony Eldridge. He was a Wall Street lawyer, several years her junior.

Had she been depressed lately?

Here Auburn and Susan exchanged glances and said, yes, of course, Ottilie had been depressed. But that was in no way unusual for Ottilie. After all, it had been five years since her last previous exhibit. She'd naturally been anxious that this show might fail, although clearly this third—and now last—series of "Imaginary Landscapes" was the best and best received to date.

Susan offered her belief that Ottilie was worried about more than the reception of her work. Ottilie had not completely gotten over her separation from Eldridge, Susan thought. I countered that as well as their emphasis on her depression—for I could easily see that Compson was leading up to a verdict of a suicide, which I didn't in the least subscribe to. I repeated to him my phone call earlier the previous day with Ottilie and how bright and charming, how not at all depressed, she had seemed.

Auburn and Susan again exchanged glances, but this time neither commented or contradicted me.

Auburn then said something he recalled as having bothered Ottilie greatly. About a year and a half ago, he'd hung two of her newer temperas in a group show here at the gallery—mostly, he admitted, to test the marketplace and to get her to show them all. One painting had been sold to a small museum in Massachusetts, a sale that cheered Ottilie a great deal; the other had been sold to a man who'd bought it as a twenty-fifth anniversary gift for his wife. The woman had had an immediate and violent aversion to the landscape, and shortly afterward had filed for divorce. The man somehow blamed Ottilie's work for the ruination of his marriage. He'd even attempted to sell it back to the gallery—which was most unusual. As Ottilie was out of town at the time and Auburn could not authorize its repurchase without her consent, he'd asked the man to wait until she returned. Instead, the customer told Auburn he'd keep the painting, then had it destroyed. Even that didn't end the matter. Since then, he'd sent strange and quite nasty letters to both Anders and to Ottilie, in care of the gallery. One letter reached her only a month ago despite Auburn's efforts to not let any more get through, and it had upset the artist greatly; upset her more than the revelation that her work had been destroyed.

She began to talk wildly, saying she ought to destroy all her work herself. It was only with the greatest of persuasion and the utmost tact that Auburn had been able to convince her otherwise—and to allow her to go along with the expected opening date of the exhibit. Still, Ottilie remained anxious, he said. In one conversation she'd had with the gallery owner, she'd gone so far as to declare that her paintings were cursed. When Auburn tried to reason with her, Ottilie had become vague, evasive, ambiguous, and yet defensive too. All he'd been able to get out of her was the odd belief that she'd somehow or other managed—through her art—to unmake human happiness, when all she'd wanted was to increase it.

All three of us felt guilty to one degree or another for Ottilie's death: Auburn for persuading her to have an exhibit she was otherwise set against. Susan for leaving her alone in the gallery that night. And me, for—well, look how late I was.

How Compson reached the conclusion he did, I still cannot fully fathom, but our testimony convinced him to reach a temporary finding of death by suicide, following acute professional and personal depression. When I attempted to point out how many easier-to-take, less hideous poisons than Prussic acid existed on the market for the potential suicide, the detective frowned, but said nothing else. When I went on to say it seemed to me—the discoverer of her corpse, after all—that she'd been pointing to a possible clue in that final, grasped-at painting, the policeman actually glared at me, then asked if I was suggesting that foul play was involved. Of course I was suggesting it, I replied. Compson responded that if he were to open a homicide investigation, I would be the primary suspect.

I remained undaunted by this news. But Auburn and Susan made me drop my request.

❖

The exhibit reopened the following day, and I promptly purchased the landscape.

I also decided to do a bit of investigating myself. Toward this end I asked Susan Vight to photocopy for me the names of the guests who'd signed into the vernissage, the names of any who'd called or written in about the show, and the gallery's usual mailing list.

The most obvious name present on the final list but not on the other two, and especially not on the list of guests attending the opening, was of course Anthony Eldridge.

I also spent time probing Susan and Auburn's memory, searching for hints of anyone who might have attended the opening night but not signed in. Each recalled several people, but they could neither recall nor had ever known their names.

It was very likely that someone who'd attended the vernissage had later returned on some pretext and somehow managed to slip Ottilie the poisoned drink. I was also fairly certain that the landscape she'd grabbed at—which I now owned—would in some way implicate her murderer.

Because of these beliefs, I went to the gallery almost daily looking for clues within the painting itself, which would remain on public display several weeks longer. This had a side benefit. Susan and Auburn would be able to tell me if anyone had spent longer than usual looking at that same painting, or had offered to buy it, or even had returned often to stare at it.

To all but the second question, the answer was no. Of course many people offered to buy it. That was easy enough to explain. Ottilie's death had been reported in all the daily newspapers. The *New York Times* ran a four-column obituary, with another two columns assessing her place in contemporary art, and naturally both mentioned the exhibit. Her death also drew the curiously morbid, who probably wouldn't have dreamed of otherwise coming. The gallery was packed day and night. By the end of the first week, all the landscapes had been sold—three to museums, the remainder to private purchasers. It was Ottilie's greatest triumph. People who'd known her for years all felt it necessary to make an appearance at the gallery, almost as though it were an adjunct to a memorial. Almost all of them seemed to go out of their way to mention this fact to Auburn or Susan, who carefully, politely (following my request) took down their names and addresses. The list of suspects grew.

I began to realize why Detective Compson had not even begun to investigate: It appeared more difficult than ever to find some clue, some lead, even a hint of one, with so many possibilities and so little to go on really, and with so much attention still focused on Ottilie.

Then I had a break. One evening I'd come to the gallery quite late, and Susan Vight immediately signaled me over. Anthony Eldridge had arrived, at last, and was still there. Still there and still so distraught that although we'd never before met (Ottilie had mentioned my name, he said), Eldridge allowed me to take him out afterward for a drink. At one of those seedy but quite good Manhattan gin joints made famous by various authors that happened to be located around the corner from the gallery, he began to speak about Ottilie, led on by my sympathy and by his own need to talk. This is what he told me.

"I loved Ottilie. I never met a woman more to my taste in every way, and believe me, I've had my share of women."

I didn't doubt Eldridge. He came from a moneyed old family in New England and possessed a fine figure and what generally these days passes for a handsome—though to me quite character-less—face.

"In every particular it seemed but one," Anthony now clarified, "we agreed, Ottilie and myself. But that was an important one—her painting.

"Of course I knew Ottilie was a serious artist when I met her. That was part of her attraction. For a year or so that wasn't a problem. Ottilie moved into my duplex, but retained her studio. She went there regularly, almost nine to five, daily, and spent after-hours and weekends with me. It was a good schedule for both of us.

"About a year and a half ago she began to change. At first I thought that she'd fallen out of love with me. We'd been together a while, and I wanted to make it official. To announce our engagement.

"Ottilie put me off. She said she wanted to complete enough work for a new exhibit. That was very important to her. And I understood why.

"It was around then that the incident with that fool Lawrence happened. Did you know that he bought something of hers at the gallery during a group exhibit, then wanted to return it, and when he couldn't, destroyed the painting he'd bought? That incident disturbed Ottilie very deeply. It was a great shame too, really, because I'd finagled for months to get her out of her studio for a few weeks and down to Barbados. It was to be our first vacation together, and I hoped a sort of honeymoon preview. Away from her work, I assumed, Ottilie would be more relaxed and far more receptive to the idea of announcing our engagement. And it almost worked. It would have, except that the day we returned, it was directly into the storm Lawrence had caused. So my plan for calming her down went right out the window.

"It was also about then that Ottilie began to express doubts about her work. She'd hardly said anything before, so I was rather surprised. But when I tried to humor her, asking why she was so anxious, Ottilie became vague—which you know was not at all like her. She did tell me that the new paintings 'weren't right,' that they were strange, almost as though done by someone else's hand. Those were her exact words, in fact.

"Odd, isn't it. Ottilie worked partly from memory, you know. But mostly she worked from her imagination. She claimed she'd never seen the original of most of the landscapes she painted in this third series. Some people who did recognize them, however, and there were a few even among our acquaintances, all said she had captured the appearance of those places to perfection. All emphasized how perfectly she'd succeeded in capturing the light for each specific time of year and day.

"I'm certain you've noticed that each painting was given a dated title—'July 14th, 1935, a quarter past noon'; or 'April 8th, 1971, nine forty a.m.' Ottilie was convinced those times absolutely belonged to each painting: She told me that the dates and times arrived in some inscrutable mental fashion simultaneously with each image. She came to believe that no landscape could exist without the exact time and date. But while that made her secure in some respects, it also frightened Ottilie, contributing to her increasingly bizarre idea that some other hand than her own was wielding the palette and brush.

"Ottilie was otherwise an unusually rational, even a logical woman. You knew her! High-spirited at times, yes, sometimes a bit distracted. But never, well…weird. Naturally I thought her explanations were a fabrication. Something meant to put me off from asking too much about her work, and afterward, to put me off from our wedding. I assumed it was all done to cover up her uncertain feelings about me. I continued to listen to her strange speech, but I have to admit, I ignored much of what she actually said, hoping she would become accustomed to giving up her independence in time to become my wife.

"She didn't. Instead she grew more anxious. She began to dread going to her studio every day. She began to fear facing her paintings.

Yet once there, she remained later every day. Soon I was having to call her to prod her back home.

"One evening Ottilie didn't come home and didn't answer after my repeated phone calls. I decided to go down to the studio and to instigate some kind of showdown. Now, of course, I see it was the stupidest thing I could have done.

"I was right about her still being at work. I used her spare key to let myself in. The landscape she'd been working on was right there, facing me as I entered. It was one of her glorious, brooding panoramas, and although not completely finished, it already bore a date and time: November 18, 1991, five minutes after noon. And here's the real surprise, I *knew* that place depicted. I also knew what the date and time stood for.

"Ottilie had painted a section of the Adirondack Mountains where my father and a friend had earlier constructed and now co-owned a large hunting lodge. You probably wouldn't know the exact area. It's immaterial anyway. But we'd been going to the lodge since I was a small child and I knew it very well. It had once been an essential part of my life, but lately I'd not gone there and it wasn't so much forgotten as no longer thought of. Oh, I was certain I'd never mentioned it to Ottilie.

"I have to admit that at first, the date and time stumped me. Partly, I believe, because I was so utterly astonished to see the locale rendered at all, and then so accurately. However, once I realized how absolutely perfect the view was, next I saw how correctly lighted and shadowed it was for midday in late autumn, how subdued and yet totally right the colors of what leaves remained upon the trees were, how even the slate gray of the sky was correct: unquestionably exact.

"I attempted to ignore the landscape and instead began to argue with Ottilie about her increasingly strange attitude and habits. Something in how aloofly she had received me into the studio must have irritated me: I suddenly let go of all my bottled-up feelings, and I have to say in memory it wouldn't have been very pleasant to witness.

"Afterward, I sort of broke down. but Ottilie wasn't angry. She'd been vindicated, you see. All she said to me was, 'Now you understand, Tony. My painting is ruining me. It's ruining us too.' That was when I looked at the landscape again and suddenly realized the significance of that particular date and time."

Eldridge hesitated so long I thought I would never find out what he'd discovered.

"You see," he finally continued, "on that date, that year, I did something shameful. Probably the only act of my life I can honestly say I am ashamed of. One of the out-of-town guests at the lodge then was a business partner of my father's from Utah. He was quite wealthy and was very free with his money. Like a lot of Westerners, he was loose with his cash, and he carried a great deal of cash on him at all times. And I happened to be particularly hard up. Desperate really. A typical adolescent stunt: I'd gotten a girl I didn't really care for pregnant and had to buy her an abortion. I couldn't let my family know. At any rate, an opportunity presented itself to me, and I stole an amount of money. Of course, the money was missed. Employees were questioned, the cash was never recovered, and finally, through the most circumstantial of evidence, one of the employees was blamed and fired.

"That made me feel even worse. I could never return to the lodge without reliving my guilt. So I stopped going. I didn't know how to pay back the man I'd stolen from later on without revealing why I was doing so. I thought of sending it anonymously to the fired employee instead, but I was never able to track him down. The time Ottilie had painted into the lower right hand edge of the landscape? It must have been the very moment I was in the guest's room, the door ajar, so I could be certain no one else was upstairs or coming up, as I rifled his bureau drawer.

"I told Ottilie all that. She appeared sad to hear my story, but was not particularly surprised. She told me that it only corroborated what she'd come to believe—that each painting she made commemorated some evil deed. I'd merely confirmed what she'd believed. I—and the affair concerning Herbert Lawrence's wife.

"Ottilie came back to the duplex with me that night. But when I returned home from the firm the following night, she'd moved out. It wasn't my past dishonesty that had impelled her move, she assured me in a note she'd left. I'd been young, in a jam, she understood. But she couldn't stop herself from painting those terrifying landscapes. She couldn't. Even knowing they were terrible. She felt only half-alive away from her studio: only fully herself when working. She told me what I'd not known, how she'd lost most of her friends over the past two years, one by one, and each of them in the same way—by unconsciously, invariably, unintentionally ferreting out and then painting for them to see the scene of some awful secret each person possessed.

"I tried to get Ottilie to see someone—a counselor, a psychologist, someone who would reason with her or help her. At the same time, I clearly could not in any way explain how she had painted that view of my family's lodge, nor the utter eeriness of her being able to so pinpoint the time and date of my misdeed. Yet even as powerfully disturbing as that incident was, it wasn't as important to me as Ottilie and I were. But she wouldn't listen to me.

"After a while she changed her studio phone number to an unlisted one. She stopped answering my letters. Sent them back unopened. That all happened less than six months ago.

"When I received the postcard announcing Ottilie's show, I thought Ottilie had changed her mind about us. I was wrong, of course. The mailing list was partly taken from her personal telephone/address book by the gallery assistant here. I couldn't know that and of course I hoped for a reconciliation. In my wildest hopes, I thought perhaps now, with the painting series completed, perhaps Ottilie would somehow be fully purged of all the eeriness and we could start anew. I thought I'd come here not on opening night, when my appearance might only spoil her triumph, but the next night. That of course turned out to be one night too late. When I read of her death, I have to admit, some part of me wasn't all that surprised. It seemed to me that success or not, she'd still committed herself to a course that could only end in suicide."

Eldridge had finished. I told him I disagreed with Detective Compson's finding of self-inflicted death. I told him that, but didn't tell him why I disagreed.

"You don't know how badly off Ottilie was," Eldridge argued. "Even six months ago. Imagine how much worse it must have gotten for her?"

It was true that I'd not seen her in that six-month period since she'd left Eldridge. In fact, I'd not seen her for a longer time before that, so he had me at a disadvantage.

"Then leave it alone," Eldridge pleaded. "Ottilie's possibly better off now. Indeed," he added, not all that cryptically, "perhaps all of us are better off now."

❖

I have to admit that after that conversation with Eldridge my faith wavered. Elements of his story seemed to reaffirm what Auburn Anders had told Detective Compson: Ottilie believed there was some secret—some evil, Eldridge said—concealed in each of her imaginary landscapes. If she believed that, and if her beloved Anthony could not disprove it, others too might have given it credence. Possibly the Herbert Lawrences had—and whoever had poisoned Ottilie Chase.

With that in mind, I decided to look up Lawrence. It's true that in doing so, I completely misrepresented myself. I phoned and told him I was writing an obituary and appreciation of Ottilie for *Art in America* magazine, and needed a description of those paintings of hers for which no photographic slides existed. According to Ottilie's own records, I told him, he once owned a work now considered lost. I asked if I could see Lawrence at his office that very afternoon. He tried to put me off, but when I hinted that what I was really looking for was information on the effect of Ottilie Chase's work on others, he reluctantly agreed to see me.

Nevertheless, as we sat in his office high over Park Avenue, Lawrence wasn't very helpful at first. As the secretary pool outside his glass door emptied and the lights went on one by one along upper Park, Lawrence poured us both a drink and loosened up. Finally, he said:

"I'm glad she's dead. Chase and her damned painting destroyed my marriage. I still haven't been able to put my life back together."

After that outburst, he didn't need much prodding to go on. This is what he said:

He'd been meeting a business associate for dinner in the neighborhood of the Anders Galley, and afterward, his friend suggested they look at the group show, as an old school friend was one of the artists represented. Lawrence himself wasn't at all interested in art, although his associate claimed to be a collector of sorts. But once inside the gallery, Lawrence had immediately been arrested by a particular landscape.

It wasn't very large, he said, yet its use of color, paint, and he guessed perspective too, lent it an amazing sense of depth. The landscape wasn't at all extraordinary—a rocky bluff into which a small gray brick building seemed almost hidden, surrounded by a scrub pine forest. A majestic ridge of high, scraggy, snowless mountains loomed over the scene, reminding Lawrence of the Rocky Mountains in that area of Colorado where he and his wife had grown up. Their twentieth wedding anniversary would be in a week, and Lawrence told me he was one of those men who never knew what gift to get his wife. He thought this would be a winner: She'd be delighted both by the novelty of the present and by the reminder of Colorado, which she always said she missed. Lawrence's colleague told him that Ottilie Chase was a well-known and well-respected artist: The work should also be a good investment. That clinched it. Lawrence bought the landscape.

A week later, when Judith Lawrence pulled off the brown paper wrappings in their house, she stared wordless at the painting for a long time. She then turned to Herbert and said, "How could you?" and fled the room. Lawrence heard her cry herself to sleep in their locked bedroom. He was astonished, and—naturally enough—disappointed by her reaction. He was even more surprised when sometime in the middle of the night, he heard—from the den, where he'd bedded down—Judith creep back into the living room. He waited as she lighted a lamp, pulled away the wrapping he'd had hastily gathered together, and then sat staring silently for a long time at the landscape.

When Lawrence got up enough courage to sidle up to her, his wife rejected his caresses—not angrily, but sadly, coldly. In an equally cold voice, she told him that now that he knew everything there was to know about her, he must be happy. When he said he had no idea what she was talking about, she asked surely he knew what the painting depicted? He said he had no idea. He'd chosen it because it reminded him of home. That surprised her, but she said it no longer made any difference. She would tell him what was painted, what he'd brought into their home and into their marriage.

She reminded Lawrence of the time before they'd married. They'd lived in Colorado Springs, she the daughter of a miner who'd died in a mine accident and of a woman who'd become bitter with loss and poverty—and with having to bring up two small daughters, Judith and her sister Lil. In contrast, Lawrence was from one of the wealthiest families in town. He'd gone to college in the East, he'd driven a foreign sports car when they met and associated with Denver socialites.

Her mother had pinned all her hopes on Lil marrying well, and when Herbert Lawrence had begun dating the lovely girl, her mother was pleased. But Lil was independent to the point of rebellion—and she was promiscuous. She didn't care for Herbert as much as she did for what he could buy her. While he was away, she went out with other men: low men, miners, tramps, almost anyone who wanted her. Her mother continually warned her that word would reach the Lawrence family. Lil didn't seem to care. Desperate, her mother confided in Judith.

The crisis arrived when Lil became pregnant by an unknown man. Instead of allowing herself to have an abortion, Lil said she would flaunt her state in the Lawrence house, say it was Herbert's child, force the marriage to occur, and thus find out what a fool in love Lawrence actually was. This was too much for her mother. She hatched a plan and had her other daughter, Judith, aid her. They would pretend they were taking Lil to a rest home where she might have the child in privacy. But the place they actually took her to was a private sanitarium located in the foothills of the Rockies—the very same building that seemed to grow out of the rock itself in Ottilie Chase's very accurate depiction. The very last sight Judith ever had of her sister was of Lil screaming, suddenly realizing what was happening and trying to flee from the two burly men who'd finally had to knock her out to get her into the straitjacket. Lil hadn't been insane when she'd gone into that asylum in the rocks, but according to Judith's mother, after losing the child prematurely, and after remaining incarcerated so long, her mind had snapped. Her mother had become guilty and visited, but she'd died years before, and since then no one had visited Lil.

Judith and her mother had meanwhile fabricated a boating accident in which Lil had supposedly drowned. No one had reason to disbelieve them. Certainly not Herbert. It was at the memorial service for Lil that Lawrence again met Judith. At first, they spoke only of Lil. But soon that topic was dropped, and as they grew closer, it was never again raised. He married Judith a year later; he'd come to love her, to see Lil's best qualities and none of her worst in her sister. In fact, he'd come to love Judith far more than he'd believed he could ever care for Lil, whose constancy he'd always been unsure of. Lawrence admitted that to Judith, in front of the damning landscape, in an attempt to win her back.

His wife didn't, or couldn't, believe him. Her secret was out and it was a terrible one. In her own mind, she'd pretended that Lil was dead. Now the seriousness of her betrayal and decades-long perfidy was upon her, right there, painted and titled with the very date her poor sister had been dragged into a living death. Judith would somehow have to make amends. Despite Herbert's protests, she filed for separation and returned to Colorado. She had the helpless harridan that Lil had become released into her custody and she resettled in Colorado Springs to care for her.

When Herbert Lawrence still thought he'd be able to change his wife's mind, he'd called Auburn and tried to sell back the landscape. When it became clear that even that would make no difference to his wife, Lawrence had flown into a rage and destroyed the painting. Since then, he'd gone to Colorado himself, trying to win back his wife. Unfortunately, once out of the asylum, Lil had lasted only a few months and had died in her sister's care. His shocked wife had taken her sister's place in the asylum.

Herbert Lawrence's unhappy tale so perfectly supported Anthony Eldridge's that I was now convinced that I possessed a motive for Ottilie Chase's murder. Luckily for them, Eldridge and Lawrence, who would have been the most natural suspects, both had airtight alibis for the night of the vernissage.

What I now had to do was to find a third crime, a crime that exactly fit the painting that Ottilie had last grasped—then, most likely, I'd find her murderer. Once the exhibit, at last, ended, my painting had been taken down and brought home. Now If I could only convince the others, Auburn Anders, Susan Vight, and most crucially Detective Compson, that the landscape must hold the answer.

Whether I could convince them or not, it wasn't going to be easy. All I really had was a date—August 13, 1999—and the depiction of a locale neither I nor anyone else who'd seen it seemed to recognize.

Here, Ottilie's tremendous skill in tempera proved useful. For there did exist something like a clue within the painting itself, although I needed a high-powered magnifying glass and patient hours of deciphering to get at it.

I mentioned before that the painting showed a body of still water surrounded by land. It could have been a bay, an inlet, or a lake—or rather one end of a lake—with an island just left of center. What I didn't mention was that Ottilie depicted not a barren, totally isolated area, but a populated one. While the painting itself was absent of human life, and unearthly still, various houses on stilts were barely visible within the pine-tree cover that grew right down to the water-lapped shingle: houses in what I could only call North American style, wooden, and with small decks, large windows, some with tottering outdoors stairways down to the water. It wasn't a style of architecture as distinguishable as, say, Cape Cod or Eyebrow, but it definitely felt to me like New England, or at least the northeastern U.S. Each house possessed its own jetty, little slatted docks for the most part that floated atop the water. At the end of most of these, held stationary with anchors, I suppose, were little boats: motor launches, collapsed-sail catamarans, rowboats, dories. One boat in the foreground was more detailed than the others as it was closer to the viewer. Inside this dinghy lay an enameled box, yellow lettering upon its side. After hours of minute discernment, I finally made out:

SEBAS O
ail & tack

"Sail & Tackle" seemed to be the most likely explanation for the second line of the two. But what was the word, or words, or—I most hoped—name, only partly revealed in the first line? Not Sebastian nor Sebastopol. But more like Sebasoon or Sebassox, or...

By now I was half-obsessed with my theory and so I spent weeks poring over gazetteers and map indexes in libraries; I even went to D.C. and checked out the Smithsonian's cartological wing. It was there that I at last discovered the single place in the U.S. that could possibly be the name on the tackle box—Sebascodegan Island, located in the northeast quadrant of Casco Bay, a hundred miles or so north of Portland, Maine.

According to U.S. Department of the Interior Geological Survey Map, AMS-7070IVSW—Series V & II—there was no lake big enough nearby to be the one painted, but instead there was a large enough inlet known as Quahog Bay, surrounded by a dozen coves and dotted with islands, several of which looked large enough on the map to be the one depicted.

The following weekend, I took color photos of the painting until I got one I deemed most accurate. I had it enlarged and took it with me in a rented car up to Maine.

I found Sebascodegan Island easily enough, but that word means "large" in the local Indian dialect, and the island was huge. So was the inland bay it enclosed. I drove miles along public and private—often deserted—dirt roads, circumnavigating the island, until I found what seemed to be near the correct spot, on the easternmost side of the island. It had to be that side, I reasoned, because the sun had been setting opposite the site from which the scene had been viewed—or in Ottilie's case, imagined.

To my surprise, I also found that the island pictured in her landscape was not one of the two—Ben Island or Snow Island—shown on the map I'd used, but instead two smaller, low-lying islets, unnamed on the map, which from only one angle seemed to cohere into a single isle. The dome-shaped copse of trees also become an evident landmark, not to be mistaken.

I remained overnight in the area, in a guest house near Cundy's Harbor, an unremarkable, poverty-blighted local fishing village. The next morning I rented a canoe, which I strapped atop the car roof. When I'd reached the land's-end point from which I'd already determined the painting must have been (mentally) composed, I took down the canoe and began to explore the two little islands by water.

Luckily it was mid-September and most of the summer and weekend homes were already closed up. Luckily, I say, as both small isles seemed much used by local picnickers during the summer. Would I, could I, find evidence here of a crime committed two years before?

I didn't on my first try, but I did on my second, more thorough attempt. It was found inside a clump of trees, the very spot Ottilie's hand had appeared to point toward during her death throes. Within the trees lay a half dozen used condoms, and a blue tampon case, among the litter at the bottom of a deep little gully. My evidence, however—unlike the rest of the junk—was older and had once been a man's leather wallet. It was once waterlogged too, I guess during high tide, and so quite moldy, and it had also been partly chewed at by some small animal. Virtually all its contents were so disintegrated as to be unreadable. However, plastic seems to possess a half-life only somewhat shorter than that of plutonium, and so after rooting about in the mess with a twig, I located a MasterCard made out to one Donald Horace Scott.

Later that day, I informally interviewed the sheriff of the town of Brunswick, the nearest police precinct that included the little island. I told him I was a reporter for *The Police Gazette* (by now I'd become inured to such pretenses) and that I was writing an article on the unsolved crimes of New England. Did he have anything to tell my readers of? At first he said no. But I prompted him. What about the disappearance on August 13th, 1999, of Donald Horace Scott?

He recalled that immediately, but he still couldn't recall much, as he'd been on vacation at the time, he said, and someone else had handled the case. It was all written up, and I might read the police file if I wished.

The contents of the manila folder were almost embarrassingly slender. A death certificate, a page of local testimony, and a preliminary finding of death by misadventure at sea.

Scott had been seen by a real estate agent in the nearby hamlet of Cooks Corner. He'd been looking for a weekend cottage, he'd told the man. He'd also told the man that his girlfriend had grown up in the area, gone to camp out on Orr's Island nearby, and loved the place. As far as the agent could tell, Scott had been alone when he picked up the key to the Glynn house, but the unnamed woman might easily have met up with him later—or she might have been totally fictitious.

Scott never returned the key to the Glynn house, and a day later the real estate agent found it still lodged in the front door lock. The cottage didn't look used, although the agent said he'd noticed a stubbed-out cigarette in the ashtray—the woman's?—on a deal table facing the view of the inlet. The sheriff later found fresh tire marks, but no car at the house. Most odd to me, however, was the date of Scott's disappearance given in the police records from the real estate agent's testimony. It wasn't August 13th, but August 11th. That two-day discrepancy baffled me at first; later on it gave me the strongest clue of all.

I returned to the site and pondered as the sun set. Since my visit there was later in the year than the date of the picture, the sun set further south than it had in Ottilie's landscape: at almost at the exact center of the picture plane. But it had been a clear week for that sodden part of Maine, and it was a similar sunset to the one she had painted, pale purple infusing the gray sky, mauve and pale magenta streaking it all.

It was almost dark and I was hungry and decided to leave the spot and thus escape the ferocity of the local mosquitoes when I couldn't help but notice a new streak of color in the sky, opposite to where I sat.

It was very thin, quite fugitive really, but unusually colored, almost cantaloupe in hue. And once I stared, directly in front of it was its cause: a tiny speck of silver outlining the fuselage of a jet plane. Could that be what Ottilie had been pointing to at the time of her death? Not the island, but the jet? And had she painted not the date of the crime, as I'd thought, but perhaps a date connected to that jet's flight?

I grabbed my photo of her landscape and there it was, the same streak, same color, although the sky around it in her painting was, naturally, far brighter. I checked my watch: 8:36. It must be a transatlantic jet from New York or Boston, flying to Europe. I knew from my own flights that all North Atlantic jets crossed the ocean substantially north to take advantage of the curvature of the earth, making for a shorter-than-direct flight. They usually crossed somewhere near Fundy or Halifax, Canada.

When I returned home, I checked with an airline travel agent. The flight I'd probably seen, she assured me, was the American Airlines 4:15 departure, flight number 414, from Logan Field in Boston, headed to Heathrow Airport, outside of London.

Now all I needed was a passenger manifest for that particular day's flight. This was more difficult, perhaps the most difficult part of my investigation. But in the end, and with me having to pay a bit for it, not impossible to obtain. After weeks, and through stratagems too tedious to go into, I finally did get it. I then compared the names of all the passengers on the jet that day to those on the lists prepared by Susan Vight.

The name jumped out at me. Alexandra Fairchild, of 20 Bethune Street, in Greenwich Village, New York.

Now all I had to do was to link her to Donald Horace Scott.

❖

There are three leading incentives for people to commit murder, human nature being, if anything, consistent: for love (or out of jealousy), for money, and for revenge. Anything else is usually pathological, and thus far less easily understood. I assumed that one of those three standard reasons would do for Alexandra Fairchild. Since she was presumably Scott's lover, love seemed to be only partly right—although he might have cheated on her, or tried to ditch her, which would make the third incentive, revenge, a good motive. But there was always the second, and strongest one—money.

I went to Bethune Street one afternoon and was surprised not to find the name Fairchild listed among the five tenants of the building. I rang the bell of the lowest floor, the one belonging to one Helena Preston. When this elderly, and as it luckily turned out, garrulous, woman answered in person, I said I was a friend of Donald Horace Scott and was looking for him. Didn't Miss Fairchild live in the building? Hers was the last address Scott had given me, a few years ago.

Helena Preston sized me up, then liking what she saw, or at least not hating what she saw, and bursting with news, although it was already fairly old news to her, she invited me inside for a cup of tea, where she gently broke the news to me about Donald's death. She added that Alexandra Fairchild had moved out of the Village flat a year ago.

"She was very broken up about poor Donald's death. And in such mysterious circumstances too. Poor dear," the woman commiserated.

I composed myself in such a way to show that while I was grieved I was even more curious. Little by little and without a great deal of my probing, she let out this information. First, her surprise that Donald had given me this particular address, as he'd never "officially" lived there. Second, her own belief that Alexandra had thrown over Scott less than three months before his disappearance. And third, that Miss Fairchild had come into "a lot of money," probably, Preston hypothecized, from a legacy, some nine months after Scott's death.

Money it was, then. More than likely an insurance policy Scott had taken out with Alexandra as beneficiary. The banal, alas, is all too often the right answer.

"She was away when it happened," Helena Preston said, nodding upward, to where I suppose Fairchild had lived. "She was in England at the time. She'd gone there looking for work. Doubt she needs to do that any more, lucky thing."

That clinched it for me. Alexandra had told the old snoop that she'd gone away two days before Scott's death, whereas I knew that her air reservations shown me that she'd gone away two days *after*: more than enough time to have murdered Scott in Maine and then driven or flown down to Boston to make flight 414.

I spent the next week checking insurance policies. There are about a dozen insurance companies of any size in the area. I thought surely Scott would have bought a policy from one. I wasn't wrong. Calling—in another disguise, as a lawyer for James L. Horace, who I claimed was Donald Horace Scott's younger, half brother—I soon found the company that had sold Scott insurance. It was for a payout of a whopping three-quarters of a million dollars. And the beneficiary was—you guessed it—Alexandra Fairchild, whom they now listed as living at the posh address of 920 Fifth Avenue, on Manhattan's Upper East Side.

This was the last piece of information I collected, and subsequently brought to Detective Compson at the Homicide Division of the New York Police Department. He looked me over very carefully after I was done explaining what I'd discovered. The procedure had lasted about two hours, with him all but grilling me, questioning every step I'd taken, every bit of logic I'd followed.

"That's a lot of work. Why bother?" he asked.

"Who else is going to bother?" I asked back. Then, to soften the sarcasm, I added, "I've known Ottilie Chase since she was sixteen years old, longer than anyone else you talked to. I *knew* she wouldn't commit suicide, no matter how depressed and anxious she might have become. And also I took her death personally."

Compson said that what I had provided was circumstantial evidence, if quite good circumstantial evidence. Even so, he would need time to prepare a scheme to do a more solid, a more "prosecutable job" were the words he used, connecting Alexandra Fairchild to the two murders. However, the fact that Fairchild was a known acquaintance of Ottilie Chase's (a fact I'd really not been aware of) would help my case. He might pretend he was asking questions about Ottilie's life, then he'd try to catch her out in some discrepancy. He was certain he could end up bringing her down to the station house and grilling her until he'd entrapped her or gotten a confession from her about Donald Horace Scott. He thought that would naturally lead to the landscape and to Ottilie's death. He was so busy planning out these varied stratagems, he didn't even thank me when I finally left his office.

❖

My work was almost complete. It lacked one more finishing touch, much the way an artist—I could picture Ottilie herself doing it—will stand back and view what appears to be a finished painting for a long time, almost as though gloating over her triumph, then suddenly dash forward and instantly add in a line here, a dab there, a tiny crosshatching somewhere else, and only *then* be sure that the work is finally done.

Because Ottilie's aged mother had not yet arrived in Manhattan to dispose of her daughter's possessions—the body had been shipped to Oregon for burial but nothing else had gone there—I suspected that Ottilie's studio was probably still intact, and, I supposed, probably not much touched, besides whatever desultory searching the police might have done. In short, it ought to have been just as it was when she had put down her paintbrushes and palette, cleaned her hands and face, removed her working smock, and cabbed uptown to her triumph—and her demise.

I phoned Anthony Eldridge and told him I'd been talking with Detective Compson, who had reopened the case as a homicide investigation. I told Tony that a break was imminent in finding Ottilie's murderer. I needed to get into her studio to check one final clue. Had the studio been sealed by the police? And if so, did he still have his key?

It had not been sealed, Eldridge told me. When he and Ottilie were still together, he'd signed a new lease for the studio drawn up in both of their names, and it was now, legally, in his name. He planned to hold on to it until Ottilie's family had emptied the place. then he'd release it back to the landlord. As for getting the key, yes, he'd loan it to me. Did he want me to join him?

"Sure. Do you really want to go there again?" I asked, fairly certain of his answer.

"I don't *ever* want to step into that place again."

So we agreed that he would messenger the key over to my home. It arrived an hour later. I waited for dark before I set off for West 27th Street.

The building contained dozens of working lofts with a plastic belt factory occupying the lowest floor. This being New York City, two keys were needed to get into the building, a third to open and operate the elevator, and a fourth for the studio itself.

Once inside, I breathed a sigh of relief, then put on one dim light—I didn't want neighbors to know anyone was present tonight.

Even by that small amount of illumination, it was easy to find what I was looking for. What I suspected—expected was more like it. It was sufficiently completed for me to recognize it, although evidently not finished enough to be exhibited. And it appeared to be Ottilie Chase's very last hauntingly eerie landscape, since it was still sitting on an easel in the middle of the studio with a drop cloth over it and the surrounding area strewn about with several tossed-down instruments of her labor. Perhaps she'd stopped work to get dressed and go to her vernissage, I mused.

It was another of her uncanny sunsets, if rather everyday in its choice of location compared to many others: the north slope of Fort Tryon Park, in western upper Manhattan, not a hundred yards from the outbuildings of the Cloisters, that medieval stone fortress brought to America and rebuilt, stone by stone, to grace the New York palisades. As usual, Ottilie had gotten the look of the place perfectly: the eroded red-brick underpass, the cement block paved path leading from the museum, the usually hidden hollow between two large, untrimmed oak trees, the path that disappeared through the underbrush. She, of course, had the date correct: October 27, 1995, at 6:37 p.m., the exact time that—after stalking a young teenage student from a local Catholic high school as she dawdled her way home—I waylaid her, at that very spot, pulling her between those trees where I bound her, gagged her, raped and sodomized her before strangling her to death. I had then pushed some leaves over lovely Holly Caputo's body, brushed the damp leaves off my clothing, and found my way to the Fort Tryon bus, back down to mid-Manhattan where I'd enjoyed a fish dinner at Howard Johnson's on Times Square, then seen a quite bad action movie.

Now, of course, seeing it, I had to wonder, naturally enough, if Ottilie was planning to mention the new painting to me after her show's opening, at dinner. Perhaps not, perhaps she was planning to ask me up to her studio for a nightcap, and then she would just spring it on me. Despite what the others, including Tony, had told me, it still wasn't all that clear to me how she herself deemed these revelations.

Saddened and upset as she must be, I couldn't help but also sense Ottilie's innate mischief in catching someone out in wrongdoing. Especially an old pal like myself. She might have been plotting how she'd get me up to the studio while she waited for me at the gallery that night. ("You like these? I've got better ones. Want to see?") But of course that was far too late, wasn't it? Auburn and Susan had already sent out a few hundred postcards depicting that other, that beautifully incriminating, landscape: a virtual invitation, never mind incitation, for someone to come murder her.

Naturally I destroyed the Fort Tryon Park landscape. I took it down off the easel, ripped it off the support she'd been using to paint it on. Once off, I cut it into fragments, which I placed in a small plastic bag I'd brought. Later on, in my apartment, I burned those fragments in the fireplace to ash as I sat listening to a Brahms string sextet. The second one, in G, with the lovely minuet? I'd just opened a fine, old armagnac I'd been saving up for just such a future celebratory occasion. The painting flamed quite prettily: all those tints and colors. Very autumnal.

You see, most of us have our dirty little human secrets: some moment when temptation was simply too irresistible. And a person like Ottilie Chase who somehow or other stumbled onto those secrets without knowing what they were, perhaps without even wanting to know, but unable to stop herself from painting them…well, poor thing, she couldn't be expected to live very long, could she? If Alexandra Fairchild hadn't poisoned her, well, I might have had to do it at a later time myself. Or someone else.

Who knows, perhaps even you might have had to do it.

About the Author

Felice Picano is the author of over twenty books, including the literary memoirs *Ambidextrous, Men Who Loved Me*, and *A House on the Ocean, a House on the Bay* as well as the best-selling novels *Like People in History, Looking Glass Lives, The Lure*, and *Eyes*. He is the founder of Sea Horse Press, one of the first gay publishing houses, which later merged with two other publishing houses to become the Gay Presses of New York. With Andrew Holleran, Robert Ferro, Edmund White, and George Whitmore, he founded the Violet Quill Club to promote and increase the visibility of gay authors and their works. He has edited and written for *The Advocate, Blueboy, Mandate, GaysWeek*, and *Christopher Street,* and has been a culture reviewer for *The Los Angeles Examiner, San Francisco Examiner, New York Native, Harvard Lesbian & Gay Review*, and the *Lambda Book Report*. He has won the Ferro-Grumley Award for best gay novel (*Like People in History*) and the PEN Syndicated Fiction Award for short story. He was a finalist for the Ernest Hemingway Award and has been nominated for five Lambda Literary Awards and two American Library Association Awards. He was recently named a Lambda Literary Foundation Pioneer and one of OUT's GLBT People of the Year. A native of New York, Felice Picano now lives in Los Angeles.

Books Available From Bold Strokes Books

Burgundy Betrayal by Sheri Lewis Wohl. Park Ranger Kara Lynch has no idea she's a witch until dead bodies begin to pile up in her park, forcing her to turn to beautiful and sexy shape-shifter Camille Black Wolf for help in stopping a rogue werewolf. (978-1-60282-654-0)

LoveLife by Rachel Spangler. When Joey Lang unintentionally becomes a client of life coach Elaine Raitt, the relationship becomes complicated as they develop feelings that make them question their purpose in love and life. (978-1-60282-655-7)

The Fling by Rebekah Weatherspoon. When the ultimate fantasy of a one-night stand with her trainer, Oksana Gorinkov, suddenly turns into more, reality show producer Annie Collins opens her life to a new type of love she's never imagined. (978-1-60282-656-4)

Ill Will by J.M. Redmann. New Orleans PI Micky Knight must untangle a twisted web of healthcare fraud that leads to murder—and puts those closest to her most at risk. (978-1-60282-657-1)

Buccaneer Island by J.P. Beausejour. In the rough world of Caribbean piracy, a man is what he makes of himself—or what a stronger man makes of him. (978-1-60282-658-8)

Twelve O'Clock Tales by Felice Picano. The fourth collection of short fiction by legendary novelist and memoirist Felice Picano. Thirteen dark tales that will thrill and disturb, discomfort and titillate, enthrall and leave you wondering. (978-1-60282-659-5)

Words to Die By by William Holden. Sixteen answers to the question: What causes a mind to curdle? (978-1-60282-653-3)

Tyger, Tyger, Burning Bright by Justine Saracen. Love does not conquer all, but when all of Europe is on fire, it's better than going to hell alone. (978-1-60282-652-6)

Night Hunt by L.L. Raand. When dormant powers ignite, the wolf Were pack is thrown into violent upheaval, and Sylvan's pregnant mate is at the center of the turmoil. A Midnight Hunters novel. (978-1-60282-647-2)

Demons are Forever by Kim Baldwin and Xenia Alexiou. Elite Operative Landis "Chase" Coolidge enlists the help of high-class call girl Heather Snyder to track down a kidnapped colleague embroiled in a global black market organ-harvesting ring. (978-1-60282-648-9)

Runaway by Anne Laughlin. When Jan Roberts is hired to find a teenager who has run away to live with a group of antigovernment survivalists, she's forced to return to the life she escaped when she was a teenager herself. (978-1-60282-649-6)

Street Dreams by Tama Wise. Tyson Rua has more than his fair share of problems growing up in New Zealand—he's gay, he's falling in love, and he's run afoul of the local hip-hop crew leader just as he's trying to make it as a graffiti artist. (978-1-60282-650-2)

Women of the Dark Streets: Lesbian Paranormal by Radclyffe and Stacia Seaman, eds. Erotic tales of the supernatural—a world of vampires, werewolves, witches, ghosts, and demons—by the authors of Bold Strokes Books. (978-1-60282-651-9)

Derrick Steele: Private Dick—The Case of the Hollywood Hustlers by Zavo. Derrick Steele, a hard-drinking, lusty private detective, is being framed for the murder of a hustler in downtown Los Angeles. When his brother's friend Daniel McAllister joins the investigation, their growing attraction might prove to be more explosive than the case. (978-1-60282-596-3)

Nice Butt: Gay Anal Eroticism edited by Shane Allison. From toys to teasing, spanking to sporting, some of the best gay erotic scribes celebrate the hottest and most creative in new erotica. (978-1-60282-635-9)

Murder in the Irish Channel by Greg Herren. Chanse MacLeod investigates the disappearance of a female activist fighting the Archdiocese of New Orleans and a powerful real estate syndicate. (978-1-60282-584-0)

http://www.boldstrokesbooks.com

Bold Strokes
B O O K S

victory EDITIONS

Drama

LIBERTY EDITION

AEROS e BOOKS

Mystery

C CRIME

Sci-fi

Sf SPEC FIC

e-Books

HE erotica

ese SOLILOQUY

Young Adult

BS BOLD STROKES BOOKS

Erotica

MATINEE BOOKS

Romance

WEBSTORE
PRINT AND EBOOKS